BEFORE
SEPTEMBER
FALLS

JESSE LEE

Lyrics from "Beautiful Day" by U2
Lyrics from "Amazing Grace" by John Newton
Lyrics from "High and Dry" by Radiohead
Lyrics from "My Neck, My Back (Lick It)" by Khia

Email Jesse Lee at jesselee55@aol.com
Cover photograph by Mary Hay.
Book layout and cover design by Jesse Lee.

P.O.D. Edition

ISBN 978-0-6151-9129-4

First and foremost, I have to thank my beautiful wife and adorable son. Kaysi, thank you for your unconditional love, support, and editing skills. And thank you Clay for making me your hero. I hope never to disappoint you.

Second, I need to thank the people whose input and support also made this book possible. Thank you Heather, David, Tori, and Megan for everything you've done. I am truly blessed to have friends like you in my life.

Last and mostly certainly least, I would like to acknowledge my grandmother. Thank you for being my perpetual example of vanity, conditional love, and self-righteousness. You are the person I hope never to become.

"Carpe diem quam minimum credula postero."

"You're so vain you probably think this song is about you..."

Carly Simon

"They say the world is round-
and yet
I often think it square,
So many little hurts we get
From corners here and there;
But there's one truth in life
I've found
While journeying
East and West
The only folks we really wound
Are those we love the best...
We flatter those we scarcely know,
We please the fleeting guest,
And deal full many a thoughtless
blow
To those we love the best...."

Anonymous

one

My nostrils are flooded with the scent of dust, cat piss, and my own alcohol drenched breath. My face is cold and blackness surrounds me, but I'm not afraid.

My face is pressed to the wooden floor and I can feel the planks leaving red lines down my cheeks. Muffled noise is all I hear and creaking, low creaking in the distance.

I squint my eyes at first, slowly, to see where I am.

The room's blurry and colors dance on the wall.

The TV's on behind me.

My head's rested against the coffee table leg and I can see my cat Tigi lying on the futon, cleaning herself. The sky's black and a slight breeze rushes through my vertical blinds.

I can't remember what happened, how this happened, how I ended up here. I remember the tequila, and the laughing, and my head starts to ache.

I sit up slowly, the booze inside me splashing back and forth. If I lie here much longer, I may not be able to keep it down.

My eyesight's slowly clearing and I rub my lashes apart.

The sound from the TV has become clearer and I stare at the screen. My bunny ears are barely picking up MTV and through the static I can see bitches shaking their asses and the pimps with their over sized bling rapping about "fucking and slapping those hos."

My living room's tiny, much smaller than modest, furnished only with the futon and table. The TV sits on the floor.

Angelina Jolie stares down at me from her *Tomb Raider* poster, her eyes inviting me to touch her large tits.

Tigi pauses long enough to meow loudly, looking at me with large green eyes. I pet her head and run my hand down her back, causing her to stick her ass in the air. Her purr intensifies and she nuzzles my hand with adoration.

I know I can't walk.

The room sways slightly then abruptly rocks back, almost pushing me down on the floor.

I hear the creaking again, this time louder than before.

1

The kitchen light is on.

Maybe someone's there.

I can't remember.

I get on all fours and crawl slowly in that direction. I crawl passed the small extra bedroom and all I can see is blackness, figures dancing in the harsh darkness.

Before I can see around the wall into the kitchen, I notice the light on in my bedroom. The door's cracked and orange light spills out from all sides onto the floor.

I start to remember, my mind jarred.

I do have guests.

I crawl to the door and press my face to the jam. The light on the bedside table's on and my brown comforter is thrown to the floor.

The mattress is on cinder blocks. Two figures are rolling on the bed, kissing.

The girl has long blond hair. She's wearing only jeans and a black bra.

Her arms and legs are wrapped around a guy on top of her and all I can see are his muscular shoulders and dark brown hair. His hips are thrusting towards her and she pulls at him hungrily.

I sit quietly with my back to the wall so that I can continue to spy on them comfortably. I rest my head to keep it from rocking back and forth and one eye never leaves them.

Sweat's begun to shine on their lean bodies and I can hear them breathing heavily.

Without words, the girl props herself up on her elbows and then her hands. The guy, his back still to me, holds her face as he kisses her, caressing her neck and shoulders.

With confidence, she stands up from the bed and walks around to the end, her back now to me. He turns over and sits with his legs straightened towards her, leaning back on his hands, a guilty grin on his face.

I can hear her giggle as she leans towards him, pushing him flat on the bed.

He lies down without protest, resting his head on the pillow, never taking his gaze off of her.

She straddles him on the mattress, first lifting one slender limb over and pulling the other close to his side. Leaning forward, with her hair cascading over his face, she kisses him softly on the lips. I strain to see without pushing on the door.

As she kisses him, I watch her ass move from side to side, rubbing her crotch against his. I can hear his breathing even louder now and he moans lightly between breaths.

The girl inches back slowly from his lap, her lips leaving his mouth and kissing his neck. Her hands are caressing his smooth chest and soon her lips are there too, her fingers lightly pinching his nipples.

He laughs nervously and lifts his head off the pillow to watch her.

Still caressing his chest with her hands, she kisses his abdomen, licking his thin happy trail.

I can barely see her face from behind her hair but my imagination gladly fills in the blanks.

With her hands on his hips, she kisses along the line of his khaki shorts and a big smile spreads across his face.

The girl leans back, resting on her knees at the foot of the bed. She flips her hair and I wish I could see her face. With determination and vigor she undoes his belt, button, and zipper, and pulls off his shorts as she stands.

She doesn't stop at his thighs or knees but pulls them completely off, leaving him naked as the day he was born.

She giggles as she drops them on the floor because he's already hard.

Straddling him around his calves, the girl leans forward over his crotch.

Most of what I see I see from between her thighs, a shadow of his cock and her face.

I can hear myself breathing.

My cock's throbbing in my shorts and all I want to do is jump in bed with them.

This is happening in my room of all places.

I watch as she kisses the insides of his thighs, his hips, and finally the tip of his penis before it starts to slide in and out of her mouth.

I can't resist the urge to rub myself through my shorts, wishing I were him. His hands gently hold the back of her head.

The girl's holding his cock in one hand as she blows him and gently massages his balls with the other.

My body begins to twitch and I strain to keep them in sight, not wanting to lose a moment.

I reach into my boxers now and hold myself, my dick harder than I've ever felt it.

My face burns from the alcohol and the excitement. I rub, slowly at first, then harder and faster.

The guy pushes his head back into the pillow, gripping the sides of the mattress with his strong hands.

Deep inside my lap I can feel pumping, throbbing, and aching. The fluids inside me are being pushed and that strong sensation comes over me. It's an urge at first, like I might have to urinate, but then I pass the moment of no return. I feel pre-cum shoot out, soaking the inside of my boxers, followed shortly by thicker, warmer fluid. The semen squirts, drips out of me, covering my hand and testicles. I bite my other fist to squelch any

3

noise I might make. I don't stop. I keep stroking and it hurts so bad it feels amazing and I keep my eyes open, watching them the entire time.

The guy on the bed moans loudly. He pushes his head farther back into the mattress, his heels digging into the bed, his toes pointing. His body convulses one last time and he shouts, "Oh, Fuck!"

I'm no longer rubbing myself, watching as he cums, but my hand's still there holding my limp dick.

His breathing's hard but his body's relaxed, his face and chest covered in sweat.

The girl sits up again, pushing her hair back and lifting it off of her neck.

He grins at her and puts a hand over his eyes.

"How you feeling?" she asks with a laugh and all he can do is mumble. "I'll be right back," she says as she kisses him on the cheek.

I get up as quickly as I can, awkwardly with my hand still in my pants.

I walk fast, trying not to make a noise.

I reach the futon as I hear the door open behind me and drop down on my stomach.

I hear her walk to the bathroom and turn the water on.

I can imagine her face in the stream, wetting her hair and hands, filling her mouth.

The water stops and I hear her footsteps as they leave the bathroom but they don't drown out into the bedroom. They grow louder as she walks towards me and my pulse begins to quicken, my heart pounding in my ears. The TV behind me turns off and I open my eyes in the darkness.

The girl takes the blanket off the arm of the futon at my feet and spreads it over me.

I hope she can't see my hand in my pants and her fingers brush my cheek as she pulls the blanket up to my face.

She walks away and I hear the door close behind her.

I strain for an hour to hear anything. I'm too tired to walk back to my seat. I lie, imagining them, picturing him holding her breasts and fucking her.

I masturbate again before I fall asleep and their lovemaking haunts my dreams.

TWO

I wake in the afternoon on June 7th, 2001, the day after my high school graduation. I lie quietly on the futon, contemplating my next move.

The blinds sway in the breeze above me and I watch them blow back and forth.

Sweat collects on my bare abdomen, filling my belly button and catching in my happy trail. One of my hands is tucked into my shorts, my fingertips in pubic hair. The other's resting on the floor.

Tigi licks that hand heartily, hungry and purring. I push her away when I remember I didn't wash my hands last night before I fell asleep.

She skips off towards the kitchen, meowing loudly for her breakfast.

I throw a forearm over my eyes and stare at the colors that dance inside my lids.

I can hear someone fill her bowl and her meowing stops while she eats.

I pick the sleep from my eyes, rub them clear, and sit up slowly. The room rocks back and forth and my cock's painfully hard, trying to push its way from my shorts.

I can feel what's left of the tequila as I stand and walk towards the bathroom, my dick like an arrow towards the toilet. I stand above the bowl, staring at myself in the mirror and holding my breath. It's something that has always proved effective in the past. My eyes are puffy and my once spiky hair is now fluffy and crunchy.

Within a few seconds I'm soft enough to urinate, trickle actually, and eventually it becomes a steady flow. I stand motionless with my hands on my hips and my cock dangles from the bottom of my torso.

I shake myself dry, milk twice for good measure, and flush the toilet.

I wash my hands and run water through my hair, slicking it back. When I turn off the water, I hear more noise in the kitchen.

Tawny stands in front of the stove, a spatula in one hand and a frying pan in the other. She's been my best friend for two years, even though we've known each other for six. She tormented me the first four and I hated her for being such a bitch. But during our junior year in high school we forged an inseparable bond that many people could never fully understand. We were each other's 'other half,' supporting one another through family bullshit, failed relationships and bad grades. When no one else would suffice, we were each other's dates for Prom and GradNite.

Tawny stands there in a pair of my boxers, a wife beater and no bra.

She's listening to her new favorite CD on my stereo, singing along, "My neck, my back, lick my pussy and my crack …"

Her straight hair's now thrown up into a messy bun.

"Wow, she cooks and sings!" I say loudly as I walk into the room, scratching my groin.

She turns quickly, drops the spatula on the counter, and hugs me.

"Well, good morning! It's about god-damn time you got up!" she says, laughing and smiling widely.

Her smile's beautiful and contagious. It's perfect except for a small gap between her two front teeth. No matter how late she stays up drinking, she always manages to be the first person awake and I'm astonished by her will power.

I sit down on a creaky old stool facing the counter that separates us as she goes back to her cooking. The counter also serves as my bar, with a large collection of half full bottles neatly lined against the wall.

"Sorry, it's just eggs and coffee. I couldn't find much in your fridge," she says with another chuckle, turning from her cooking to pour me a cup.

She drops two scoops of sugar in and puts the mug in front of me.

My fridge is and probably always will be empty. Working in a restaurant allows me to eat on a regular basis for free and smoking helps me keep my appetite low.

"Hey, is Jared still here?" I ask after my first sip of coffee, realizing I haven't seen my other guest.

"No," she pouts, sticking out her lower lip a little too far. "He had to work today. Did you know he gets paid double for working on a Saturday?!"

"Yes, I did know that," I answer a matter of factly.

Jared's a year younger than us and goes to Mountain High School. I met him through a mutual friend and in the year we've known each other, I've always admired him.

He's one of those guys that all the girls want and all the other guys want to be. He carries himself so unconsciously it makes me sick and secretly I hope some of it will rub off on me.

"So… how was your night?" I ask, continuing my thought, already aware of the answer.

"Well, you might need to change your sheets," Tawny answers with a wicked smile.

She's finished with the eggs and scoops them onto two mismatched plates. After pouring herself a large glass of water from a jug in the fridge, she sits on the stool next to mine.

I'm dying for details, more than what I saw, but I wouldn't dare ask.

"You know, I always had a feeling you and Jared would hit it off," I finally decide to bring up after a couple silent bites.

"He's so cute! I didn't exactly think we were going to, you know, like each other so much. But thank you very much for inviting him to our graduation last night! Oh, and thank you for letting us borrow your room!" she answers through a mouthful of food.

Tawny and Jared had never met before last night but I'm not surprised how quickly things transpired. He'd known about my graduation for weeks and was glad to come.

His ex-girlfriend and our mutual friend, Michelle, was going to be there too, which I had hoped wouldn't be a problem. I've known her brother Brandon since elementary school and we were best friends for years. We met in Sunday school at the First Presbyterian Church of San Soledo and were inseparable.

But attending different high schools, Brandon goes to Mountain High and I attend Desert Valley High, then losing interest in church drove us apart. As our friendship started to dwindle, Brandon's sister started working at the same restaurant as I do.

Michelle, who's a year younger than Jared and also attends Mountain High, is the sole reason we became friends.

"No problem," I continue. "I just hope Michelle doesn't find out though."

With that, Tawny drops her fork with a loud clang and stares at me.

"Jared said the same fucking thing!" she practically screams, her face flushing. "Why? They broke up! She's a big girl and knows perfectly well what happens when people split. They date and on occasion sleep with other people."

She tortures me with a short moment of deafening silence, staring at me with rage in her eyes and continues to inform me, "We didn't have sex though, if you were wondering."

I was.

I sit quietly, feeling guilty, realizing I should have kept my mouth shut.

"Who broke up with whom anyways?" she asks, her voice calm again as she picks her fork back up.

"It was Jared's decision. It had something to do with his grandmother. She's a devout Jehovah's Witness and Michelle isn't, so you can probably imagine where it went from there," I inform her, cutting myself short intentionally.

It's none of my business really and none of hers either.

"Yeah, I guess I can see where that could become a problem. He loves his family. Organized religion can have its way of breaking up relationships," she reaffirms, filling her mouth with eggs.

I jam the last bite of eggs into my mouth and take my plate to the sink, tossing it in on top of the frying pan.

I know exactly what she means.

I was raised in the church, devoutly attending until the ripe old age of fifteen, a Presbyterian, one of God's 'Frozen Chosen.'

Tawny slowly finishes her eggs, not looking up at me as I stand across the counter from her. I can sense, even feel her frustration. I lean down on my elbows and our faces are level.

"I'm not trying to pick sides or point fingers. I understand why she would be upset. Hey, you used to work with us! She considered you a friend!" I plead.

Tawny looks back at me solemnly as I speak. She had in fact worked with us last summer and the two of them got along very well.

"Yeah, I know. But I no longer work there! And that was a year ago! And didn't you introduce Jared and me knowing I'd find him attractive?" she says, standing up and taking her empty plate to the sink.

I turn away, guilty.

It is my fault. I knew exactly what I was doing.

"So, what do you want to do with the rest of our day?" I ask, desperately trying to change the mood.

I have five hours until work and I have no money to go out and do anything.

"Well," Tawny answers, staring out the window above the sink into the warm sunshine outside. "It's too damn hot to go jogging, so let's just lay out."

We leave the dishes in the sink, egg caked to the frying pan and spatula. I can't afford patio furniture, so towels protect us from the hot wood beneath our backs. My patio overlooks a large dirt lot filled with weeds and scattered Joshua trees. The thermometer above the door reads 110° and the usually busy highway below is completely silent. I take off my shorts and lie down in my boxers. Tawny reties her hair.

"Why don't you get out naked?" Tawny asks, looking down at me.

I shield my eyes from the sun and simply shrug my shoulders. In high school, during our lunch breaks, we'd suntan when the weather was warm enough. We found a spot between two of the modular classrooms, hidden from the world, and we'd lean back in classroom chairs wearing nothing but our underwear.

I slide my boxers off, a little self-conscious. Tawny and I've never been naked together.

She pulls off the wife beater that was see-through anyway and drops the boxers to reveal that she wasn't wearing panties either. I avert my eyes respectfully, determined not to stare.

"It's ok, you **can** see me naked," she laughs, lying on the towel next to mine. "I just don't want us to get tan lines!"

"I know I can, I just don't want the sun in my eyes!" I defend myself a little too urgently.

She responds with a simple grunt, sliding her sunglasses on and smiling.

The hot sun illuminates my pale skin, reflecting onto the sliding glass door and the awning. I can smell the tequila, like pepper, seeping through my pores and I'm beginning to wish I had taken a shower before deciding to come out in the direct heat.

The silence is peaceful but my thoughts haunt me and I'm relieved when Tawny decides to speak up.

"I saw your mom yesterday at the end of the ceremony. She looked pissed!" she chuckles.

My mother was there, with my grandmother and grandfather. My sister couldn't make it because of work but it wouldn't have mattered anyway.

"Yeah, well, she didn't seem as pissed as your mom! She looked at me like I was crazy when I told her you could stay the night!" I laugh back at her.

My mom didn't appreciate the fact that I didn't pose for a picture after the ceremony and Tawny's simply doesn't trust her.

Her mother's a reclusive bitch that excommunicated herself from the rest of the family and her father is a pussy-whipped geek that will never stand up for himself.

"Hey, how much money do you have left over?" Tawny asks after laughing hard about her mother.

"A little," I lie.

It's completely gone.

I received two thousand dollars cash for my graduation, five hundred of which was from the grandmother I never got around to thanking. Knowing I'd be tempted to spend it, I paid upfront for the first three months rent.

"You're going to need roommates eventually, right?" Tawny continues to ask.

"Yeah I will. I talked to Brittney and she said she might be interested," I answer.

I'll never be able to pay the entire rent on my pathetic salary and Brittney, a waitress I work with, can definitely relate.

"What about Mark?" Tawny asks, sitting up.

Mark is Brittney's boyfriend, for the moment anyway. I sit up to face Tawny. Her skin glows gold in the sunlight and I still avoid looking at it

"What about him? Brittney said she's talked to him about getting a place of their own and he hasn't budged. He works at Thrift City, in the loading docks, and spends all his free time online!" I say, defending myself.

Honestly I just want an opportunity to fuck Brittney.

"Well, if I wasn't going to Washington in September, I would so move in with you!"

"Thanks. But where would I sleep? You'd keep me up every night with all your noise making!" I quickly respond, grabbing her knee and squeezing it. She hates it when I do that.

Tawny squirms and giggles and finally curses at me to stop.

I'm tired of the sun in my eyes and I roll over onto my stomach. My chest and abdomen are turning red and my ass definitely needs color.

"You should put some sunscreen on your tattoo," Tawny says as she turns over too, motioning towards my back.

She was with me three months ago when I got the words 'Carpe Diem' tattooed between my shoulders. She held my hand as I tried not to cry.

"I'll be ok," I mumble into the towel that now smells like B.O. I need a shower and I hope the stench is not strong enough for Tawny to smell.

My mom cried the day I came home with the small tattoo, ashamed that her son would do such a thing to his temple of God. I told her as we were leaving that I was going to get it done as an eighteenth birthday present to myself and she didn't take me seriously.

The sun has begun its descent and soon I'll have to leave for work. Tawny will go home to her overbearing parents and I'll be left alone.

Completely alone.

It's a sensation I'm still becoming accustomed to. I enjoy my solitude but my newfound responsibilities are almost too much to handle. Like a weight on my chest, I find it hard to breath. Despite all the good times I know I'll be able to make for myself now, I'm terrified. I quietly hope and pray that Brittney will move in with me. While celebrating our graduation last night, I was also trying to drown out my irrational fears that were still there when I woke up.

I hope Tawny leaves soon. I'm dying for a cigarette before getting ready for work.

She hates it when I smoke.

THREE

San Soledo, California is located north of Los Angeles, twenty miles shy of the Kern County line. My mother moved my sister and me here when I was only four years old. She began attending community college with our child support, money anonymously transferred from an undisclosed bank account. When she graduated with her nursing degree she thanked the two of us for our support.

She forgot to mention the person that was earning that money.

I'd love to let him know what he paid for.

I've never known any other home than this desert. With a population of only 45,000 people, it's considered small compared to the metropolis of Los Angeles. Proud of their rural and individual way of living, so many people claim to be 'cowboys' despite driving Escalades and BMW's.

I got a job at The San Soledo Restaurant and Saloon at the end of my sophomore year of high school. In the two short years I've been there I've gone from bussing tables to serving them. I finally settled into the position of Maître D.

It's one of our valley's few nicer establishments, a family owned business. An escape from chain restaurants that have been developed simply to extort us of our money, I feel at home amongst my coworkers that are like family.

Close to my home and school, it was a great choice for my first job, even though I've had to endure country music on a daily basis.

After our sunbathing, I quickly help Tawny gather her things.

I light a Marlboro the moment she walks out the door and the nicotine hits me like a cookie for a fat kid. I smoke it slowly as I go about getting my clothes ready for work.

A black shirt and a black pair of slacks paired with a dark red tie.

It's hot outside but the colors suit me. With my dark brown hair and pale skin, everyone laughs at how 'gothic' I tend to look. I'm comfortable with that and I probably do it on purpose for the mere fact of being individual.

I've only lived in this apartment for a week and already all my boxes are unpacked.

My closet is half full and my dishware is minimal.

I live on coffee, Frosted Mini Wheat's, raisin bread, and cigarettes.

I have an old computer that was given to me by a friend of my mother. I use it to play *Tomb Raider* and jerk off to stolen dial-up speed porn.

I own two sets of sheets and only one set of towels for my bathroom.

After finishing my cigarette, I take a shower. I hesitate at first but finally give in to the urge to masturbate. I buy sweet smelling conditioner for this reason because it reminds me of the first time I violated myself.

I grew up being taught it was a sin and when I finally partook in what all the other guys had been doing for years, it changed my world.

I was fifteen, squatting in the shower with a handful of my sister's conditioner, slowly rubbing myself. When I finally erupted, I sat there shaking for what felt like an eternity, consumed with the greatest feeling I had ever experienced.

I have another cigarette after my shower and walk around the apartment nude to air dry. Living at home with two women limited my privacy and now I take advantage of it whenever I can.

I still sleep with underwear on though, always scared that someone might walk in on me.

I quickly drink another cup of coffee and brush my teeth. I open the rest of my windows after dressing and tie up my Doc Martin boots. I lock the front door behind me as I leave.

I live in the upstairs apartment of an old complex and take the stairs two steps at a time as I hurry down. My red Jeep Wrangler is parked out in the sunlight and the air inside is stifling.

I bought the ten-year-old car shortly before I graduated for $4,500, all the money I had saved bussing tables. I have yet to take the top off and I want to replace the tape player with a CD changer. Until then I'll just make mix tapes.

I smoke two more cigarettes on my way to work and listen to a U2 tape. Rebecca, a waitress I work with, made me copies of all their CD's.

Until high school, I lived a fairly sheltered life and it'll take some time still before I catch up on all the pop culture I missed out on.

I arrive at the restaurant fifteen minutes to five and park in the back.

Brittney's the first person I see as I walk in and punch my time card. She simply smiles as she hurries passed, grabbing plates from the kitchen.

I set my keys down in the office and walk out into the bar.

Michelle greets me with a hug. She's a foot shorter than I am so I have to bend over to embrace her. She has a slim body and shoulder length blonde hair.

"So, did you party hard last night?" she asks with a big smile. She was there for the ceremony but declined to attend any of the parties. With two years left to go, she's one of those over-achieving academics that has other things better to do than drink.

"Yes, I had a great night. Thanks for the card by the way," I tell her, really not sure if she even gave me one. Apparently Jared hasn't talked to her yet.

Brittney was at the ceremony as well, waving at me from the bleachers. I couldn't find her after we threw our caps though, probably because Mark impatiently urged her to leave.

I give Dana, the bartender, a kiss hello and she calls me Mijo. She's a few years older than my mom with curly blonde hair and olive skin.

I wave to people I know in the bar.

I take the reservation book from next to the cash register and walk to the podium at the front of the dining room.

Every bar stool is occupied, the happy hour chafer is empty, and the dining room is already loud with conversation. Nearly all the candle lit tables are full and the reservation book before me shows there will be many more people passing through. The phone rings moments after I take my place and I answer it with a smile.

"Good evening, San Soledo Restaurant," I speak clearly, putting my vocal skills to the test.

"Hey Penis," Tawny's jovial voice rings back.

"Would you like to make a reservation or just annoy me while I work?" I ask as a group walks in the door.

"Hmm, I would definitely not like to make a reservation. I just wanted to let you know I'm stuck at home tonight. My mom is being a cunt."

"Well, I am sorry to hear that. Just let Jared know because I don't think I can entertain him the way you do. I don't want him coming over later all ready for action."

"Why not? That would be hot!" she snickers.

"Yeah, okay. I gotta go," I say quickly and quietly, hanging up the phone to greet the group that now stands before me.

"There are five of us and we'd like a table over near that window," one of the women says to me. She's in her mid fifties with small glasses and shoulder length graying hair. This is the best part of my job and I breathe in deeply, expecting the worst.

"Do you have a reservation?" I ask coolly, already knowing the answer. I turn from her to stare into my book as if I have something important to read.

"No, we didn't think they were necessary," she continues, readjusting the purse hanging from her shoulder.

I count to myself... one... two... three... scanning my book and trying to figure where I could seat them. When I reach ten I turn to her with a smile.

"I'm sorry but all of these tables are reserved. I do have another table this way," I say as I grab menus and a wine list.

The group looks at me for a moment in quiet protest but I continue to walk away, leaving them with no choice but to follow. I walk passed the stairs that lead down to the wine cellar to a table across the room from the one they requested. I set the menus down, along with the server's ticket and turn back to them.

The gray-haired woman, apparently the leader of her middle-aged pack, stares straight at me as if I might have made a mistake.

"Do you think you might have another table? Something nicer?" she asks with a frown.

Their side of the room's empty with a very boring view of the abandoned patio. I simply shake my head, my smile never faltering. They slowly sit down, adjusting their seats and not saying a word until I leave. I briskly walk away and into the kitchen to inform Brittney that she has a table.

Like any other night, I seat tables, serve cocktails, and open bottles of wine. Rebecca's also serving and so is Eric, Brittney's ex-boyfriend. She tends to dip her pen in company ink but luckily it doesn't affect their work environment, for the most part. Tawny calls twice more, encouraging me to run out the door and never return.

An hour after I start my shift, Michelle walks briskly up to my podium.

"Brittney's in the office crying again. Go take care of it," she says diligently and annoyed, slipping behind the podium to answer the phone. I hand her the wine cellar keys as I quickly head off to the office.

Brittney can be a little dramatic and crying at work is something she's made a habit of. She's seated in the only chair facing the computer in the corner, her face in her hands and her elbows propped up on the desktop. Drops of mascara have smeared her cheeks and one dripped onto her white tuxedo shirt. Her hair's pulled back into a ponytail, showing off her beautifully tanned skin and piercing blue eyes.

I've had a thing for her since we met my freshman year of high school. She was a sophomore.

There's a powerful presence when she walks into a room. She may go away to college someday but I'm happy she's stayed. She isn't the skinniest or sexiest girl I know, but her personality outshines everything else. Seeing her like this now makes me want to hold her and tell her it'll all be ok. Or at least go hit whoever it is that made her cry.

"Sorry to interrupt but I do have some more tables coming in that I was planning on putting in your section," I tell her, smiling.

"I'm sorry," she says apologetically, wiping the tears from her cheeks. "I shouldn't let it bother me, but they're just being so fucking mean! I can only do so much and they don't seem to notice how busy I am. They even told me I'm the worst waitress they've ever had!"

Before she finishes the sentence I know exactly what table she's referring to.

The middle-aged table, especially the ringleader.

I can just imagine that bitch getting her kicks out of belittling Brittney.

"I'll take care of them," I say reassuringly, resting a hand on Brittney's knee. "Just go get their food."

I follow her into the kitchen and walk into the dining room. I move purposefully, not arrogantly, right up to their table.

With my biggest and fakest smile, I ask, "How is everything?"

My newly found independence fuels my passion to impress Brittney.

"For one," my familiar friend with the gray hair starts, "Our water glasses are empty! I've already asked twice for another martini and I'm starving! Please tell the kitchen to speed it up a little!"

When she finishes, the woman looks down at her watch and then back up at me with raised eyebrows, expecting me to grovel. I quickly excuse myself, reassuring her I'll personally take care of the matter.

Heading back to the kitchen I see the martini sitting at the end of the bar getting warm.

"Dana, would you please make me a fresh one of these?" I ask her with a quick smile. "Brittney, if you'll hurry with those entrees I'll refill their waters," I continue as I pick up a fresh water pitcher.

I fill it with ice and water and covertly step back into the office.

I close the door behind me. Snorting, trying to be quiet, I hawk a loogy into the water. Thick, yellow and transparent, a large wad of spit now sits on top of the ice. I shake the pitcher hoping to disperse the chunks and even use my finger to twirl it together. I leave the office, pick up the bitch's fresh cocktail and walk briskly back to the table. Brittney's still in the kitchen placing their food on a tray.

I set the cocktail down first and the woman doesn't even look up or acknowledge me with a 'Thank you.' In slow motion, I refill every single glass at the table. And one by one, they sip the cool refreshing water. I save the bitch for last, who instantly puts down her alcohol to drink the water like a dog locked outside in the heat. She leans her head back and pours it down her throat.

Suddenly she stops.

"What's the matter, Joyce?" the man next to her asks.

Joyce sets down her glass and puts a hand to her mouth. Her eyes are wide and her cheeks are quickly reddening. She spit's the mouthful of water back into the glass and exclaims, "There's spit in my water!"

And there it is, a large yellow glob resting on the surface.

Brittney walks up behind me and sets her tray of food down on a stand next to the table.

I quickly grab the glass, aghast and embarrassed.

"That's not possible! I just filled this pitcher myself!" I stutter, pretending not to see the rest of my spit stringing through the ice. "It's probably some food from the dishwasher!" I continue as Brittney starts passing out their plates. "Give them a round of drinks on the house and I'll get you a fresh glass," I yell, running back to the kitchen.

The rest of the evening proceeds uneventful. Brittney never verbally thanks me or acknowledges what I did but her kiss on my cheek tells me she knows and is grateful.

No one else stays after work to drink and when the entire restaurant's empty, I join Dana at the bar. She sits quietly, filling out her closing paperwork, smoking Virginia Slims. I flip through the satellite radio stations, smoking my cigarettes. We quickly fill the air around us with a blue haze.

I settle on the alternative rock station and Dana finishes her paperwork around 11:30. She takes a joint from her purse and holds it up for me to see. All I do is nod my head and she lights it.

The blue haze quickly infuses with the sweet, grassy aroma of pot and The Smashing Pumpkins roar from the overhead speakers. After taking a long drag, she hands the joint to me. The drug hits me hard and I quickly get tunnel vision.

The last thing I expect from Dana is a conversation and she quickly takes the joint back from me.

"You know, my mind only makes sense when I'm on pot," she quietly whispers, the smoke leaking through her nose.

"Uh, yeah," I respond, not really hearing what she just said.

After the long night, I don't feel philosophical.

"Mijo, what do you want to do when you finish college?" she asks, handing me back the joint.

"Well, I don't know..." I start, taking a long drag and holding.

"No really, what makes you happy? I remember when I was young, I always wanted to be a dancer. I'm forty-two now and can still dance but back then I was amazing. My mama would have never agreed to it though," she blurts out, watching as I take another hit.

"An actor! I want to be an actor," I let out with the smoke.

"An actor? That's great! You definitely have the look for it."

"Yeah, maybe. But everyone thinks I need something else to fall back on, as if they know I won't make it," I think out loud, the sadness hitting harder than usual.

"That's such bullshit! Everyone has a purpose in life! We all know what we're meant to do! Like when you were on stage during those plays in high school, you felt something inside didn't you? Something God wanted you to feel?" she asks quickly, dragging and not noticing as I roll my eyes at the notion of God.

At this point we're both feeling hazy and neither of us takes offense to the openness of the conversation.

"What do you mean?" I ask, lost in my tunnel that is now turning over and over.

"Don't let anyone discourage you from getting those feelings. The feelings that make you happy, that make you feel complete. I regret everyday the fact that I never became a dancer. My mama made me get a 'real job' and get married. I've been married four goddamn times! When you get to a certain age, you start counting down the days because you realize all the time you've wasted. Don't ever be embarrassed by your dreams or you'll start thinking like everyone else. You have to protect them and hold onto them," she whispers, leaning in close for the last few words, as if it were a secret and the whole world was on top of us trying to listen.

I stare at her for a few moments and I can see a tear welling up in the corner of her eye. She puts out what's left of the joint and brushes passed me as she stands up to turn off the lights behind the bar.

"Well, we should probably get out of here. You'll be back in the morning for brunch, right?"

"Yeah, and Brittney's serving," I answer as I stand up from my stool.

"Do you want to sleep at my place tonight?" Dana asks without hesitation, picking up her purse and turning off the lights. "I hate sleeping alone."

She walks slowly back to me and we stand there looking at each other in the dark.

I consider my options.

I can stay with her tonight and probably fuck her, but is that how I want to lose my virginity?

Do I want to make a fool of myself and tell her I've never had sex before or make a fool of myself by keeping my mouth shut and showing her I haven't?

Her mascara's caked on and I can smell Crown Royal on her breath. I don't want to know what she'll look like in the morning.

"No, thanks though, but I have to go home and finish unpacking," I say, knowing it sounds like bullshit the moment the words leave my mouth.

"Well, ok then Mijo. I'll see you in the morning," she says, sounding disappointed as she leans in and kisses me on the cheek.

Her kiss burns my skin long after she walks passed me and out the door. I set the alarm and lock up, lighting another cigarette as I walk through the warm night air to my Jeep.

I promise myself I'll think about it all in the morning.

FOUR

I learned to play billiards when I was seven. My sister taught me. I'll never be as good as her but I'm not as bad as some people I know.

I hadn't played for years before I started working at the restaurant. Brittney and everyone else had a tradition of playing Wednesday nights and I quickly adopted the custom. The pool hall 's a place of many firsts for me and I've adopted it as yet another place to call home.

The place is called Frank's and cigarette smoke lingers in the air between the twenty tables.

The Wednesday after my graduation's no exception, aside from the fact that I don't have school tomorrow.

Michelle picked me up for work and when our shift ends we drive straight there. Tawny and Jared said they'd come, a fact I'm beginning to dread. I begged them to keep the public displays of affection to a minimum.

We walk in wearing our disheveled tuxedo shirts and glance around the haze.

"There they are!" Michelle says, taking me by the hand and dragging me to the table.

Brittney notices us first and greets us both with a hug and a kiss. Mark simply nods.

"It's about time you two got here! Ty's kicking my ass," Rebecca says from the table where she's playing against her son.

She also greets us with kisses, smearing dark lipstick on our cheeks. She has a cigarette in one hand and a pool cue in the other.

Rebecca's forty, with shoulder length auburn hair and large breasts. Her husband's a very popular CPA and, surprisingly, not a jealous man. She always says she serves tables because she wants to; I just figured she was tired of sitting around while John worked late hours.

I went to high school with Rebecca's son, Ty, but we were never friends. We existed on different sides of the social spectrum but he still greets me with a warm handshake. He looks like his mother, olive skin and an Italian nose, and is probably what Sylvester Stallone looked like forty years ago.

"You wanna beer?" Rebecca asks, filling up her glass from an already half empty pitcher.

She's the only person amongst us over the age of twenty-one so we don't need to be asked twice. The bouncers never question us and we smoke inside even though it's illegal. Vic, the owner, continues to get cited and the smoking ceases for about a week. The ceiling fans are always on so the air's ventilated for the most part.

I sit in a chair at the cocktail table directly across from Mark. Rebecca's so excited to see me she sits on my knee to watch Ty make his next shot, which of course goes in. I take a Marlboro from her pack on the table and inhale deeply. She hates when I tell people that she gave me my first cigarette.

My mother's always been jealous of our relationship, even though we act more like siblings. She fears Rebecca will replace her.

Michelle takes Rebecca's pool cue and finishes the game against Ty.

I see Tawny and Jared walk in the door as I finish my cigarette. I quickly excuse myself, practically pushing Rebecca to the floor, and rush to greet them.

"Hey you two," is all I can get out, hugging them both.

I hope they read the distress in my eyes because I know everyone at the table is staring at my back.

Tawny reluctantly lets go of Jared's hand and I finally breathe relief.

"Can we stay at your place tonight?" she asks with a devilish grin as we walk back to the pool table.

"Sure. I have to work tomorrow night but you can stay and hang out if you want."

When Tawny and I reach the table, Jared's already talking to Michelle. I may never know the details of the break up but at least they're civil. With hesitation, she actually hugs Tawny.

Michelle doesn't know, not yet anyway.

Smoking cowboy cigarettes and drinking pitchers of over-priced beer, typical in a town with not much to do. There's a Karaoke machine in the corner, across the room from the jukebox that stands alone on its own platform collecting dust.

After Michelle kicks Ty's ass, I take his place. I'm pretty sure he lost on purpose

"Now I'm going to show you how to lose properly," I tell her with a smile, lining up the cue ball as she racks.

"Yeah, I'm sure about that," she yells back at me over the Jimi Hendrix blaring from the overhead speakers.

I hit the ball and it strikes the triangle hard, sending colors everywhere. As I step aside to let Michelle shoot, I notice Jared and Tawny sitting close to one another, flirting.

Throughout the game, they can't take their eyes off each other. As if the world around them doesn't exist, he touches her knee here and she grazes his thigh there. I can feel the tension.

I smoke two cigarettes, trying to focus on the game. I don't want to bring any more attention to them. Brittney and Rebecca are chatting loudly. I win the game only because Michelle's staring at them too, her suspicions flying.

"What's wrong?" I ask, leaning in close and acting as if I don't already know.

She doesn't look at me but focuses on Tawny, who's now sitting on Jared's lap, talking across the bar table to Mark.

"Nothing," is her response and she forces a smile.

They're like an elephant standing between us, crushing the table and creating chaos. It's something Michelle doesn't want to talk about, let alone look at.

Brittney and Rebecca take over the pool table and I sit next to Mark. He's the same age as me and went to the same high school as Jared. Up until now I haven't spent much time with him, something I think Brittney's doing deliberately.

"So, how long have you and Brittney been dating?" I ask with Michelle sitting on my lap.

"A couple months," he answers cautiously.

It's been a popular suspicion that this new romance started before things ended with Eric, but we may never know. He pulls out a pack of clove cigarettes and offers me one.

"Cool. She seems really happy," I lie, leaning in close so he can hear me over the loud music.

He doesn't respond, just lights my cigarette and continues to watch Brittney.

Michelle's pretending to watch the game too but I can tell her patience is waning. Ty's now sitting next to Tawny and the three of them are laughing and joking. Jared leans around her to talk to him and Tawny rests her hands on him with ease, a gesture that hits home.

"I have a great idea!" Michelle shouts, standing up quickly.

She pulls me from my chair and starts to drag me in the direction of the karaoke machine.

"Sing us a song!" she begs.

"Yeah! Sing some U2!" Rebecca calls after us, laying her pool stick down and dragging on her Marlboro.

She jumps up and down excitedly and Brittney follows us over to the small stage.

I flip through the book, finding the only U2 song I know by heart, and enter the numbers into the dusty keyboard.

The jukebox goes silent and the room glances over in my direction, obviously annoyed. Some don't even bother and they continue with their games.

I stand quietly, holding the microphone and the clove that's slowly burning between my fingers. I drag the sweet smoke and it burns my throat. I lick my lips and they taste like cinnamon. The opening notes for "Beautiful Day" begin and I close my eyes, letting the smoke creep from my nostrils.

"The heart is a bloom..." I start, the mic against my lips and my other hand stretched out to the side.

I slowly rock my hips to the music and the words scroll down a big screen behind me as well as a tiny monitor before me.

I can hear Rebecca cheering over the music and as I open my eyes I can see her dancing to the song, her hands raised above her head.

"It's a beautiful day!" I belt out, the music picking up pace.

I kick my feet and sway back and forth vigorously. My voice is awful and the speakers are unforgiving. Those watching are unsure of what to make of my display and I finish the song with both my hands in the air, my head tossed back.

Rebecca, Brittney, and Michelle cheer loudly and I take another deep drag from the clove.

"That one was for you Rebecca because I too have a boner for Bono!" I rasp into the microphone.

The outburst is greeted with silence and looks of disgust and as I step down the jukebox turns back on, disregarding my moment of bravery.

The evening soon comes to an end. Tawny and Jared decide they have better things to do. I give them my key and they leave while Michelle's in the restroom.

Rebecca tires quickly and leaves Ty behind. Michelle promises him a ride so they stay to play another game.

Brittney refuses to leave and when Mark finally realizes that threatening to go without her won't make a difference, he exits. His absence is an obvious relief to her and she sits close to me, sharing a cigarette.

It's nearly one in the morning when we decide to leave.

Michelle and Ty play two more games and when she offers me a ride home, Brittney reassures her that she'll do the honors. We push through the drunks outside, bid farewell, and go our separate ways.

The air's warm. Brittney and I sit in her car.

"My buzz is wearing off," she moans, blowing the smoke from another shared cigarette out her open sunroof.

"Well, do you wanna try and get something? It's gonna be difficult, just the two of us."

"I have an idea," she says, starting the car.

The familiar twinkle resonates in her eyes and she flicks the butt out the window as we pull out of the parking lot.

The grocery store on Seventh Street is open twenty-four hours and we walk into the harsh fluorescent light. My buzz is wearing off too and the quick decline of being awake for the shift from drunk to sober is peaking around the corner. Brittney walks with determination straight to the liquor section and grabs a large bottle of Goldschlager.

"Want anything?" she asks, her face straight and innocent.

I grab a bottle of Jose Cuervo and we walk back to the front of the store. We set the liquor down and it runs along the treadmill to a cashier in his forties. He doesn't look up at us, just runs the bottles across the laser scanner. The register beeps, reminding him to ask for an ID. He glances over his glasses at Brittney, his eyebrows raised. She doesn't say anything, just smiles and sticks her chest out. Her top's a light purple color and the V-neck drops dangerously low. I didn't notice until now that she's not wearing a bra and the cool air has hardened her nipples. The cashier notices too and completely forgets what he was going to ask. We quickly pay with cash and Brittney glances back at him one more time as we walk out the door, blushing.

"Here, you can drive," she says, tossing me the keys. "I want to drink."

I slip in behind the wheel of her new Honda and Brittney cracks the lid off her bottle the moment I turn the key.

"Where do you want to go?" I ask.

"I don't know. Just drive," she says after swallowing a mouthful.

The streets are completely empty now and the stars are blurred by the streetlamps.

I'm not sure where to go but the one thing for certain is we don't want to go home. I settle on the next best place. My heads pounding and I'm jonesing for tequila, so I figure, *"Why not?"*

Within ten minutes we're parked on the outskirts of town by the reservoir. We're elevated and can stare down at the city lights. Joshua Trees and tumbleweeds surround us. Brittney's favorite Dashboard Confessionals CD is playing over and over on the stereo, carried out through the open windows.

I turn off the ignition and the headlights and crack open my bottle.

This spot's deserted and the only other sound than the music is the power lines humming overhead.

"Mark and I used to come here," Brittney comments nonchalantly before taking another swig from her already half-empty bottle.

After wiping her mouth, she looks over at me with glazed eyes. I can feel my face flush from the first swig of Jose and my head's already starting to spin.

Brittney stumbles towards me, trying to keep her balance, leaning over the emergency brake to kiss me. Her mouth's warm and wet and tastes like cinnamon. I suck on her tongue longingly. My courage quickly builds and I slowly reach a hand up and run it through the hair at the base of her neck.

With one surprisingly quick motion, she's straddling me in the driver's seat. She holds my face as she continues to kiss me and I grope her ass, pulling her crotch closer to mine. We kiss vigorously, as if Mark's watching, and he may be the only reason we're here.

Brittney starts unbuttoning my shirt and I lean forward to help her pull it off my shoulders. I lean the seat back, giving us more room, and she pulls my undershirt over my head.

Our carnal need for one another slows as "Screaming Infidelities" starts to play and Brittney turns the stereo up. I lift her blouse off and her skin quickly pimples in the cool breeze. She leans forward, pressing her bare breasts against me and I wrap my arms around her as we kiss.

I can see her figure in the faint light from the stereo.

He large breasts are still young and perky.

She stares into my eyes and I'm unsure of what to do next.

I've heard so many horror stories about guys that fuck chicks while they're drunk and then get accused of rape later, and even though I hate his guts, Mark's still her boyfriend.

But what kind of a guy would turn down this kind of opportunity?

To lose his virginity at an infamous make-out spot in the front seat of a car?

As far as I know, Brittney knows I'm a virgin.

While I sit contemplating my choices and their consequences, she senses my hesitation.

"Let's stay here for a while," she says, slipping off my lap. The song fades into another. "Jesus, it's getting fucking hot," she continues to complain, kicking off her shoes, followed by her pants.

Her skin is no longer pimpled. It's glazed with sweat and I can smell the liquor on her.

I follow suit, kicking off my boots and sliding off my pants. Brittney glances over at me and we both lounge in our underwear.

"It's such a great view from up here. It almost looks beautiful if you try and forget all the bullshit," she says after an awkward silence.

She lifts her feet onto my lap and I massage them as she stares out the windshield. She lights a clove from a pack hiding in her glove compartment and I take out a Marlboro. We're in a world all our own, a world where none of my rules or fears should matter but do.

We continue sitting in silence, drinking and smoking. There's so much I want to say to her but she seems so content with the silence. Her bottle's two-thirds gone when I finally reach halfway through mine. My mind is spinning. I feel everything around me losing equilibrium and I scream inside because I can't control it.

"I have to pee," Brittney finally says and we both laugh.

She starts rummaging through the glove compartment for something to wipe with.

"Here, take this," I offer, handing her my undershirt.

She smiles warmly, takes it, and steps out of the car.

She closes the door behind her and I watch as she stumbles along the dirt, barefoot. I close my eyes and lay my head back. In the distance I can hear the faint dribble of urine. She returns to the car after a few minutes and sits with the door open, one leg outside. She tosses her head back against the headrest.

"God, I'm so drunk," she mumbles, her eyes closed and her body lifeless.

I steal the opportunity to look her over in the light and I glance down at her panties. They're cotton and thin, probably from too many washes, and I can see her pubic hair.

She's nicely shaved into a small triangle and even though it's not exactly funny, I start giggling.

Brittney opens her eyes, sees me staring, and pulls her leg in, closing the door.

"What's so funny?" she asks, looking at me angrily in the sudden darkness.

"Nothing. I was just thinking about how I heard you pee," I lie and it seems sufficient because she starts to laugh too.

Her anger is quickly gone and she looks at me with that familiar smile that stops my blood.

"You know, I've always liked you. You're so funny," she says between laughs, placing a hand on my thigh.

Her fingers are warm and send chills down my spine.

"I didn't know that. I've had a thing for you for years," I respond, placing a hand on top of hers.

"I know," she answers back, turning her gaze from me and staring back out at the city lights.

She doesn't say anything else, just continues to stare.

"Well, why didn't we ever do anything about it?" I finally ask.

I didn't mean for the words to actually come out but the tequila's loosened my consciousness as well as my jaw. Brittney thinks to herself for a moment and finally looks at me again, running her fingers through her hair.

"I don't know. I guess the timing has always been wrong," she says with a shrug and I know that's true.

I've longed for her for years but we've never been single at the same time. Whenever I felt the courage to say something, there was always someone in my way and the fact that I wasted time dating other girls when I could have had her breaks my heart.

"And plus, if anything ever happened and we broke up, it would ruin our friendship," she continues, averting her eyes.

"Nothing like that could ever happen... will ever happen," I say quickly, looking at her with determination.

She doesn't respond or even look at me. She stares down at our interlaced fingers. I know she's thinking about Mark and what she'd be doing with him and I want to scream *Choose me! Pick me! Let me make you happy!*

I want to be selfish for one minute and take her away from everyone else.

"I think we should run away," I say instead, the tequila still slowing my thinking process. "We can start tomorrow. We'll sell all of our stuff and just leave. We can travel and get odd jobs along the way." I sound ridiculous but she smiles anyway.

"I've always wanted to travel. We could see the world," she responds, almost excited about my proposal. "Mark isn't going anywhere. If I stay with him, we'll probably end up living with his parents. I need something else."

We sit in silence for a while and all I want to do is hold her.

I want to take her home and make love to her.

Then I want to wake up tomorrow and leave forever.

I don't think she'll ever leave though. She loves the comfort of this place, of this life.

The CD's still on repeat and we've heard it three times already. The breeze is picking up, blowing hard through our windows. Without saying anything, I stand up through the sunroof, pulling Brittney with me.

The wind blows straight into our eyes, running tears down our cheeks and drowning out our laughter.

We may not be able to leave everything behind but this moment, this moment of joy and childish dreaming, is ours.

We kiss like we did earlier, holding each other. It means more to me now because I know that she wants me, has always wanted me, and is here with me instead of Mark.

We spend the entire night under the stars, Brittney straddling me again in the front seat. She lays her bare chest against mine.

Before she falls asleep, she whispers in my ear, "When we have sex, I can only cum when I'm on top."

I can't stop thinking about her words and I stay awake to watch the sunrise on the horizon before us.

FIVE

Brittney doesn't say a word to me in the morning. She remains quiet the entire way home, only breaking the silence to yawn and stretch. It's nearly eight o'clock when I pull up in front of my apartment and she slides across into the driver's seat when I get out. We kiss lightly on the lips and she gives me a half-hearted goodbye, leaving without a second glance. I hope she's only in such a mood because of the Goldschlager.

Tawny and Jared have already left and my sheets are again thrown to the floor. The front door's unlocked and my key's on a note on the counter.

> We woke up early. We're out to breakfast and then
> an early movie.
> We're at Denny's if you get home in time.
> XO, T&J

The handwriting is unmistakably Tawny's, messy and feminine. I crumple it up and toss it in the trashcan. I wouldn't mind spending time with them but my head's splitting and my feet can no longer carry me. I fight jealous feelings because I know they're unreasonable. They have every right to spend time alone together.

I smoke a cigarette while watching MTV and fall asleep as the sun starts to rise higher in the sky.

I wake shortly before three and take a shower. Brittney has to work and I want to call and see if she's feeling well enough to. I decide to take her flowers and leave them at the restaurant instead. I quickly stop at the grocery store and pick up a bouquet of red roses and two packs of Marlboros.

Only Dana is there when I show up at three thirty.

"Do you work tonight?" she asks and then notices the flowers. "Who're those for?"

"Brittney," is all I say and walk to the office.

I sit at the desk and pull a piece of paper from the printer. She'll be arriving at four o'clock and like the child I often times feel like, I want to be gone before she shows up. I stare at the paper for a moment, unsure of what to write.

Would a thank you be too forward?

Do I want to tell her to dump Mark?

26

Or should I leave the decision solely up to her and not influence it at all?

> *Dear Brittney,*
>
> *I had a great time last night and I hope you enjoyed it as well. I just want you to know that I really do have feelings for you. I regret having never told you and I wish I had the balls a long time ago to do what we did last night. I know you love Mark, or at least I think you do, and I'd never want to do anything to destroy that. So, whatever you choose, I'll have to be happy with it. No matter what, I'm still your friend.*
>
> *Love, Jason*

I stare at the letter, not happy with it. I want to rip it up and rewrite it.

You have to go with your first choice because spontaneity is rarely wrong.

Or at least I think.

I fold it, place the flowers on top, and walk out. I say goodbye to Dana, who still looks at me funny. As I pull out of the driveway, Brittney drives in wearing her sunglasses, waving at me suspiciously.

She never thanks me for the flowers. I work with her the following weekend and she doesn't say more than five words to me.

Maybe she's still torn about what to do, I tell myself, childishly hoping for a miracle.

Mark shows up towards the end of her shift and they have dinner at the bar. She laughs at his jokes and kisses him affectionately, squashing all my dreams of ever having her.

I haven't heard from Tawny in a week when she finally calls me. Her parents have relatives in town and she's being forced to spend time with them. That also means that she's had to go a week without seeing Jared. It's nearly ten in the morning when she calls me and having already called Jared, they both want to go to the beach. So like always, I volunteer to drive.

"I'll pick you guys up at eleven," I tell her, lighting my morning cigarette.

"Good, and don't be late," she insists, hanging up.

I slowly get out of bed and walk naked into the living room. I worked a wedding reception last night and I still stink like beer and cake. I turn on MTV and walk into the kitchen to make coffee. I yawn as I turn the faucet on and I barely hear a knock on the front door. I quickly pour the water into the brewer, switch it on, and hurry to answer it. Whoever it is bangs again, louder this time.

I peak through the hole and see my sister, Janine. I quickly grab a blanket off the futon, shouting, "Give me a sec!" while wrapping it around my waist.

She's standing there impatiently, wearing her sunglasses and gym clothes. Her hair's nice and pulled back, obvious that she was on her way.

Janine's four years older than me, very health conscious, and always ready to criticize other people for not taking better care of themselves.

"Hey little bro. I just wanted to stop by and see your new place," she says with a forced smile, stepping passed me and looking down at my attire.

I close the door behind her and lean my weight against it, waiting for the onslaught.

"Very nice," she practically scolds, taking off her glasses and looking around my small dark space.

"Yeah, well, I can't afford a place as nice as yours," I defend myself, quickly walking into the other room to put on some clothes.

"Eventually," is all she says and I can hear the smirk on her face.

She moved out of our mother's house shortly before I did and part of me thinks she resents me for it. She'll be graduating from law school in a year and then she'll be marrying her fiancé Heath, a criminal justice major and prison guard.

"Well, I like it. It fits you," she says, sitting down on one of the stools in the kitchen.

I pull on a pair of shorts and hurry back to the kitchen. The coffee's nearly done

"Want a cup?" I ask, grabbing myself one from the cupboard.

"You know I don't drink that shit!" she scowls, staring at me as I light another cigarette. "And I can't believe you're still smoking! Did you know mom quit?" she asks with an actual hint of joy in her voice.

I haven't talked to my mother since my graduation but I have been curious about how she's been.

"Her birthday's coming up in a couple weeks. I was wondering if you had anything planned?" Janine asks, drinking some iced tea from the bottle she brought in with her.

I've thought about throwing a surprise party, just another excuse to get drunk.

"Yeah, I think we should throw her a big party! Hell, you only turn forty once, right? We can invite all our friends and a couple of hers. It'll be fun," I respond, anticipation actually beginning to build.

"Did you know Brian moved in with her?" Janine continues immediately after me, looking down at the counter and instantly bursting my bubble.

"When?" I ask, shocked.

"Right after you moved out," she continues, knowing I won't be happy.

"Why!?"

"She said she was lonely without us. She said she needed someone else there with her."

"Jesus Christ, is she certifiable? If she were so lonely I would've bought her a fucking monkey! That guy's an asshole!" I fume as I finally fill my coffee cup.

I've always hated my mother's choice in men and the latest is no exception.

I glance up at the clock and remember that Tawny will soon be waiting for me.

"Sorry, but I have to get ready. I'm going to the beach with Jared and Tawny," I continue, not offering an invitation.

"Really?" she asks, sounding disappointed. "Have you fucked her yet?" she proceeds, making me uncomfortable like she always does when she talks about sex.

"No, I haven't. She and Jared are kind of a thing," I sneer, quickly finishing my cup of coffee and pouring another.

"Oh well. Eventually. One of these days you'll get your cherry popped," she says encouragingly, patting me on the shoulder.

I want to pull away. I want to cower.

I promise to call, then quickly push her out the door. We've never been too physical about our affection for one another and I can't remember the last time I told her I loved her.

The clock now says ten-thirty and I know I'm going to be late.

I finish dressing in the Jeep, pulling on my shirt and sandals. My contacts are dry and itchy and I want to scratch them. I haven't taken them out for a week and I can feel the calcium starting to build. My sunglasses help shield them from the sun but do little against the breeze coming in through my open window.

I roll into the McDonald's parking lot at eleven-fifteen. Tawny and Jared are sitting on the tailgate of his beat-up pickup truck that's parked next to her old Toyota. She's wearing her sunglasses but I can see her forehead wrinkle into a frown as I pull up.

"I know. Get in," I say with a smile, leaning out my window.

The smile doesn't warrant a response from Tawny and they both climb into the backseat, leaving me by myself. Jared's carrying his skim board and he drops it behind the backbench.

"You're late, fucker!" Tawny finally says as I pull out onto the street and I have absolutely no argument.

The hot summer air blasts us after I get on the freeway. I have yet to take the top off and with the windows rolled down I can barely hear my own thoughts. The wind is a good excuse to stay quiet because a conversation would be too difficult.

Tawny never gives up on something easily and her silence is my punishment, so I let her simmer down. I can barely hear the new Incubus tape I made, even with the stereo on full blast. Tawny and Jared don't waste any time and they start making out, free from the restraint of seat belts.

I've always enjoyed driving and today is no exception. The rolling hills along the freeway are green and there are surprisingly few cars out for a weekday. The wind gradually becomes cooler and I can taste the salt in the air. Within an hour I can see the ocean in the distance, vast and blue. The sea shines, welcoming us.

"I brought my skim board, if you want to give it a try," Jared reminds me as I finally pull into the beachfront parking lot.

There isn't a cloud in sight and the beach is nearly deserted. Except for a handful of surfers, the ocean is completely ours. We gather our things and Tawny takes us both by the hand as we walk out onto the warm sand. We skip and laugh like little children. After dropping our things down a safe distance from the wake, Jared wastes no time taking off his shirt and sandals and running to the water.

"I wanted to leave without you! You promised!" Tawny says to me as she strips off her clothes.

She's wearing a dark purple bikini that beautifully accents her tanned skin.

"I know. I'm sorry. It won't happen again," I reassure her, taking my shirt off as well.

The sun instantly starts to cook my pale skin. I wish I'd brought sunscreen.

"I won't hold my breath," she cuts me off, pulling her sunglasses back over her eyes.

She turns and walks away from me, sinking the point like a knife.

The air becomes warmer the higher the sunrises. Jared and I spend two hours taking turns with the skim board. I fall flat on my back my first try, smashing my head into the soft sand. Tawny's laugh is all I can hear over the crashing surf and she stands watching us from the sand.

Jared drops the board with ease, steps onto it gracefully, and slides across the water as if he were weightless. I wade back and forth through the surf, admiring him and jealously wishing I had a fraction of his talent. A talent that comes from self-confidence and pride; two things I have very little of.

I continue falling and right when I think my ass might not be able to handle another blow, I finally stay on the board. It doesn't last long and I quickly sink into the soft sand, but both Jared and Tawny cheer me on. I can feel my face blush with embarrassment and Jared slaps me on the back.

"Finally!" they both shout and I continue practicing.

Tawny leads Jared by the hand back towards our belongings and I'm once again left by myself. I continue for a while longer then give up. I got up once and stayed on my feet, which is completely satisfactory for me. Giving up is in my nature and the fact that I actually attempted this for two hours is practically unheard of.

Tawny spreads out a blanket and they're sprawled out by the time I get back up on the sand. Jared's on his back and Tawny's tucked against his chest, resting her head on his bicep. I lay my towel a short distance from them and can watch them without being seen. I lie on my stomach with my face resting on its side. I can feel the jealousy now more than ever, wishing I was either of them, and I can't help but think of all the people I could have brought with me. Brittney instantly comes to mind and I'm pained to think that I turned her down.

I wake suddenly on my back and the sun is much lower in the sky. I've slept for an hour and my companions are no longer on their blanket. I look around frantically at first, disoriented. My skin burns, my face feels tight and my brain hurts. I finally notice them out in the water and I stand to get a better view. Jared stands waist deep in the water and Tawny's holding onto him tightly, her legs wrapped around his waist. They kiss slowly, romantically, and the sun lights them up like that scene in *From Here to Eternity*.

I take my time walking out to the water, being sure to catch their attention first. I wade out far enough to sit down and the cool water sooths my shoulders as the tides rush in.

"Hey there sleeping beauty!" Jared yells as they notice me.

He walks towards me with Tawny flung over his shoulder and she screams and laughs as the water splashes up at her.

"We're fucking starving! Let's get some lunch!" she shouts between bouts of laughter.

Jared sets her down on the sand and we race back to our belongings. We quickly grab everything and race to the parking lot, dragging towels and t-shirts behind us. We don't bother putting anything back on except our sandals and as we pile in Jared starts to tell us about a local fish market he knows of.

"Just pull out and turn left," he directs me as I push into first gear.

We ride along the coast for a short distance, watching the sun as it picks up speed, racing towards the horizon. I find one open parking spot in front of the restaurant and we can clearly see the ocean across the busy highway. Tawny finds us a table while Jared and I wait in line for fresh fish and chips.

The last open table is under a canopy and we can watch the sunset as we eat. Like a watercolor painting that envelops all the senses, it's one of those evenings that leave an indelible mark on the memory. A memory that can quickly be brought back by a familiar smell or sound.

We talk loudly and laugh at each other's jokes. The round table is the perfect size for us and we all sit at even distances from one another. Jared tells us a story and Tawny laughs uncontrollably.

"Well, my friend went to bed and I wasn't tired, so I decided to stay up and watch some TV in the living room," he begins, talking through bites of fish. "That show *Real Sex* was on HBO and I figured, what the hell? So, I took my dick out and started jerking off," he continues, acting out the motions in front of him.

Tawny's beside herself, snorting and choking.

"How old were you?" she manages to ask.

"About fifteen," Jared says after thinking for a second, which makes Tawny laugh even harder.

"To make a long story short, I'm getting close now. I mean, my parents didn't have HBO so my access to porn was very limited. All of a sudden, I hear something and there's my friend's dad, standing in the kitchen getting something out of the fridge. He kind of stares for a second, shakes his head, and walks away."

"What did you do?" I ask, not quite as entertained as Tawny.

"Nothing. I went limp and went back to bed."

We all laugh at his story and share more embarrassing, sexually charged tales. I suddenly realize something I hadn't told them and blurt it out faster than I can think.

"I almost fucked Brittney," I say and both Tawny and Jared stare at me. "About a week ago. That night at the pool hall. We ended up driving out into the hills over the reservoir and we spent the night there."

I quickly push pieces of fish into my mouth, waiting for responses.

"What about Mark?" Tawny asks, obviously hurt that I hadn't already told her.

"He pissed her off and went home early. God, I wanted to have sex with her so bad. What's my problem?!"

"Well, why didn't you?" Jared finally asks, cutting into the conversation.

"Because he's a pussy," Tawny answers for me, leaving me no room to respond. "You should have! You could have lost your cherry with a hot girl in a perfect situation! It would have been something to brag about!"

I know it's all true.

"I was afraid. So many bad things that could have happened were running through my mind. We haven't even talked about it! I brought her flowers to work the next day and she didn't even acknowledge them! God, I even put a love letter on them!" I confess, dropping my face down onto the table, embarrassed. "I told her that I respected any decision she made, but I really just want her to break up with Mark and be with me!" I continue to mumble pathetically.

"Don't beat yourself up about it and stop being such a pussy. I plan on helping you lose your virginity this summer, even if it's the last thing I do before I leave," Tawny encourages me as she lifts my face off the table.

She takes me by the hands and continues to lift my spirits.

"You need to learn to be assertive and take what you want. She wouldn't have turned you down if you had tried. You just had to take that first step."

I take my eyes off her face long enough to glance over at Jared. He's quietly eating his food, obviously ignoring her.

The sun's completely dropped beyond the sea as we make our trek home. The sky above us is dark red and orange and the cool night air is refreshing as it rushes in on us. Tawny and Jared quickly fall asleep, cuddling in the back seat. I find it strange that she pushes me so hard to lose my virginity when in fact Jared's still a virgin. Maybe that's the excitement. Apparently she hasn't pushed him yet.

All good things come in time.

SIX

I have had very few friends like Tawny. Other than the people I've gone to school with most of my life, Jenny Jones has known me since I was four years old. We met in church shortly after moving into the neighborhood and my mother helped us exchange phone numbers. I've always teased her because her name sounds like a porn star's.

Shortly after *My Best Friends Wedding* came out we made a promise to each other that if we weren't married by the time we turned thirty we'd marry each other. It was a promise that Tawny and I would have never made but since Jenny and I were childhood sweethearts I figured it couldn't hurt.

In all honesty though, I knew I'd never marry her and secretly hoped someone else would first.

After Sunday school, we attended kindergarten, elementary school, junior high, and high school together. We never went further with our childhood crush. I've always known that she harbors strong feelings for me. Keeping her at a short distance is my only way of not hurting her. I don't feel the same way.

When Jenny calls me nearly a month after our high school graduation, I'm pleasantly surprised. After fourteen years, we've never gone more than a day without at least talking to each other on the phone. I haven't made an effort to call her either, so I can't hold it against her. She's excited and wants to see me and offers to pick me up for dinner.

Over bread sticks and diet soda, Jenny talks quickly and barely leaves room to breathe. She looks as good as she ever has, maybe a little thinner, with a hint of something new in her voice. Her piercing blue eyes and long brown hair are by far her greatest attributes and I can't help but feel guilty for not calling.

"I've met someone," she exclaims, the smile on her face widening. "The night of our graduation," she continues, her eyes growing larger and larger.

Finding a compatible mate has always been a problem for her and I've served as a safety net in case Mr. Right never came along.

"Wow! That's great!" I say after a moment of hesitation.

That same feeling of jealously I get when I spend too much time with Jared and Tawny starts to rise to the surface and I ignore it as best I can.

"My parents brought me here after the ceremony. They insisted I spend time with family because my grandparents were up from the valley," she continues, holding my hand across the table. "I want you to meet him so badly. You'd love him and your opinion means so much more than anyone else's. He's a soup cook and came up to the table to ask for my phone number. I was surprised my dad didn't shoot him!" she finishes and falls silent, waiting for my response.

Her father's never been a big fan of me and was probably thrilled with the prospect of another potential son-in-law.

"I'm happy for you," I respond as the waiter returns to our table with food.

"When you get the chance," Jenny tells him after he sets down our plates. "Could you tell Jose Jenny is here to see him?"

The server frowns and leaves without a response. The name Jose sticks out like a lightning rod and I bite my tongue.

"He's so good to me. He's from Mexico and has lived here for about ten years," she quickly adds, probably to keep me from asking the obvious.

"Wow," is all I can say and I feel stupid for it.

Her father's also not one that I'd think would be okay with his daughter's involvement in a biracial relationship.

From where I'm sitting I can see the swinging door that enters the kitchen. Soon after our server enters, another man exits. He's tall and thin with much darker skin and jet-black hair. He has a young face with soft features, not at all the 'Mexican' I had pictured. He glances around the dining room slowly, notices us, and starts to walk in our direction. Jenny stands before he reaches our table and greets him with a warm embrace.

His walk is slow but confident, with a faint swagger to it. He greets Jenny with a kiss on the lips and a smile. Nothing obscene, but quicker than I would have. She turns back to me, her arm in his, and I stand to shake his hand.

"Jason, this is Jose," she says, the smile on her face widened to the breaking point.

"Jenny's told me so much about you," he says while shaking my hand.

His hands are large but soft, with manicured nails. I glance down at them quickly, surprised by the softness of his grip and the limpness of his wrist. There's a slight accent in his voice that he hides well and he speaks slowly, choosing his words.

The three of us sit back down at the table and I finally find the words I was looking for.

"I'm really happy to meet you. I'm sorry it's taken a while, I've been busy," I say with a smile as sincere as I can muster.

They smile back at me and then at each other. Jenny holds tightly onto his arm and he kisses her again, this time on the forehead.

"I get off work soon. Do you two want to come over and hang out for a little bit?" he asks after a short uncomfortable silence.

"Yeah, that would be fun," Jenny answers for both of us.

I respond with a nod. Jose leaves us to finish his shift and the server brings our check. I pay for the meal with a large wad of one-dollar bills and we wait outside for Jose, smoking Marlboro's.

We smoke three each before he finally comes out.

I'm cramped in Jenny's coupe, my knees tight against the dashboard. The convertible top's down and she follows Jose's junker pickup back to his house. The night air is warm and refreshing as it rushes through my hair.

"I need to tell you something important," Jenny begins, her voice full of worry and hesitation.

I look at her, waiting for the news. She glances at me quickly and puts her eyes back on the road, the hesitation even more obvious.

"What?" I ask, almost annoyed.

"Jose's bisexual," she says quickly, falling silent and cringing as if I'm going to yell at her. "He recently got out of a long term relationship with a guy and wanted to try something new," she proceeds. "It's not a rebound thing, it really isn't. I think we're falling in love."

I have no idea where to begin. As a logical person I want to intervene and warn, but as a friend, I quietly support.

"I've talked to his family on the phone and his mother cried when she found out he was dating a girl. She was so overjoyed and wouldn't stop telling him to marry me.

My mind's racing and I can't stop on one idea. This is not the Jenny I've known most of my life. An irrational and naive girl has replaced the cautious and timid Jenny. I want to question his legality, warn about his motives and shake sense into her. Right when I think I can continue, she drops another bomb on me.

"There's something else I have to tell you," she begins again when I show no signs of responding. "I lost my virginity to him."

My chin drops.

I feel like I'm the last virgin on the planet. When we were thirteen, we made a pact with our church youth group that we were all going to wait until marriage to have sex. I'm left standing alone, with my dick in one hand and a porn magazine in the other.

"Wow..." I lie, "That's great news... just give me a second to absorb it all."

We stop abruptly in front of Jose's house and I'm pulled back into the reality of where we are.

Jenny closes the top on her car and we get out. The neighborhood is one of the oldest, probably the first in the area and the duplex Jose calls home was definitely the first built. He lives in the back half and his truck is already parked near the garage. His front door stands open and Jenny leads the way inside. I follow her in through the kitchen and the fluorescent lights are still flickering to life. The inside of the building's almost as run down as the outside and the furnishings aren't much to brag about. Jose greets us in the living room.

"Please, make yourselves at home," he says as he exits down a hallway to his bedroom. I sit on a couch next to Jenny.

"I'm sorry for springing all of that on you so suddenly," she tells me under her breath. "He's a nice guy, you'll see."

Jose returns after a few short moments, wearing a pair of blue jeans and a t-shirt one size too small for his thin frame. His hair's wet and slicked back and he seems much more at ease. Before sitting in a chair across from us he turns on the CD player, which starts playing Madonna's *Immaculate Collection*. He turns her down to a whisper and the music's barley audible.

"Jack and Cokes?" he asks the moment his ass hit's the chair and he's back up, headed into the kitchen.

We both mumble our approval and he quickly returns carrying three glasses. The whiskey's cheap and tastes like shit and the cola's not Coke. We sit quietly, sipping.

"So, Jenny tells me you two went to high school together," Jose starts, finally breaking the ice, the ice I was terrified to step on for fear of never finding the surface again.

"Yes. Actually, Jenny and I've known each other for a very long time," I tell him, looking at her and smiling.

"Yeah, it's been like fourteen years. We used to play Ewoks on the playground," she continues for me, grabbing him by the hand.

She talks like Drew Barrymore did in *E.T.* and I can't help but find her adorable.

"Jason was my very first boyfriend. His mom helped us exchange phone numbers. We've been inseparable ever since," she says, placing her other hand on my knee.

That sentence is only half true; she hasn't called me in nearly a month.

We sit quietly until the silence becomes awkward.

I quickly down my cheap drink and Jose runs to get me another. Jenny does the same and before we know it, round four comes along and we're wasted. I become more lucid, more comfortable, and my conversation becomes more at ease, less strained.

"So, do you have a girlfriend?" Jose asks, the whiskey bringing his accent closer to the surface.

He's sitting on the couch with us now and has an arm wrapped around Jenny's shoulders. She leans into him and has her feet propped up on my knees.

"No, you got my number one girl. I'm still fishing," I respond, smiling widely at Jenny.

My face burns from the alcohol and the heat and the embarrassment. I'm starting to feel stifled, so I motion to the window.

"Do you mind?" I ask, standing up.

Jose shakes his head and I quickly slide the window open. The cool air that rushes in chills my arms and I pull off my t-shirt. Sweat has pressed my undershirt to my flesh and I pull it free. He looks at me and I avoid his eyes.

"Feel better?" he asks, smiling.

"Much," is all I can muster, sitting down and laying my head back.

My legs are hot and my jeans are drenched with sweat. I feel like a whore in church; I didn't know I was this drunk. I open my eyes wide enough to see Jose kiss Jenny's neck and she replies with a giggle. I empty my glass and when I stand to get another we hear voices enter the kitchen.

Our collective attention turns to see two men walk in through the dining room. They're both older, in their mid forties. One's white and the other's Hispanic.

"You two are home early!" Jose says, standing quickly and a bit frantically. "Jason, I'd like to introduce you to my roommates," he continues. He turns and waves me forward.

I step towards them, leaving Jenny alone on the couch.

"This is Greg and Miguel," Jose announces proudly, his accent completely present.

"It's really nice to meet you," Greg says with a broad smile.

He's almost as tall as me but much thinner.

"Nice to meet you," Miguel says, shaking my hand. His accent's thicker than Jose's.

"Is he...?" Greg begins to ask Jose, pointing directly at me.

"Oh no! He's a good friend of mine," Jenny finally speaks as she stands.

"Oh well!" Greg whines, pouting. He leans in close and whispers, "If you were gay, I'd gladly teach you a couple things."

I laugh, completely wordless. I was just propositioned by a man old enough to be my father and everyone around me finds it funny. My head's rocking back and forth and I can't find the humor in it.

"I hope we're not interrupting anything. The club was dead so we decided to come home early," Miguel says, eyeing me suspiciously and holding Greg's hand tightly.

"You kids have a good night now," Greg says, leading Miguel down the hallway.

They whisper and laugh like school girls and are soon out of sight. We can hear Madonna in the sudden silence, moaning like a virgin.

"Well, I need a refill. Anyone?" I ask.

Jenny and Jose hand me their glasses.

The kitchen's small and badly lit and I stumble around for the two simple ingredients. For every ice cube I get in the glasses, I drop two on the floor. I'm afraid if I bend down to pick them up I'll eat shit. I was right about the whiskey too; the plastic bottle has a label written in Spanish. I fill the glasses too high and spill down my arms as I struggle with all three simultaneously. I stop in the doorway to the living room, suddenly uncomfortable and out of place.

Jenny and Jose are kissing vigorously on the couch where I was just sitting. Jenny's hips are turned towards him and she has a leg wrapped around his thighs. He gropes her up and down, from her tits to her ass, and moans while jamming his tongue in her mouth. She, on the other hand, gently rubs his neck with one hand while her other has a firm hold of his cock through his jeans. Their eyes are closed and they don't see me, so I simply watch. My pulse is beginning to race and my dick's throbbing. I want to turn away, act like I never walked in on this, but the moment I go to turn, Jenny's eyes open.

She doesn't stop when they meet mine. Her mesmerizing blue eyes hold me by the balls and she stares at me longingly, continuing to rub Jose. His lips leave her mouth and start kissing her neck and then her chest. She stares at me and I know what she's thinking. She's thinking about me and she's thinking about my cock. I'm so hard now she can see the bulge growing in my baggy jeans.

I clear my throat, my threshold reached, and Jose turns from her breasts to face me.

"Here you go," I say, handing over the drinks.

I sit quickly, hoping to hide my painful erection.

"Thank you," Jenny says, her eyes still focused on me.

She sips gratefully, pushing her hair back from her neck. Her legs are still wrapped around Jose's thighs and she makes no effort to move them. I've never seen Jenny like this; I've never seen this side of her. I squeeze myself into the cushions, as far as possible from them.

Again, we sit in uncomfortable silence. I feel like a lost tourist in a foreign country. I sip my cocktail and listen to a barely audible dance track on the stereo. My head continues to spin and I close my eyes. The warm summer breeze is continuing to blow and it refreshes my burning cheeks.

"I like this song," I exclaim before I realize I'm thinking it, trying to hear "Like a Prayer."

"Yeah, it is a really good song to dance to," Jose replies, his voice low and calm.

Jenny stifles a giggle and I open my eyes.

"Jason's one of the best dancers I know! I loved dancing with him at all the school dances!" she manages to say, standing up. "But you should have seen him when he first tried!" she continues, the laughter falling out like rocks.

She sways back and forth awkwardly, offbeat with bent knees. Jose laughs at her imitation of me and I can't help but chuckle.

"Well, show us how you dance now," Jose exclaims, the smile on his face more expressive and full of desire than I've ever seen.

"Yeah, get up. You only danced with me once at prom!" Jenny agrees, pulling on my wrists.

I reluctantly stand, slowly. I brace myself for a moment and wait for the blood to finish its trip back to my head. Jose uses the remote to turn the music up and restarts the song.

Jenny pulls me in close and our crotches touch. I bend my knees enough for our thighs to rub against one another and we fit like a jigsaw puzzle. She wraps her arms loosely around my neck and I place my hands on the small of her back. We sway slowly at first but the pace becomes more passionate, more intense. She leans her head back with her eyes closed and instinctively I lean in to kiss the spot on her neck where it creeps onto her chest. She leans forward into me and lifts a leg to wrap around my thigh. I hold her up by her ass, my other hand running through the hair at the back of her neck.

My mind races and the animal instinct that pursues this pleasure is galloping free. Before I can say anything, Jenny reaches back and pulls Jose to his feet, who doesn't hesitate for a moment. He walks into her, pressing his body against her back. I step away, still dancing, but at a distance. She sways her hips into Jose and he kisses her neck where I had and whispers in her ear. His hands slide up and down her torso and one finally rests on a breast.

I'm nervous again and unsure of what to do. I close my eyes and my thighs continue to lightly brush against Jenny's. The song comes to an end and silence, deafening and terrifying silence, ensues.

I open my eyes to find Jenny and Jose staring at me. I look back at them imploringly.

"You don't have to be anywhere tonight or... tomorrow morning, do you?" Jenny asks. Jose's arm's still wrapped tightly around her.

"No," is all I can say.

"Jenny told me you were still a virgin," Jose finally speaks, looking at me strangely, almost longingly.

I smile and shrug weakly.

My physical actions don't come close to what I'm going through internally. I have a pain in my chest. Figures start to dance before me and I ask myself *What are they getting at?!*

I know the answer but I don't want to hear it.

"I have to pee," I blurt out and quickly turn.

I stumble to the hallway, almost falling twice before I find the comfort of the small commode. I lock the door behind me and lean against it, confused, scared, and strangely aroused.

I want sex, I need sex, I want sex, and I need sex.

My hunger for fucking is so extreme right here and now I want to jerk off and squirt cum everywhere.

But having Jose look at me the way he did sends chills down my spine, chills that I can't quite understand.

I turn the sink on to splash water on my face.

This will not be a pussy tag team situation.

Jenny wants me. Does Jose?

I suddenly remember late summer nights with Brandon and Jenny. When we were in junior high and we'd try staying up all night. We'd lay in my bed, the three of us, joking and laughing, never quite making it to sunrise. Our innocence was never interrupted and we never crossed lines we could have so easily, too early.

A low knock interrupts my thoughts and I ask who it is.

"It's me," Jenny's voice whispers. "I'm coming in."

She slowly opens the door. Her expression's worried and full of genuine concern. Before I have a chance to say anything, she speaks.

"You don't have to do this if it makes you uncomfortable Jason. I love you and I always will, no matter what happens tonight. But this is something I've always wanted," she ends with a whisper, stepping close to me.

The bright vanity lights illuminate her eyes and they paralyze me. I pull her into me. I kiss her hard. My lips and tongue take turns making love to her mouth.

Jenny 's always wanted me but knows she can't have me. Despite all the voices in my head telling me to stop, I kiss her back. I kiss her deeper and stronger than I've kissed anyone and when we finish, she leads me back into the living room.

Jose's sitting on the couch smoking when we walk out. He smirks when he sees me.

"Well?" he asks, smiling.

"Yeah," Jenny answers, smiling too.

Jose kisses her softly and walks passed us to a closet in the hallway. He returns with a thick blanket and two pillows. Jenny kisses me. She helps Jose unfold the blanket and when everything's arranged, she turns out the light on the end table. We're guided by the light from the kitchen, a soft yellow glow. I'm exhilarated, drunk, and completely helpless.

Jenny starts to undress and then Jose. I kick off my sandals and drop my jeans, leaving my boxers intact. After I pull off my undershirt and let it fall to the floor, I lie on the blanket next to Jenny. Her arms are outstretched, one around Jose's shoulders and the other around mine. We lie there for a moment in our underwear, quietly smiling and anticipating what's about to happen.

Jose leans in and kisses Jenny. He rests a hand on her abdomen and the other holds the back of her head. She turns to face him, leaving me unsure and completely self-aware. I kiss her shoulder and run my hand down her hip to her thigh. The arm that was around my neck is now reaching behind her. She runs the hand slowly in front of me and grips me through the fabric. She holds me tight and strokes me slowly, pushing all the breath from my lungs.

Jose reaches behind Jenny and unhooks her bra. While he removes it, I pull her panties off. Jose and I slide out of our underwear and she watches with a smile on her face. Her hand's on me again, this time flesh on flesh. I press myself against her back and my cock is so stiff it hurts.

I reach a hand around and place it on her breast, between her hard nipple and Jose's hairy chest. He pushes a hand in her groin.

The deeper into this I descend, the more my mind becomes clear, warning me to stop. The alcohol's wearing off and I have a conscience I wish I didn't. And as we lie there, our bodies swaying and humping against each other, I feel something.

Not an emotion or a sensation, but a hand.

A strong, large hand tightly gripping my thigh.

I know it is Jose's hand, not Jenny's, and my mind races for an explanation.

If I continue, I'll have sex with Jose.

Do I want that?

Do I want this for my first time?

I feel my body tense and I stop kissing Jenny's shoulder.

"I don't think I can..." I start to whisper, suddenly realizing that my mouth has conjured the words my mind was shouting.

Jenny stops kissing Jose and he pulls his hand off of me. They lie until she turns flat on her back. Jose and I lie parallel to one other. I can see his naked body in the dark, his dark and uncircumcised cock resting a short distance from mine.

"Is everything ok?" Jenny finally asks.

I can hear irritation in her voice and they both stare at me as if I'm crazy.

"I'm sorry. I can't do this... have sex like this," I blurt out, propping myself up on a pillow.

"It's ok. We don't have to have sex. We can... do other stuff," Jose says this time. He reaches his hand back across, placing it on my hip. His thumb massages my pelvic bone while the other four fingers grip the side of my ass.

This is for Jose and this is for Jenny and I'm not ready.

I pull myself free of his grip and stand up.

"Where are you going?" Jenny asks, watching as I collect my clothes off the floor.

"I'm gonna go sleep in the other room. You guys keep doing this, I can't. Not tonight and not like this," I answer, and just like that, I leave the room.

I find the bedroom in the dark. It's a large room with two full size beds in it. In the nearest bed I can see two figures sleeping and I walk quietly passed them to the other bed. I drop my clothes on the floor and pull my boxers back on. I slip under the covers and lie completely still. The only noise I hear is my heart pounding in my head.

I can think in my solitude.

42

Should I have stayed?

Does this guy have any diseases?

So many thoughts cloud my mind and chase sleep away. So I stare at the ceiling, aglow from a nearby street lamp.

After what must be an hour, the door creaks. Soft footsteps approach and I can see Jenny standing above me. She sits on the mattress and leans in close.

"You can come out and sleep with us. We're all finished," she whispers, placing a hand on my chest.

"No, I'm good," I answer back awkwardly. "Thanks though."

Jenny hesitates as if she might leave but instead starts pulling the sheets off me.

"Well, I can't leave you like this. You deserve to finish too," she says out loud, pulling the sheet completely off.

She straddles me at the knees and slowly pulls my boxers down. I prop myself on my elbows and watch as she takes me into her mouth, sucking and bobbing.

This is my first blowjob.

The sensation's different than what I've expected. I've seen this so many times in pornos. I've always wanted to know what it felt like.

At the same time though the woman always has that look on her face, that gagging and choking look, that turns me off. I close my eyes and place my head back on the pillow, instinctively running my fingers through her hair. I hold her head as it bobs up and down.

Images flash before my closed eyes.

I imagine cumming on Jenny's face and tits.

I picture her hungrily lapping it up as I ejaculate.

But that unpleasant face with the sunken in cheeks and the eyes that yearn for the hung stud to hurry up come into view.

This goes on for ten minutes until I finally ask her to stop, to give up.

"Are you all right? Did it feel good?" she asks, wiping saliva from her chin.

I can hear doubt in her voice, self-loathing even. I was the one who couldn't cum and she's the one disappointed? That's something I'll never understand.

"Yeah, it felt great. I'm just tired I guess," I lie.

Jenny kisses me quickly and leaves the room without another word.

I lie in bed for two more hours, until the sun starts to rise in the distance. I watch the dust dance in the rays of faint light and finally dress in the pink haze. I walk into the living room and Jenny and Jose are still sleeping. I sit on the couch and light a cigarette, holding an ashtray in one hand. I watch them sleep, listening to them breath. Shortly after I start my second Marlboro Greg comes out of the bedroom. He's shirtless and wearing a pair of black pajama pants. His chest is sunken in and he has a small potbelly.

"Don't worry, you didn't wake me," he says as he walks into the kitchen. "Do you want coffee?" he asks and I answer yes.

Five minutes later he returns with two mugs.

"I just put sugar in it," he says as he sits on the couch next to me.

I say that was perfect and hand him my pack of cigarettes. He slowly takes one out and lights it, watching me as I stare down at Jenny and Jose.

"If you love her, you should tell her," he says, blowing his first puff of smoke into the air.

I simply look back at him, dragging deeply on my cigarette.

seven

We quickly leave after Jenny and Jose finally wake.

I don't say goodbye.

I don't say a word to Jenny and we smoke on the way to my apartment. When I get inside my answering machine's flashing. Janine doesn't think she'll be able to help with my mother's birthday party, a trivial event that slipped my mind.

"I've been so busy with work," she says, an excuse that can be easily interpreted to mean she doesn't give a shit.

So for the last week of June, as it slowly slips away, I'm left with the sole responsibility of the party.

In all honesty the party's more for me than anyone else. My place is way too small for a large gathering and my mother knows my friends. She prides herself on being the 'cool mom,' when in actuality my friends just want to get away with the things their parents won't let them.

And rightfully so.

With four days left before Saturday, I have a lot of shit to do.

I take a shower and brew a pot of coffee. I take out my contacts and put on a pair of broken glasses. I rinse out my favorite mug, chipping crystallized sugar off the bottom. I light a cigarette and sit down at the counter with my little black book.

I call Tawny and she says she'd be glad to come, even help me set up.

I call Michelle and Brandon and they say of course they'd be there.

Rebecca says she'll bring Ty with her.

Even Brittney says she'll be there and I hope that does not include Mark.

I call my friend Karen and she says she'll be there with her boyfriend Kyle. She's another one of my hopeless obsessions. We bussed tables together for a year and like I always seem to, I waited too long to confess my adoration.

Over hamburgers and fries, late Halloween night of our junior year, I told her I wanted to be with her.

"I love you," I blurted out, trying my hardest to be taken seriously dressed as James Dean.

"Oh," she said simply, averting her eyes. She looked amazing as Marilyn Monroe. "I just started seeing someone." We won the prize for best-dressed couple.

I continued eating, as if what I said never really happened. And at the end of our senior year, she moved to Long Beach, following Kyle.

Two cigarettes and three cups of coffee later, I start a list of people my mother would want there, friends of hers.

I call her fat friend Sue, who'll be there with the husband half her size.

My orthodontist Joan says she'd be delighted to come. She became friends with my mom after taking care of my braces for six years.

My mother's best friend Ramona can't make it. The long drive from Lake Arrowhead is too much on her young kids and I completely agree.

I wait until the very end to call Brian, my mom's live in boyfriend, to give him all the details.

As the phone rings, my heart starts racing. I hope he doesn't answer the phone. The longer the phone rings the more I want to hang up.

"Hello?" my mother's voice says just before the answering machine clicks on.

"Hi mom," I say in a typical monotone drawl.

"Hello sweetheart!! It's been so long since you've called!! I was beginning to think you'd forgotten about me," she wails, trying her utmost to unsuccessfully make me feel guilty.

"Sorry. I've been busy," I say even though I wouldn't be able to tell her what's kept me so busy if she'd asked. "Umm, is Brian there? I have to ask him something."

"Oh... sure. Hold on a sec," she hesitates.

My mother acts completely unaware of my disdain for her current lover and is obviously surprised. I hear her call his name and I can also hear his daughter's voice in the background. I silently prepare to make this conversation as short as possible.

"Hello?" he finally says in an awful southern accent. Its origins are unknown; he was born and raised in southern California. I can hear him suck back the chewing tobacco that just dribbled down his chin.

"Hey Brian," is all I can muster, forcing myself to smile.

"Hey there Jason Boy! How ya been?" he responds, the definitive good ol' boy.

"I have to ask you something. Or actually, tell you something. I'm planning a surprise party for my mom's birthday on Saturday and I was hoping to have it over there."

"This is a little late notice, don't you think?" he says after a moment.

I can hear the tobacco rolling around behind his lips.

"I know. I'm sorry. It's her fortieth and I wanted to do something special. Don't worry about any of the booze or food, I'm gonna get everything. I already called all her friends too, so you just need to be there... with your daughter of course."

Her inclusion will smooth any possible problems. I'm negotiating with the man and it isn't even his fucking house! It's more my house than his!!

"Alright then. Just let me know if there's anything I can do to help."

When we hang up I wait to see if my mother might call back but the phone never rings and I'm relieved because the hardest part's over.

The clock says one and I'm drained. I jerk off in bed and take a nap with cum drying on my thighs. I have to work at five.

Tawny comes over early on Saturday. We drive across town to the grocery store Jared works at. The air's abnormally still, the warmth settling around us. After getting a cart and running inside, I tell her about Jenny and Jose.

"I can't believe you," she says, laughing hard. "You had another chance to get laid and you didn't take it? Even though, having sex with them doesn't sound like something to brag about," she continues, still laughing and slapping me on the back.

"Get off my ass," I tell her defensively. "For one, if I had decided to have sex that night I would have been expected to fuck both of them. And for two, who are you to talk? Have you slept with Jared?"

She keeps walking and a small smile starts to spread across her face.

"Not yet," she says after a well thought-out pause.

I throw chicken wings in the cart.

"But I'm sure it will happen soon. I've decided not to push him. He's a virgin too. He's taken all the steps and he only has one left."

The small smile grows the entire width of her face and she puts an arm through mine as we walk along filling the cart.

It's soon overflowing and we can't think of anything else to buy.

Cases of beer.

Bottle after bottle of booze.

Boxes of cheap wine.

Frozen snack foods.

Chips and dips.

Birthday cake.

As we were anticipating, Jared's working behind one of the registers.

"Let's go to number five, that guy's fucking hot!" Tawny says loudly as we walk towards him.

"Ooh, I agree!" I say in a flamboyant voice.

"Good morning," Jared says pleasantly. Tawny smiles flirtatiously, batting her eyes.

"Good morning to you handsome," I say loudly.

Tawny laughs.

The store manager turns from his desk and watches us. Jared starts to fidget nervously as he scans our items. His register beeps loudly as he runs the alcohol and he looks up at me.

"ID please."

I haven't shaved in a week and hopefully my youthful face has a hint of maturity. I pull out my wallet and hand him my driver's license.

"Thanks," he says and continues to scan our items.

I tell him to get me three packs of Marlboros and Tawny starts to complain. The grand total comes in a little over four hundred dollars and I slide my debit card. I will now officially be three hundred and ninety seven dollars overdrawn until Tuesday.

We say goodbye and walk away. Before we step out of the store, Tawny turns and makes the blowjob motion with her hand. She rolls her eyes and pushes her tongue against the inside of her cheek, moaning loudly. Jared starts to laugh uncontrollably and waves us off.

We show up at my mother's house shortly after noon and I barely recognize it. She's been living there for five years and has always been diligent about tidiness. Her garage is now overflowing with boxes and tools and Mike's ridiculously big truck is leaking oil all over the driveway. The lawn I once kept green and trim is now overgrown and browning.

Tawny and I both load up on grocery bags and walk to the front door. After I kick it twice, Brian's daughter Jessica answers. She's an awful spitting image of her father, nine years old and helplessly dressed in Wranglers.

"Hi Jason!" she says with a big smile and I try to hug her without dropping everything.

"Hi. Is your dad here?" I ask, walking inside.

Tawny impatiently follows right behind me. The living room is ransacked and the couches are covered in clean laundry waiting to be folded. Brain's done nothing to help prepare for the party.

"He's outside in the pool," Jessica answers as she sits back on the couch, watching *Scooby-Doo*.

After three trips back to the car, the kitchen counter's completely covered. Surprisingly, this is the cleanest room in the entire house.

I walk outside, completely unprepared to talk with my least favorite person.

The 'pool' is actually more like a large bucket. It came with the house, is above ground, four feet deep, and only fifteen feet wide. Brian's floating in the middle on a pink raft in nothing other but a pair of white briefs and a cowboy hat pulled down over his eyes.

"Umm, Brian..." I say loudly before we get too close.

He slowly lifts the hat off his face and squints at us in the harsh light. His skin's red from too much sun and he looks much older than he really is.

"Well howdy," he says with that annoying twang, the ever-present dip shoved behind his bottom lip.

He slips off the raft and into the water, placing the hat atop his little head.

"I just wanted to let you know we're here and we're gonna start getting ready."

Tawny is silently standing by my side.

"And this is my best friend, Tawny."

She waves.

"It's a pleasure to meet you," he says, climbing the ladder out of the pool.

His ass crack is completely visible as are his genitals. We can see his shriveled dick and patch of pubic hair as he walks towards us, hand outstretched for Tawny to shake.

"No, the pleasure is definitely mine," she says as she shakes his hand, trying not to laugh.

Brian's barely as tall she is and his build is small and thin.

"Wow, he's a keeper," she whispers to me as I lead her back in through the sliding glass door.

"Yeah, my mother has impeccable taste." I wish he'd leave but I have no choice.

Jessica tells us my mom's having her nails done. She'll be back around three.

I get dust-covered coolers from the garage and Tawny cleans off the couches.

Tawny starts to hang streamers and blow up balloons while I prepare the snacks. By the time three rolls around, all I have left to do is cook the chicken. I grab my cigarettes and head for the front door but at exactly 3:03 my mom walks in. She pauses, staring over her sunglasses at me, and shrieks.

"Happy Birthday," I utter meekly, my hands in my back pockets and a cigarette hanging from my lip.

"I was wondering why you didn't call me!" she continues to yell, her eyes welling with tears.

She throws herself into my arms, her large purse smacking me in the side.

"My sexy girl!" she shrieks even louder when she notices Tawny.

It's been less than a month since our graduation and she acts like she hasn't seen my friend in years.

The sliding glass door opens and I can hear Brian's tobacco before he even enters the room. He pulled his jeans on but forgot his shirt. His skin's dark and taught and the bull-riding scar on his chest is stark white. It must make him feel at least two feet taller. My mother's slightly shorter than him but when they kiss her large red hair makes her look taller.

"Hey sexy! Happy birthday!" he slurs as he kisses her.

"You already gave me a happy birthday this morning, cowboy," she says with a loud laugh that makes my teeth grind.

She kisses him erotically, making no effort to restrain herself on our behalf. I can just imagine the taste of his mouth and I can practically feel his dark saliva drip down my throat. Tawny and I avert our attention.

"So, when's this party supposed to start?" my mother finally asks when they detach.

"People should start arriving around five."

"Who'd you invite?"

I quickly list off all the invites, starting with her friends. Her smile grows bigger and bigger and she quickly takes Brian by the hand and drags him upstairs.

"We gotta get ready," he yells back to us.

Tawny opens us both a beer and follows me outside. I light a cigarette and sip heartily on the bottle. Within a minute we can hear grunting from upstairs, followed by my mother's loud voice.

"Give it to me!" we hear her scream.

"Jesus, isn't his daughter inside?" Tawny asks.

"Yes, yes she is," I say, not at all surprised.

Janine and Heath arrive shortly after the noise upstairs ceases. She's wearing her typical nicely starched blouse and black slacks. Heath on the other hand is wearing a pair of ripped blue jeans and a shirt unbuttoned to the middle of his chest. Their attraction surpasses me and I'll never fully comprehend the combination.

"Hey bro," he says as he embraces me.

He hugs like Jared. I squeeze him back, relieved he's here.

Janine cordially greets Tawny, a little hesitant. She hugs me quickly, waving at the lingering smoke.

"You're such a bitch!" I tell her loudly.

"Hey, I've been busy," is her only response.

The four of us walk into the house together, preparing ourselves for what's to follow.

My mother's friends show up before any of mine. Sue arrives with a big container of potato salad and I wouldn't be surprised if it was all for herself. Joan has a date and even people from my mother's church show up. **This** is going to be more fun than I had expected.

"I hope you don't mind," Heath says to me after we've already had a few beers, "but I invited my cousin. She should be here soon."

"She?" is all I can say, hopefully.

The house fills up quickly.

I put some of my mother's favorite CD's in the player: Garth Brooks, Tim McGraw, The Eagles, Journey.

I fill the rest of the trays with my own: Incubus, U2, Tool, Soundgarden, Nine Inch Nails.

I don't think anyone notices the music anyway and even the elderly guests, those in their forties, are enjoying the alcohol.

Michelle arrives with Brandon and Jenny follows right behind them. Rebecca and Ty walk in at the same time and I'm overwhelmed. I've already had twelve Bud Lights by sundown and I'm starting to spin.

"Is that all you got?" Brian asks when I pull the trays of chicken wings and finger foods from the oven.

The look on his face makes me seriously doubt his IQ.

"I'll cook a couple steaks too," he says and he quickly runs outside to light up the BBQ.

Tawny makes a funny face at the sight of red meat and I laugh out loud.

Ty brought a bottle of tequila and we start taking shots.

One shot ignites my lips.

The next numbs my mouth.

The third fills my lungs.

And the last burns my stomach.

Once the last shot goes down for Rebecca, Tawny, Ty, Heath, Janine, Jenny and finally myself, my mind's completely numb. Everyone's words slur and I walk around in a trance, trying to stay on my feet. I greet people I don't think I've ever seen before. When Karen arrives I hug her warmly, smelling the familiar scent of her hair. I shake Kyle's hand, suspending the urge to hit him. Michelle watches me quietly, laughing at how silly I act. I feel so good, so smooth, so in control. Brandon sits by himself, sipping on a can of Pepsi. When Heath's cousin arrives I greet her with a kiss on the lips and she smiles at me. Her name's Morgan and she's tall. She has short, bleach blonde hair that's spiked. I wanna fuck her. Brian brings the steaks back in and I remember to take the rest of the chicken wings out of the oven. They're dark and dry and we all laugh. My mother excitedly talks to everyone, bragging about how thoughtful her son is and how wonderful it is of him to throw this wonderful party. We're already in full swing when Jared arrives. He changes out of his work clothes and I quickly do three more shots with him. Voices become loud hums and my skin's boiling. I step outside with Tawny and pull off my shirt. I light a cigarette. I'm in the small pool, cooling off my body, laughing and trying to keep my head above the surface while removing the remainder of my clothing. The Marlboro remains lit somehow. I can hear Tawny's loud snorting and I can see her stripping off all her clothes, throwing them out onto the grass. Jared's in the pool with us and then Jenny and all of our clothes are out on the ground. The moon's shining brightly and the air's still and hot. Morgan jumps in the water too, with all of her clothes on. She runs her wet hands through her short blonde hair, ruining her spikes. The party quickly spreads into the backyard and smokers quickly surround the small iron picnic table, watching us, laughing and pointing. I can hear Janine scream and I turn in time to see Heath lifting her over the side of the pool. She pulls him in with her. I can see flashes of cameras and hear more laughter followed by screaming from Janine. Heath starts to step up the ladder but Janine pulls on his soaked pants. They fall to his ankles and he shakes his dick at us. His penis is pierced twice and Janine squeals for him to stop. Her eyes shine brightly and I can see how much see loves him. I can see something that I've never seen in her before, all thanks to him. She quickly gets out of the water and runs in the house. Heath follows after her, laughing. Like a force of nature, Tawny and Jared start kissing, holding each other tight. Morgan finds Jenny and me and we take turns, the three of us, kissing and caressing each other. My contacts are slipping off my eyes and I have to squint to watch Jenny as she jams her tongue in Morgan's mouth. Tawny dares Jared and me to kiss and we peck quickly. She squeals with excitement. Rebecca shouts at us and Jared and I jump in the air, our cocks flopping above the water's surface. Another flash blinds me and someone now has a picture of me in all my naked, drunken glory. At the back of the crowd, beyond the bright flash, I can see Michelle. Her eyes are filled with tears and she quickly leaves, pushing passed people to get back inside. Ty follows close behind her and soon they're out of sight. Tawny gets cold and we leave the pool, running naked across the grass, picking up our clothes as we go along, heading to the garage. Tawny and Morgan put their underwear back on. I fish through a bag of my old clothes and find two pairs of board shorts for Jared and me. I toss our clothes in the dryer and we stumble into the house. The door opens into my old room. Tawny and Jared drop onto my old bed. They start to kiss, ignoring the absence of sheets. A pile of Jessica's shit is in the corner. Soon my room will be painted pink. I take Morgan by the hand and lead her out. Brittney walks in the front door and I rush to embrace her. She 's by herself. I take her hand with my free one and lead the way into the kitchen. My mother's chatting loudly, smoking in the house and breaking her own rule. I open both ladies a beer. We watch Brian play drinking games with his friends. One of them had a bull riding accident and walks funny. He's short and skinny and his ten-gallon hat is nine gallons too big. He dares another drinker to show her tits and in exchange he'll show her 'The Flying Squirrel.' The crowd cheers him on and she quickly pops out her breasts, shaking them wildly. The cowboy stands on his chair and drops his pants. He grabs his testicles and stretches his scrotum upwards, the tip of his dick peaking out from the elastic sack. My mother reaches across the table and grabs his balls and the crowd goes wild, Brian jumping forward to stop her. She laughs and chuckles, spilling beer all over him. I have to pee and Morgan follows me to the bathroom. In the short time they've been here Karen and Kyle have had too much to drink and are wrapped around the toilet, leaning on each other for support. I lead Morgan upstairs and we go into my mother's bathroom. While I stand peeing she sifts through the medicine cabinet. I finish and turn in time to see her swallow a handful of pills. My mother's depression medication. She pulls me in close, gripping me by the front of my shorts. I instantly go hard and press against her. She kisses my neck and I watch it all in the mirror. While she sucks on me I reach into the medicine cabinet and pull out a jar of prescription strength painkillers. I swallow four of them dry and they tear at my throat. As she starts kissing my chest, I admire myself in the mirror, fingering the dark brown hickey that is now forming on my neck. I hear my name over the voices down stairs and pull Morgan up just as she starts to kiss my happy trail, her hands caressing my cock through my shorts. Brittney's downstairs, still holding her purse, looking up at me. She has to leave. Mark's waiting for her. She just wants to say goodbye. I boldly take Morgan by the hand and lead her downstairs. I walk Brittney outside and she hugs me quickly, not acknowledging Morgan. As I watch her walk to her car, I notice Michelle sitting in her car across the street. Ty's sitting next to her. Morgan goes back inside and I run over to say hi. Nothing is all Michelle says when I ask what she's up to. Her eyes are wet and her cheeks are red and I can tell she's been crying. Ty looks at me like he wants to hit me. Are you sure I ask and she just nods her head, forcing a smile. I walk away, aware of what the problem is but unsure and unequipped at the moment to repair it. Morgan's in the kitchen with Heath and she greets me with a kiss. They were talking about me, I can tell. Heath walks away and sits at the picnic table next to Janine, who's talking to her friends. Jenny walks up to me and I can't remember when I saw her last. In the pool? I'm leaving she says and walks away. What the hell why don't you stay I ask and she says she feels like a third wheel. Morgan looks at me and we watch Jenny walk out the front door. I take Morgan by the hand and we walk into my old room. Tawny and Jared are making out and they don't even take notice. I pull two blankets from the linen closet and we walk out into the backyard. Heath and Janine cry catcalls after us as I lead her to the far end of the yard. The large trampoline my sister got for her sixteenth birthday is still sitting there out of view of the patio and we stumble on, spreading out the blankets. It takes us no time at all to find each other and Morgan's kiss is deadly. She sucks on my tongue, pulling at the tendons underneath. She instantly goes for my shorts. I pull a blanket over us as she pulls them down and her grip is tight. I stumble with her bra and she pulls her pants off, never letting go of me. She pulls me on top of her. Fuck me she whispers and I continue kissing her. The painkillers are numbing my senses and I can barely feel my dick. Fuck me she says again, desperate this time. All I can concentrate on is kissing her and when she realizes I don't have the willpower to follow through, she forces me in her. Warm, wet and inviting. I slide in and I wait for the music to start playing. I wait for the orchestra to rise and the scene to quickly cut to the morning. The music never comes and all I can hear is Morgan's grunts as she pulls at my hips, whispering, harder, faster. In the distance I can hear my mother again, screaming and talking dirty up in her bedroom. The lights are on. They stole away a moment to get some. I instantly go soft. Frustrated, Morgan climbs on top of me. She thrusts her hips, trying hard to keep my ever-softening dick from sliding out. With no luck, she lays off. I have no response for her. I stare at the stars, waiting for it all to end, praying for the credits to roll. She turns her back to me and I can feel her masturbating. After a couple minutes she's silent and still and quiet and probably asleep. I turn, reluctantly, and wrap an arm around her. She doesn't push me away. My head is spinning and I fear if I fall asleep I might fall and break my neck. The yard goes silent and the house goes quiet. The only thing I can hear is Janine throwing up in an upstairs bathroom. The window's open and I hear Heath soothing her. My mother comes out to water her plants at three in the morning. She didn't bother to dress. She's robed in little more than a short teddy. I glance at her and she is oblivious to us, naked and wrapped up in blankets. I'm a jackass.

I'm no longer a virgin. I wonder what happened to Jessica, I hope she's ok. I start whispering the chorus from a Radiohead song to myself, "Don't leave me high, don't leave me dry..." and the music starts playing, faint and inviting...

EIGHT

I'm still awake, damp under our thin blanket when the sun begins to rise. My mother's house is completely quiet and the only sound I hear is Morgan's faint breathing. I still hold her tight, our nude bodies exchanging and absorbing all the heat they can.

I didn't want the evening to end the way it did. I didn't want to spend the night outside, drunk, holding someone I barely know. Under the circumstances though, I feel like I owe her this much.

Why not?

After all, she was willing to do what I couldn't, so I figure it's a fair trade.

With the sun come the mosquitoes and with the mosquitoes come the birds. I try as quietly as I can to find my underwear. I reach around without letting go of Morgan. The trampoline springs squeak and I feel her body tense.

I freeze, hoping she won't wake, not wanting to face the embarrassing moments to follow. But she yawns and stretches, rolling from her side onto her stomach. Her short spikes are now fluffy, crunchy bunches of white hair. Her mascara's smeared as if she was crying.

"Good morning," is all she says to me.

We both fumble around under the sheet, trying hard to keep our bodies covered, desperately searching for our underwear. After we dress and fold the blankets, we make our way across the backyard. The patio's scattered with trash and the rusted picnic table is covered with empty beer bottles.

The sliding glass door stands ajar and we quietly step inside. The stale smell of alcohol invades our senses and my stomach continues to churn. The house is still and empty except for a few guests that passed out on the floor. Karen and Kyle are still in the bathroom, lying on the floor with their feet sticking out into the hallway. The door to my old bedroom is open and Jessica's sleeping under a big pink blanket thrown on top of the bare mattress. We collect our car keys and slip out the front door unnoticed.

I walk Morgan to her car and the silence between us is excruciating. I should be embarrassed. I feel guilty that I have nothing to say.

"Well," I mumble as I move in to hug her goodbye.

She embraces me softly, kissing me on the lips. She steps down into her car and drives away, never looking back. I watch her leave.

The keys in my hand feel different and I look down at them. I've been tossing them around and now notice that one of them is missing. Tawny must have stolen my house key because the ring it was on is completely missing. I don't want to go back inside to look for it so I'll take my chances.

In ten minutes I'm home. Tawny's car and Jared's truck are parked out front.

I hope they're either awake making breakfast or still asleep because walking in on the alternative would be a little awkward. It would be a slap in the face to the guy who couldn't keep it up just hours ago.

As I step into my humble abode I'm gratefully met with silence. I walk around slowly, kicking off my shoes and pulling off my dirty shirt. I start a cup of coffee and walk to the bathroom.

Stepping down the hall, I notice my door's slightly open. I fight the temptation at first but in the end succumb to desire. I push the door open, lifting it by the handle so the joints don't squeak. I open it just far enough to squeeze my head inside. In the pale morning light I can see their naked bodies. My heart starts to race. I quickly shut the door.

After urinating and pouring myself a cup of coffee, I lie down on the futon. The clock on top of the television just turned eight. I quickly empty my cup, turn on the television, light my first cigarette of the morning, and lay back with the ashtray on my abdomen. I listen to an infomercial about a home gym system and watch my smoke drift to the ceiling. Shortly after snuffing out what's left, I fall deep asleep.

A loud knock finds me in the darkness. The next time it comes I'm jarred awake. By the third intrusion, I'm slowly stumbling to my feet. The clock says eleven and my apartment's excruciatingly hot.

I quickly pull the front door open without checking the eyehole first and warmer air rushes inside. Michelle stands there in sunglasses, wearing a small tank top and a pair of board shorts.

"Good morning," she says with a weary smile. "Want to get some lunch?" she asks, pulling off her glasses.

Her eyes are swollen and squinted in the harsh light.

"Sure, come in while I change," I mumble, stepping back and quickly walking into my bedroom.

My bed is empty, the sheets on the floor. I quickly pull off my shorts and boxers, dropping them on the floor as well. I put on a clean t-shirt and a pair of ripped blue jeans without underwear. Michelle's sitting on the futon when I step back into the living room.

"Ready to go?" she asks.

We walk out and silently get into her Firebird.

"I thought we'd get some sandwiches and take them up to the dam," she finally says as we pull onto a busy street.

"Sounds good," is all I can say.

I'm hung over with horrible morning breath and my oversized sunglasses aren't helping keep the sun away.

"Thank you for inviting me over last night. I had a good time," she starts, unenthusiastically. "I was tempted to get naked with y'all in the pool..."

I thought she might step on ground I wasn't ready for so I change the subject.

"I have to tell you something," I begin and it instantly peaks her interest.

She braces herself, holding the steering wheel tighter, answering with a simple, "Mm hm?"

"I lost my virginity last night," I say through a smile I try to hide.

It sounds far better than what actually happened. Michelle will understand the importance of the news almost more than anyone. I met her family at the church I spent my entire childhood attending. She took the same vow as Jenny and I. She stares at me over her sunglasses in a way that I can only interpret as shock.

"With who? With that blond chick... Heath's cousin?" she asks as we pull into the sandwich shop parking lot. Apparently this wasn't the news she was expecting. "Wow, I'm... happy for you."

"Thank you," I say, holding the door open for her. "It was a little unexpected but you know how those things happen."

No, she doesn't. Jared was the only guy to ever see her naked.

We don't talk again until after our sandwiches are ordered and we're back in the car.

Michelle tosses them on the back seat and turns the radio to a low hum.

"Are you gonna start dating?" she asks after finding the right station, which is playing the new but overplayed Evanescence song.

"Probably not. I didn't make a great first impression." I finally spill my guts because I'm more honest than I wish I was.

Michelle gives me a puzzled look and I can't help but continue.

"I couldn't keep it up."

I'm waiting for an on slot of laughter. Instead, she sits quietly for a moment, carefully choosing her next words.

"Well, just blame it on liquor dick," she finally says with a smile.

It isn't a mocking smile but an understanding one. I finally let out a breath of relief because at least the first person I told didn't laugh.

The dam is completely deserted when we arrive and the sun's directly above us. Michelle stops her car shortly beyond the main parking lot, up an overgrown dirt road. The road comes to a small clearing that forms a low cliff fifteen feet above the water. We set out a blanket and eat our sandwiches with our feet hanging over the waters edge. The stereo remains on, blaring through the cars open windows.

We listen to The Cranberries while we eat, rebels in the sun.

"I have to ask you something," she finally starts again after taking a few bites of her sub.

"Ok. Go ahead," I say, stopping to look at her.

"Why didn't you tell me about Jared and Tawny?" she asks, hesitating between each word.

"I didn't think it really mattered," I say after a pause, more than half-tempted to act like I had no idea what she was talking about.

"Didn't matter?" Michelle responds with a chuckle that tells me she didn't find it funny at all. "You think it doesn't matter? You're one of my best friends, and Tawny and I used to work together. I should have at least had some sort of warning before I saw them naked together... with you of all people!"

"I know. I should have told you. I just didn't think it would do any good or make any kind of difference. You two aren't together anymore!" I tell her defensively, setting down my sandwich.

It's quickly covered in ants but I don't care.

"Well, if it weren't for you introducing them in the first place, none of this would have happened," she scolds me, setting her sandwich down too.

Frustrated and bewildered, she stands.

"Did you know they would like each other when you introduced them? Please, tell me that much! Were you hooking them up?" she asks, staring down at me with her hands on her hips.

I can't answer.

I simply stare out at the water because we both know the truth.

Michelle remains silent. She's fighting back tears and knows arguing with me would be useless. The damage is done. She's made me feel like shit and that's sufficient. Before I have a chance to apologize she kicks off her sandals, pulls off her tank top, and drops her shorts on the blanket beside me. I watch as she jumps out over the water. She doesn't look back at me, says nothing, and splashes through the still surface. She resurfaces, sucks in a lung full of air, and starts to swim away.

I stand and do the same. I have no boxers on so I strip naked and jump into the green water. Everything is cold and refreshing and I can hear the music from the car echo through the valley. Michelle doesn't call back to me and I wouldn't dare yell for her to wait. For the first time in my life, I feel like I've truly betrayed someone. So without words, I quickly catch up to her and we swim across the water, side by side.

We climb a sharp incline to get back to our clothes. The sun's warm on my bare skin and the cold water was unforgiving. I step carefully, trying hard to avoid a collision with the sharp rocks beneath my feet. The effort is useless and I cut my foot anyway.

Our clothes are crawling with ants.

"Shit!" Michelle exclaims, picking up her shorts and shaking them off.

I pick up my jeans and do the same. When they appear ant free, I slip them back on, spilling blood inside. I toss my shirt and sandals in the back seat. Michelle does the same with her clothes. We leave the remainder of our lunches and drive away. The breeze that rushes through the open windows chills my skin and refreshes my mind in a way that it hasn't been in a long time. The sun has started its descent and we both have an evening of work ahead of us.

"Let's drop by my house so I can get ready. You can take a shower if you want and I'll take you home to get your clothes," Michelle says after it's obvious we're not going back to my apartment. "I'll get you a Band-Aid too."

She turns and looks at me, smiling the smile that I love most about her. Hopefully Brandon's home.

Michelle's parents aren't home when we pull into the driveway but her brother's pickup is parked on the street.

"What time did Brandon leave last night?" I finally ask.

I don't want to ask him myself. We walk across the lawn to the front door.

"I'm not really sure. He and Jenny went out for coffee and I stayed with Ty for a couple hours. He was already asleep when I got home," she says as she unlocks the front door, leading the way inside.

It's completely still and dark in the cramped living room. All the blinds are drawn and the air conditioner is on full blast. Michelle quickly walks back to her bedroom, knowing I'll make myself at home. After helping myself to a glass of her mothers Diet Coke, I go see if Brandon's still asleep.

His door's closed and I knock lightly as I push it open.

"Hello? Brandon?" I ask, peaking inside.

In the dark I can see him lying in bed. He sleeps on his back, rigid like a corpse with his hands to his side. His computer's on and humming.

I get two Band-Aids from the medicine cabinet and rinse my foot in the sink. The cold water stings as it rushes across my open flesh.

With no one to keep me company while Michelle showers, I take my soda out front to have a cigarette. The sun instantly starts to burn my bare skin, which is now pulled taunt from the sudden loss of moisture. The smoke feels wonderful as it fills my lungs but burns as it meets the hot air around me. I sit quietly in a warped wooden chair and put my feet up on a large flowerpot.

My muscles ache from the impromptu exercise and my lungs still burn from breathing heavily. If I close my eyes, I still feel as if I'm rocking back and forth in the water. Michelle steps out onto the porch just in time to see me flick my butt onto the grass.

"You should really quit that shit. Honestly, you've been doing it long enough," she scolds, drying her hair with a towel. "The shower's all yours."

Michelle walks back inside. She's wearing her black slacks and a white sports bra. I follow back into her room.

"No, I'll be alright. I just have to throw on fresh deodorant," I respond as I lie on her bed, grabbing a *Cosmopolitan* off of the bedside table.

I'm not interested in reading; it's merely a way of averting my eyes from her flat stomach and muscular back.

"Ok, suit yourself," she answers without looking at me, pinning her hair up and watching herself in the mirror.

"Have you registered for your classes yet?" she asks with a bobby pin in the corner of her mouth.

"Not yet. I can wait till the day term starts if I want to."

"Yeah but you might not get any of the classes you need."

The word *need* rings in my ears and I suddenly remember that I haven't even met with a counselor yet. Most everyone, including myself, would be staying local to attend junior college. Only the lucky few will leave town.

Mental note, call counselor's office.

I shake my shirt out once more before putting it on and slide carefully onto the burning hot passenger seat. The sun's already far along its descent and I don't have much time to get ready. The silence between us is foreboding and Michelle insists on listening to music. The new Bush CD is a good thing.

When we finally pull up in front of my apartment I sprint up the steps. I dress quickly and brush my teeth. I'm back in the car in seven minutes and we're on our way.

The sun sets as it always does and we watch the red glow slowly fade to dark purple while we fold napkins. Only five tables are occupied tonight and I quickly become bored at my podium. Rebecca busies herself helping the patrons and Dana keeps the beers full in the bar.

It won't get any busier and is all downhill from here.

"Should we catch a movie tonight?" Michelle asks, her eyes never leaving the napkins in front of her.

"Yeah, that'd be a great idea. I'll call the theater and see what's playing."

We continue chatting about school, music, and movies. That's what I like most about our mundane nights working together, the abundant and seemingly meaningless conversations that I'll never forget.

As the occupants in the dining room dwindle, the bar quickly fills up like all other Sunday nights. It's a last chance effort to enjoy what's left of the weekend. Dana comes looking for us, like she always does, disrupting our hiding place.

"Quit wasting time with those napkins. We have plenty!" she scolds. "I need ice. Now."

I escort Michelle out to the storeroom. We carry buckets and set them down in front of the ice machine. I hold the lid up and she starts to scoop. We make a simple one-man task even easier for two.

"Did you know," Michelle begins to ask, breathing hard with each exertion, "that I used to have a huge crush on you?"

She looks at me with a smirk and continues. "Yeah, when you used to come and hang out with Brandon. I would have so much fun just following you guys around and watching you. God, one of the big reasons I continued going to church was to be around you!"

She finishes filling the buckets and I close the lid. The ice is overflowing onto the floor and I'm frozen in place until a sudden urge becomes uncontrollable.

We attack each other. I scoop Michelle up by the ass and slam her against the ice machine. She moans loudly and instinctively wraps her arms around my neck. Her ankles lock behind my back and we jam our tongues into each other's mouths as if our lives depend upon it. All her bitterness and disdain comes out in that kiss as she digs her hands into the back of my head, holding tightly onto my hair. Holding tightly onto a moment. I start groping her like an animal, kissing her neck and feeling around under her apron.

Michelle giggles as I grope her and I pause. The noise brings me to a level of clarity. I knock over a bucket of ice and I'm standing in a large puddle, pressing my crotch against hers. With water soaking through to my socks, I know I have to stop. If I continue I'll regret it.

Michelle notices my hesitation as if it's a relief to her as well and she loosens her grip on my hair. We stand there, staring into each other's eyes for what feels like an eternity. Then we burst into laughter

"Thank you..." she says, kissing me softly on the lips.

I step back, letting her down to adjust her apron. I need to walk it off. I quickly go outside.

The dirt lot behind the restaurant is empty and dark. With trembling fingers I pull out a Marlboro. I sit on a knocked over trashcan and inhale slowly. My groin aches and I gently massage it to ease the pressure.

Like a scene from a movie that's oddly familiar, our intense moment came and went in just a few seconds. I can still smell her hair. The way her shampoo mixes with sweat is so intoxicating. My lips are sore from her aggressive kiss and the hair on my scalp is screaming in indignation. But none of it matters as I sit here quietly, grinning with satisfaction.

The rest of the evening flies by uneventful. I help Michelle clean the last of the tables and we quickly bid farewell to Dana. As she usually does, Rebecca turns down an invitation to join us. We leave them at the bar smoking cigarettes and drinking Cabernet with the sign turned to CLOSED.

"So, is there anything in particular you'd like to see?" I ask, getting in the car.

"There are a few starting soon, so we can decide when we get there," Michelle says, glancing at the times I scrawled down.

We chat on the way to the theater, evading the topic I can't stop thinking about.

We settle on a movie we've both wanted to see about a bisexual love triangle between three over-privileged college students. After buying Michelle a large bottle of water and a diet soda for myself, we walk into the nearly deserted theater. There are only three other couples in the room and an old man in the corner. We sit patiently, listening to the latest music blaring from speakers in the ceiling and watching local advertisements flash across the screen.

Within minutes the previews begin and in the dark I'm able to do what I've been dying to.

Michelle looks beautiful in the pale blue light, the colors dancing across her wide eyes. My curious, longing stares are too obvious and she turns to face me.

She doesn't blush or look away, but smiles.

It's an understanding smile, a reassuring and comforting smile. We'll never continue where we left off but the thought of what could have been is satisfying enough. As the previews end and the studio logo rolls up the screen she takes me by the hand and never lets it fall.

"I really enjoyed it, even though every one else walked out," Michelle declares later as she pulls up in front of my apartment. "I wonder if the book's as good."

"I don't know," I say.

The excitement from holding Michelle's hand faded fast and now all I want is a cigarette and some sleep. After a quick kiss on the lips and a fond farewell, I run up my steps three at a time. I light a cigarette the moment I unlock the door and burst inside.

My body screams for sleep. My eyes can't stay open much longer and my contacts are tearing at my pupils. I strip off my clothes and plop down naked on the futon. I'm dazed, staring at the smoke as it lingers in the air in front of me. It changes shape and shade in the dim lamplight. I fall asleep the moment I drop it in the ashtray.

I'm asleep for only an hour when I hear another knock. Unlike this morning, the breeze coming in through my constantly open window is cool and my skin is chilled. My knees are drawn to my chest and the knife stabs at my aching head again. I check the peephole this time. In the dark I instantly recognize Jared, wearing his apron and tie from the grocery store.

"Hang on a sec," I shout, pulling on my boxers before I open the door.

"Hey, had a good day at work?" I joke while hugging him.

His apron is covered in dust and food and his eyes are redder than mine.

"Yeah right. My feet are fucking killing me!" he says as I step back to let him enter.

I blink my eyes hard, trying to clear the calcium from my lenses. I close the door. Jared kicks off his shoes and tosses his apron and tie on the floor.

"Were you asleep?" he asks.

"Yeah but its ok," I lie as I light a cigarette and offer him one.

"Wanna beer?" I ask as he takes a cigarette from the pack I hold out to him.

"Sure. I can use one."

I walk into the kitchen and pull out two Bud Lights. Jared sits at the counter across from me, moaning in pain as he climbs onto one of the stools.

"So, are you in pain from today's work or last night's?" I try joking as I hand him his beer, knowing he had to have been more successful than I was.

"Yeah, well, I hope you don't mind that we spent most of the night here," he answers, blushing slightly.

"So you two... you know?" I ask, raising my eyebrows.

I know they had sex and that he lost his virginity but I need the confirmation from him. I can still smell them. The scent of his semen lingers the air.

"Yeah. We did."

"So, how was it?" I ask, trying hard not to act too interested.

I hope for an opportunity to brag.

"Good. Real good," he says and takes a swig of beer.

He looks at me with a smirk and asks, "What about you and Morgan? You two did, right?"

"Yeah. Out on the trampoline. Froze my fucking balls off," I answer with the same machismo grin, prideful only on the outside.

"Nice man, real nice," he responds, high-fiving me.

And in that moment we confirm one more step into manhood, witnessing each other's new venture into an ever-widening world.

We finish our beers and open two more. We walk back into the living room and I'm fading fast. Jared's exhausted so we crash on the couch, putting our feet up on the coffee table.

"You want to watch a movie or something?" I ask when it becomes obvious we have nothing else to talk about.

He stands and walks over to my small stack of DVDs.

"How about that one movie about the guys who get together just to beat the shit out of each other?" he asks.

I nod and he puts it in the player.

We sit in silence, a mutual acceptance of fatigue. We smoke the rest of my cigarettes and finish off the six-pack. Shortly before the end of the movie I fall asleep, my feet still propped up and my head resting on the arm rest. When I wake in the morning Jared's gone and the television's still on, the DVD menu playing over and over.

nine

July begins three days after my mother's party and the fourth falls on the very next Saturday. I work four days this week, each day completely lost in thought. I've only told a handful of people about losing my virginity and Dana was the proudest, kissing me on the cheek. I'm nineteen and determined to make up for one night's disappointment.

I don't get to see Tawny again until the fourth. We talk on the phone and when I do tell her about what happened with Morgan she demands every single detail. I embellish and quickly change the subject.

"Good, he's not too bad for a virgin. He does need to trim back some of that bush though. It's growing out of control!" she says after I ask her about Jared. "He's seen his share of porn because at least he knew where to put it!"

I spend the rest of the week leading up to the fourth trying to decide who I want to get into bed with next. I've awoken a hunger, a yearning that will not be fed with masturbation. One person, one name, one face keeps coming to mind and no matter how hard I try to put her out, Brittney haunts my dreams.

The restaurant's closed on the fourth and I sleep late into the afternoon. I'm awoken only by the phone ringing in the distance. I stumble out of bed and crawl to it.

"Hello?" I croak, lying on the floor.

"Get your ass out of bed nigga! You're gonna to come play pool with us before we go to Rebecca's party tonight!" Tawny yells.

She's referring to herself and Jared and I've completely forgotten about the party.

"I'll meet you there," I say, dropping the phone back on its jack.

I crawl to my room and pull a pack of cigarettes from a dirty pair of jeans. Rebecca has very simple gatherings and we'll get to drink. Ty's decided to make an event out of the holiday.

I dress in khaki shorts, leather sandals, and a black wife beater. I slip on cheap Elvis sunglasses before rushing out the door. The air is dry and hot and I decide to put the top down on my Jeep. The air doesn't cool as it rushes through my hair but it quickly dries the sweat on my brow.

I can't see anything as I step into the pool hall. Unlike in the evenings with crowds and bright lights, the only light comes in through the windows and only three tables are being used. Tawny sits at a small table watching Jared play against an older gentleman. She notices me instantly.

"Poopy! Poopy! Poopy! You big boy! I'm so proud of you!" she screams, hugging me. "Attention everyone! It's official; Jason is no longer a virgin. So please feel free to jump his bones," she continues, turning to everyone in the room.

No one seems to notice and she drags me over to Jared's table.

"Hey man," is all he says as he greets me with a half hug, half handshake.

He doesn't stand near us and turns back to his game, obviously upsetting Tawny. We sit down at the table and I pull out my Marlboro's.

"Must you?" she scolds, frowning.

I flip her off with my lighter hand, ignite, and inhale deeply.

"What's going on here?" I ask under my breath, pointing back and forth between her and Jared.

"I have no clue! I haven't seen him since we fucked and he hasn't called me all week. I finally caved, called him first, and he told me he's been busy," she whispers back, her cheeks blushing.

"Is he coming with you tonight?" I ask.

"Of course. I'm hoping he'll stay the night too," she says, watching Jared.

She completely ignores the fact that she should at least ask first.

"That's cool. I'm gonna to give it another try with Brittney, so maybe we can crash at Rebecca's."

When Jared finishes another game we decide it's late enough to go to Rebecca's house. It's almost six and I didn't want to play anyway. I'm too distracted thinking about Brittney.

As we file out and walk to our cars, I turn to watch Jared kiss Tawny. It's short, almost forced. He doesn't hold her hand or say one word to her. They follow me the short distance to Rebecca's house and we're the first guests to arrive. We park on the street and I wait for Tawny and Jared before I walk to the front door.

Rebecca's husband John answers and their dog Cowboy barrels up behind him. He greets me with a handshake and as I enter the German Shepherd almost knocks me over.

"It's about time you got here Jason! Rebecca keeps saying she needs your help!" John jokes as he holds the door open for Jared and Tawny.

After introductions, he goes back to watching a volleyball game on ESPN. I lead the way into the kitchen and Jared awkwardly follows Tawny.

Rebecca and Ty are behind the counter when we enter the room. Ty's opening cases of beer and icing them in a cooler. Rebecca busies herself with snacks. She leaps with joy to see us and greets us with wet kisses and hugs. Ty looks up and nods his head in our direction, a sufficient acknowledgement from him.

"Thank you for coming early," Rebecca starts to say as she walks towards the sliding glass door that leads to her backyard. "I need you to do me a favor."

Tawny, Jared, and I follow her outside.

They have a decent size backyard compared to others on their street. It butts up against a city park, the same city park everyone gathers to watch the annual fireworks show.

"We'll be able to see the entire show from out here!" Rebecca exclaims wildly, holding Tawny's hand.

She's wearing a tight white shirt that's practically see through in the harsh setting sunlight. I've seen the views and the fireworks from here before.

"If you lie on the grass and look up it feels like the fireworks are falling down all around you," she continues enthusiastically.

Jared and I stand patiently, waiting for our instructions.

"I need you to hang that banner," Rebecca finally tells us, pointing to a rolled up red, white, and blue ribbon in the corner.

She shows where to hang it and goes back inside with Tawny in tow. Jared doesn't say much to me and quietly goes about helping me erect the decorations. We hang it from the roof, stand back to admire it and walk back inside. Jared's lost in thought, distracted and worried.

"Are you alright?" I ask, concerned.

"Yeah. I'm just tired," is all he says.

Tawny and Rebecca have already set out the food and I help Ty carry the coolers out onto the patio. When we finish Ty, Jared, Tawny, and I sit in the living room with John to finish watching the game. Rebecca rushes upstairs to change into something nicer. I try my hardest to get into the game, but sports have never been a favorite pastime of mine. The anticipation of seeing Brittney is much more consuming.

At seven-thirty more guests arrive. People from the restaurant, including Eric, Matt, Noah, and then friends of Ty's, only a few of which I recognize from high school. By the time the sun's completely set the house is bursting. Rebecca's constantly running back and forth from the kitchen getting food.

Ty opens case after case of light beer.

When the game ends, someone pulls out the Playstation and Jared quickly jumps in line. When Tawny finishes helping Rebecca she sits quietly beside him. I mingle, patiently waiting for one person to show up.

After a few beers Jared's mood changes. He starts laughing and joking. I hear Tawny laugh extra loud at one of his jokes. She calls me over.

"Jason, you have to hear this shit," she squeals between bouts of laughter.

"Yeah, it's pretty funny," Jared says, watching the video game and waiting his turn. "The night of your mom's party, after we all went swimming, you gave me a pair of board shorts to wear. I was in your old room with Tawny then walked out to take a piss."

Tawny's already laughing hard and it's getting annoying.

"Well, the shorts were like two sizes too big so I had to hold them up. I walk out of the bedroom and bump into your sister on the way to the john. She looked at me strangely so I explain, 'Wow, Jason's a big guy!' She just stared at me, like she thought I had just taken it up the ass from you or something!" he finishes with a chuckle.

Tawny's rolling on the floor hysterically and the entire crowd laughs. I can't hold back laughing either, but I dread having to explain it later.

Rebecca starts a game of Uno, which will inevitably go on all night and I sit down next to her. John stands in the kitchen, looking on, and we have to use two decks of cards because of all the people crowded around us.

I can see the couch from where I sit as well as the front door. Tawny's face is expressionless as she plays with her hair. Jared's turn has finally arrived and he's enthralled in a game. They sit next to each other, completely detached, and when he scores she sits motionless.

Something catches her eye and she turns her gaze to the front door. I follow it in time to see Brittney walk in, alone. I can't resist smiling myself. Tawny quickly rushes over and greets her with a hug followed by excited chatter. After a few seconds, Tawny turns and points in my direction. Brittney's gaze follows her finger and her eyes meet mine.

She waves and mouths the word "Hi."

I take this as a positive sign and instantly want to get her alone. I excuse myself from the game and walk outside to have a cigarette. The park beyond the brick wall is already full of spectators and the show's only an hour away. I light a Marlboro and turn to watch Brittney make the rounds greeting everyone. They're all pleased to see her, especially Rebecca, who insists she sit down to the game. Brittney promises she'll be right back and walks outside, unnoticed.

"Hi there," she says, greeting me with a lingering hug and a long kiss on the lips.

They stay as if they might do more but she eventually pulls away. Up close I can tell that she's been crying and her breath smells like rum. She takes the cigarette from between my fingers and drags on it slowly.

"Where's Mark?" I ask as casually as I can manage.

I down what's left of my beer and open one for Brittney and another for myself.

"He didn't want to come. Fuck him," she says as she continues to smoke my cigarette.

We say nothing more. I watch her quickly empty the bottle. She flicks the butt over the brick wall and walks back inside. I feel like a dog following her. I'd love to be her dog. I'd wear a collar if she made me and walk around naked on all fours eating raw meat out of a bowl if she requested it.

Brittney walks passed the card game and I can see that my cards have been re-distributed. I don't care and I follow Brittney into the kitchen. She picks at the food, eats a couple of crackers and opens another one of the beers that's being iced in the sink. We quickly finish four more each. The hour passes and the timer above the stove buzzes five minutes to nine.

"Time for fireworks!" Rebecca yells.

The crowd turns to look at her and she directs us out back. She bullies everyone out of the living room and notices us alone in the kitchen.

"Come on you two!" she insists, attempting to pull us outside. We simply laugh and plant ourselves against the counter.

"I'm too drunk to walk!" Brittney moans as she waves Rebecca off and sits on the floor, leaning her head against the cupboards beneath the sink.

Rebecca gives up and rushes outside with Jared and Tawny, who're holding hands. She turns off all the lights as she goes hoping it will help the view and we're left completely alone in the dark.

I fill a glass with Jack Daniels I find hiding above the fridge and add Coke for color. I plop down next to Brittney and instinctively she rests her head on my shoulder, slipping an arm through mine. I take a drink of whiskey and my courage quadruples.

"Brittney," I begin, looking down at the top of her head. She turns her face to mine, brushing the hair out of her eyes. "Why didn't Mark come with you, really?"

"We got into a fight," she starts, hesitating. "And I wanted to see you... without him."

She turns her face away, as if she might cry just looking at me. Her grip on my arm tightens and she digs her face into my neck. The confusion and the whiskey raise a demon in me that simply can't be controlled.

"So... what's this all about?" I ask harshly. "Hanging on my arm like this? You've barely spoken to me since... that night, and now I'm supposed to feel sorry for you?!"

She's stunned, stiff, and unsure of what to say. She sniffles and I can just imagine the tears rolling down her cheeks. She looks up at me and her big wet eyes stare longingly.

The fireworks begin, bathing the kitchen in rich blues and blinding whites. Her face glows in the illumination and I find the opportunity too perfect to turn down.

We grab at each other, pulling our faces together. My mind races and I push away all doubts. I won't stop this time! I close my eyes and kiss her deeply, the colors flashing beyond my eyelids. The booms and cheers invigorate us.

I pull Brittney away from the cupboards and onto her knees. Our chests, abdomens and groins are flat against one another. I feel myself engorge and the friction with my shorts is almost too much to bear. I hold her as tightly as I can and she doesn't pull away. She holds my face firmly in her hands and it feels like home.

I open my eyes as the fireworks show reaches its finale, a spectacle of gold and red. Brittney's cheeks are smeared with mascara and her lids are tightly shut. We're engulfed in a warm glow and tears begin to drain from my eyes. Like all my fleeting dreams, darkness suddenly surrounds us and I'm left with reality.

The cheers from outside echo loudly through the empty house. And instantly, Brittney pulls away. She looks at me, both scared and satisfied, and we stand up as well as apart. Everyone quickly re-enters the house and the lights come back on. Brittney does exactly what I thought she would and denies what just passed between us.

The game of Uno is continued and the Playstation is turned back on. It isn't long before Brittney's cell phone rings and she leaves without saying goodbye.

I know it's for the best.

She wants me, but won't let go of Mark. If only she could us have both. If only she would try.

The crowd only stays till midnight and almost instantly Rebecca's house is empty. John heads upstairs after kissing his wife goodnight and patting me on the back. We can faintly hear Ty upstairs with some girl and Tawny's watching TV with Jared on the couch. They're much closer than earlier, wrapped around each other.

Rebecca and I slowly clean up and when we finish, we sit at the counter and drink red wine. U2's newest CD is playing on her computer and we're smoking inside despite a strict rule not to.

"Did you enjoy the fireworks?" she asks, filling my glass to the brim.

"Umm, I wasn't exactly paying attention," I mumble, shuffling a deck of playing cards.

We start playing a mind game, a card game we're usually very good at. When I pull out a card, she'll need to guess what it is simply by looking into my eyes. It's silly and immature but funny when you're three bottles of wine to the wind.

"Really? What were you and Brittney doing?" she asks with a smile.

I hold up a card, press it to my forehead, and stare at her.

"Three of hearts," she says quickly, sipping wine.

"Close," I answer, turning it around for her to see. "Three of Diamonds."

"Are you two dating or something? What happened to Mark?" she asks, guessing King of Spades when the next card is actually Ace of Spades. "You know she's always had a thing for you."

"No, we're not together or anything. And she's probably off fucking him right now anyway," I mumble, the mental picture of them making love burning itself onto the inside of my lids. "Of course I know she likes me. I've had a crush on her for years. But she can't make up her mind and I won't wait around."

She guesses correctly once out of twenty, getting close almost every time.

"I know what you mean," Rebecca says, taking the cards from me.

We share a cigarette and she blows smoke out her nose. She does understand, reassuring me in a way only a mother and a true friend can.

69

"Remember that blonde chick from my mom's party?" I ask after missing severely on my first guess.

"Yeah, the one you were making out with?" she retorts with a smile.

"Well, I lost my virginity to her," I admit, feeling my cheeks turn a deep crimson.

I guess Queen of Hearts and it's really a King of Spades.

"Kind of close," Rebecca says with a smile, setting down the cards and picking up her wine glass. "I'm happy for you. How was it, your first time?" she asks.

"Ok, I guess. It could have been better." I light another cigarette.

"Ty lost his four years ago," Rebecca starts to share, making me feel even more insignificant.

It always makes me feels uncomfortable when she talks this openly about her son, for obvious reasons.

"It was some older girl and he said it was amazing. You wore a rubber, right?" she continues, grabbing my forearm with concern.

"Of course," I lie.

Rolling on a condom had never crossed my mind and the only ones I had were at home in my nightstand.

"Good. I told Ty if he got some girl pregnant I'd kill him! He said she put it on and I kept my fingers crossed for a year!" she finishes, emptying her glass of wine.

She quickly fills it back up.

"How was your first time?" I ask.

"Awkward," she says after thinking for a moment.

"It was uncomfortable. I didn't bleed that much and I didn't cum. Jesus, I didn't do that for years!" she continues with a chuckle. "It was with some guy I went to the senior prom with. I was one of the few virgins I knew. So I figured why not. Ryan, that was his name, was really nervous and only lasted a few minutes. I'll give him credit for effort, but then he almost fell asleep on top of me."

We both laugh loudly.

We continue our conversation into the living room. I carry my glass and an ashtray and Rebecca carries what's left of our bottle of Cabernet. Tawny and Jared are silently sleeping and we attempt to watch *The Postman Always Rings Twice* on HBO. Despite our best efforts to keep quiet, they soon wake. Jared excuses himself to the restroom, closing the door tightly behind him.

"Sorry if we woke you," I whisper.

"It's ok. We're gonna go crash at your place. Jared has to work early tomorrow but wants to spend the night with me," Tawny says, stretching and yawning.

I can hear disappointment in her voice and I know this isn't exactly what she wants. I retrieve my key for her.

I hug both Jared and Tawny goodnight and watch from the front door as they walk out into the brisk night air.

"What's wrong with her?" Rebecca asks.

She's only half interested because she's watching Jack Nicholson finger Jessica Lang.

"I'm not sure," I tell her, still watching them go.

When the movie finishes another quickly follows and Rebecca's living room is filled with smoke. Three empty wine bottles are sitting on her coffee table.

I stand slowly as Rebecca starts cleaning up our mess and I walk to the bathroom. I'm too tired and inebriated to stand so I sit down to pee. It's a few moments before my bladder begins to empty and when it does sharp pains shoot through my penis. Tears collect in my eyes and words like 'fire' and 'razorblades' shoot through me head. I brace myself until it's empty and I place a hand over my mouth to keep from yelping. I can barely breathe when the last drop falls from my urethra and I hold myself tenderly.

I'm shorter than normal and as I feel my shaft, I can feel inflammation inside. My urethra must be raw and as I inspect the head, yellowish green fluid oozes from the hole I'm spreading open. Unable to do anything about it now, I put my withered dick back in my shorts and carefully walk out of the bathroom.

Rebecca's putting our glasses in the dishwasher when I sit down at the counter.

"Are you ok?" she asks, stopping everything.

She's genuinely concerned.

"My stomach hurts," I answer quickly, tempted to tell her the truth.

"Oh. Well, have some warm milk," she says, filling a tall glass.

She microwaves it for thirty seconds and hands it to me. Milk is my least favorite beverage and warming it simply makes it that much more repulsive.

We sit down on the couch again and I quietly sip on my milk. I struggle to keep my eyes open and Rebecca covers me with a blanket. She kisses me softly on the cheek and goes to John.

I can't fall asleep at first. It's quiet and dark with the TV off and I stare at a curio cabinet full of porcelain dolls. I count the eyes to help me slumber. Somewhere around four I finally fall asleep. It doesn't last long because I awake at five and throw up. I rush to the bathroom and reach the bowl just in time. The milk has curdled with the wine and now smells like rotten cheese, coming out my mouth and nose. After emptying my system, throwing up every last drop of milk and dry heaving uncontrollably, I lie back down and fall into a deep sleep.

Ten

I wake up feeling sick the morning of July the 5th. I'm disoriented and hung-over, my mind slowly trying to catch up with what my eyes are seeing. I eat breakfast with Rebecca and John. They talk while reading newspapers and I struggle to keep my toast down. Ty comes down looking exactly how I feel and we all drink coffee with our eggs.

I leave right after finishing breakfast. The sun is torturous and my headache's worsening by the minute. I have tunnel vision and at the end the only light I see is my bed, faithfully calling my name.

Like always, my apartment is dark and hot. Tawny and Jared have already left and I take off my clothes, leaving them where they fall. The breeze coming in through my window's hot and does nothing to cool me off. I can feel sweat dripping down my back and collecting in the small patch of hair just above my ass.

I drop down onto the mattress and my nose is met with the stale scent of sex. I haven't changed my sheets in a month and my face is in dry remnants of lovemaking. With all my willingness to change them, I'm too tired. I turn over and pull my face as close as I can to the window. I quickly fall asleep with the drapes blowing back and forth across my cheek. I sleep for the rest of the day, sweaty and alone.

I meet Tawny for an early lunch the next day after seven phone calls coaxing me out of my cave. We meet at a Mexican grill on the new side of town, near the mall. She's wearing short shorts and a tank top, her eyes hidden by her sunglasses. I'm wearing my typical white t-shirt and blue jeans. My black rubber sandals are so old holes will soon be rubbing through the soles.

"Is Jared meeting us?" I ask after we sit down at a table facing the parking lot.

"I didn't invite him," Tawny responds a matter of factly.

Before I have a chance to inquire why, she continues angrily.

"That friend of yours has problems. He doesn't tell me what's wrong and just blows me off!! Have I done something?"

"Umm, I don't know," I stammer, thrown off guard. "Didn't you guys have sex the other night?"

"Yeah. We went back to your place and did it," she says, not lowering her voice as the waiter approaches.

We both order grilled salmon and throw our menus at him.

"It was weird though. When he was done he just rolled over and went to sleep," Tawny continues, sipping her water. "It was like he felt guilty or something."

I have my suspicions but I keep them to myself. I know this is the only reason she invited me to lunch.

"I have something for you to give to asshole for me," she finally says after taking off her sunglasses.

Her eyes are swollen and red. The envelope she hands me is thick and the front simply says 'Jared.'

"I'm going to say it before he gets the chance. We're wrong for each other and it was going to end soon anyway," Tawny begins again, tears glossing her green eyes.

She's more emotionally involved in this than I thought, probably even more than she thought she'd be. I change the subject.

"I have something to tell you," I start, regretting every word.

She stares at me blankly, waiting.

"I think I have an STD or something. It's been getting worse," I finish.

In just one day it's gotten much worse and much more painful. Just sitting and waiting for my lunch is awful and I haven't jerked off in two days. I can't go on like this for much longer.

"What's wrong? I mean, what are the symptoms?" she asks with a shocked expression, taking my hand from across the table.

"It hurts when I pee and the inside of my cock's sore," I say, blushing. I continue, completely embarrassed. "And I have secretions."

"You should have it looked at," she says, absorbing it for a minute.

There's a hint of a smile on her face but she quickly wipes it clean.

"But I don't have any medical insurance!" I tell her defensively.

I lost my coverage the day I moved out of my mother's house, her way of teaching me a lesson that I'll never fully comprehend.

"Go to the County Clinic. I'm sure they have free testing," Tawny says quickly and condescendingly, unintentionally mocking me the way she always does.

The server quietly sets down our food, fills our waters, and leaves.

Tawny sits silent for a moment but starts to giggle. What at first comes out faint and muffled soon grows into full-blown laughter. She laughs so hard she has to hold her stomach, trying to stifle the noise with her other hand.

"What!?" I demand with a mouthful of fish.

"I'm sorry honey," she says between bouts, wiping tears from her eyes.

"But I can't help see the humor in it. First, you're nineteen and just now losing your virginity. Second, you didn't seem too excited about it, which makes me think you couldn't keep it up or something. Now this?!"

"Ha Ha," I yell at her through a mouthful of food. "For you information and for humor's sake, I couldn't keep it up!"

Tawny laughs so hard I hope she falls on the floor.

I spend the rest of lunch recounting in embarrassing detail what actually happened that night. She laughs more and so do I. The laughter takes my mind off the problem at hand and I'm quietly hoping it's nothing penicillin can't cure.

After lunch we stop in Barnes and Noble. I have a couple hours to waste before work. Tawny rushes straight to the fiction section in hopes of getting the latest from Anne Rice and I peruse the magazine rack. I flip through a few fitness newsletters and soon find myself standing in front of the entertainment section. A single copy of *Backstage West* sits in the very front. Without thinking too much of it, I pick it up and flip through it.

As I look through the auditions, I'm discouraged by words like 'attractive' and 'muscular.' I've always wanted to act but I've done absolutely nothing to realize my dream. Other than a few acting classes and two open casting calls, I've made no effort. My eyes rest on a small ad in the corner, almost dismissible in the fold.

Need an Agent?

Open auditions in Hollywood with well-known Agency West.

Looking for unique talents. All Actors and Actresses welcome.

Call Sheba Williams at 323-555-0750

Below the ad is a list of open days and the very last day is tomorrow. The thought's intimidating but what do I have to lose?

"Found it!" Tawny's voice calls out from behind me. She waves the very book she was looking for with a proud smile on her face. She glances at the magazine in my hand and continues, "You finally gonna go for it?"

"Yeah, I was thinking about it. Wanna go with me to Hollywood tomorrow?"

"Sure. I have nothing else to do."

I quickly look through the theater section for a book of monologues. I should at least have one piece prepared.

I spend the whole night at work looking through the excerpts, standing at my podium with the book open next to the phone. I decide on a piece of a guy trying to talk his girlfriend out of killing herself. I know it's morbid but it suits me. After reading it over a couple times, I finally decide to make the phone call I've been dreading.

I find a number for the local County Clinic in the phone book. The machine operator directs me to a menu that informs me the next free STD clinic is a week away. They only take the first ten desperate patients so I'll have to be there at five in the morning.

Tawny's waiting out front when I get to her parent's house early the next morning.

"Look at you. On time and everything. Good boy!" she jokes as she climbs in.

In an hour we're battling traffic. Tawny brought her CD player and adapter so we listen to Tool.

The 405 is packed and we slowly make our way south. We chat about movies and music and the many high school memories that are still fresh in our minds.

We take the 101 into Hollywood and drive slowly down Sunset Blvd, admiring the city in all its trashy glamour. We find the building on the corner of Vine St. but park two blocks away.

"Well, good luck," Tawny says, hugging me.

"You're not coming up with me?" I ask, scared without her.

"Of course not. I hate actors," she says with a devilish grin.

She hops from the Jeep and runs across the street to a store with an **XXX** sign in the window.

As I ride the elevator up to the eleventh floor, the anticipation starts to grow in my chest. I'm wearing a button-up black shirt tucked into my cleanest pair of blue jeans. I can feel the sweat collecting in my armpits and groin. I recite the monologue over and over in my head and I only have half of it memorized.

The elevator stops on no other floor and finally dings, the doors flinging open. I step into a large waiting area with a receptionist sitting directly in front of me.

"Can I help you?" the girl from the front desk asks, leaning around her flat screen monitor.

Her voice is beautiful and her annunciation is meticulous. She has shoulder length blonde hair, tan skin, and long legs that unabashedly stick out from under a very short black skirt. I glimpse light pink panties when she crosses her legs. She smiles at me sincerely.

"Umm, yeah," I stammer. "I'm here for the audition, casting thing."

I feel like a retard as I hand her my crumpled up *Backstage West*. She simply glances at it and picks up her telephone.

"Please have a seat," she says.

She hands me a clipboard and gestures to a nearby leather sofa. As I sit she quietly talks into her phone, glancing over at me. The walls are adorned with large movie posters and signed headshots, all of which must belong to clients.

Attached to the clipboard is an application. I write my name, a description of myself, and then glance over a list of talents. I don't exactly have any talents so I check off the ones that I might be able to learn.

Horseback riding, check.

Rifle shooting, check.

Singing, check.

Of the hundred listed I check twenty-seven. When I finish I sit quietly, nervously waiting my turn.

The phone rings and the pretty blonde answers it. She stands and motions for me to follow her.

"They're ready to see you now," the girl says, holding the door open for me, a door with Sheba's name etched into the glass.

The room is sparsely furnished and well lit with floor to ceiling windows that look onto another glass building.

"Please, sit," Sheba says to me from behind her desk, not looking up as I enter.

She's in her early fifties with dark skin and black hair braided tightly down her skull. Her assistant, a white guy in his twenties, is standing next to her. He reaches out for my clipboard as I sit down and sets it in front of her. She begins to look at it and after an eternity of sitting quiet, finally looks up at me.

"So, what brings you here today?" Sheba asks with a big fake smile, as if she has absolutely no idea.

"I saw your ad in *Backstage West*," I stutter.

"Well, I see you didn't bring a résumé or a headshot, so James here will be taking a picture of you," she continues, glancing back down at my talents.

James pulls a camera from a filing cabinet and motions for me to stand against the wall. Before I have a chance to smile, the bulb flashes and the camera's quickly put back.

"We'll be working on a quick scene today," Sheba says while standing, handing me a sheet of paper.

"Ok," is the only response I can muster.

"You'll be reading the part of David, a crazy college frat guy. And I'll be reading the part of Clay, a new roommate you're showing around the house," she continues as she walks across the room.

James guides me in front of a tripod and I stand on an "X" taped to the carpet. He adjusts the height and glances into the lens. Sheba isn't paying attention and is still glancing over my application.

"Umm, can I have a couple minutes to look this over?" I ask, holding up the dialogue.

"No, you can't," she responds blankly. "This is not high school drama. James."

James turns back to the camera and the red light blinks on.

"July 8th, 2001. First audition with Jason," Sheba says over James' shoulder. "Let's begin."

I glance down at the paper in my hand. My palms are sweaty and my heart's pounding loudly. I have the first line and I can barely see it.

"Hey man," I begin, trying my hardest to sound laid-back and crazy.

"Yo. Thanks for showing me around," Sheba says in a flat monotone voice, making me feel like Kenneth Branaugh.

"No prob boss. This is the beer fridge and this is the food fridge," I continue, reading and mimicking towards two invisible refrigerators.

"Feel free to eat anything you like but keep in mind, whatever you put in there, we might eat," I continue and when the script calls for a chuckle, I try to sound realistic.

"Cool man. So, where are all the chicks at?" she continues, looking at me over her glasses.

"Hold on a sec man, we'll get to that. We have keggers every Friday and Saturday so there will be plenty of pussy around. We have rules when it comes to the ladies and the bros too," I continue to read, putting up three fingers.

"First rule, you have to carry a condom on you at all times, just in case a brother needs one. Two, never bang another brother's conquest. And C, if a sock's hanging on a door handle, that means stay out."

Reading the dialogue makes me feel like a fucking idiot and I can't wait for it to stop.

We still have the bottom half of the page to read when Sheba interrupts me.

"That'll be sufficient," she says, setting her paper down. I stand nervously, on the spot.

She stares at me, then continues. "You're more of a serious type of actor I imagine. Who would you mold yourself after if you had the choice?"

"Anthony Hopkins," I blurt out.

Silence of the Lambs is my favorite movie and Sir Hopkins sounded like a suitable answer in my head.

"What do you think of Sean Penn?" she asks, still staring at me blankly.

"Umm, I don't know," I say like an idiot.

What the fuck do I care about Sean Penn? I think I've only seen two of his movies.

"It says here that you can sing," Sheba moves on, picking up my clipboard. "Would you mind singing a piece for us?"

My pulse runs cold. I wish I hadn't checked anything. The one thing I can't do. I can sing in the car, in the shower, and in the middle of church. But singing in front of the camera is a totally different story.

"Ok," I respond again like a broken record.

I could've said no or said it was a mistake but instead I choose to make a fucking idiot of myself. I clear my mind and sing the first song that comes to me, the last song I would expect myself to remember.

"Amazing Grace..." I start.

My voice is awful and out of tune.

"...how sweet the sound, that saved a wretch like me..." I continue, wishing I had gone with "Beautiful Day."

Before I finish the first verse, Sheba interrupts me again. She's laughing now, shaking her head.

"That is definitely enough," she says. "If you can't get paid to do it, do not put it on your résumé."

I'm quiet, crushed, embarrassed, and humiliated. I just put myself on public display and was reduced to this fucking bitch's humorous joke. Right when I think I might cry, she speaks up.

"Do you have any questions for me?" she asks.

"No."

"Well, thank you for coming in and have a nice afternoon."

James holds the door open for me and I quickly walk out. I sprint passed the receptionist and push the down button. I don't want her to see me cry.

The door dings open and I step inside. I hold the **Door Close** button and the tears roll down my cheeks. I hold the button all the way to the lobby, avoiding any interruptions. I wipe my eyes as I walk across the lobby and out the front doors.

Tawny's waiting for me when I walk up. She's smiling wildly and has a black plastic bag on her lap.

"I got you a present Poopy!" she says as I climb in next to her.

She pulls out a large video box and tosses at me.

"*Bath Time Beavers*! Doesn't it look super?"

The cover's plastered with naked people in various sexual positions, every one of them in a bathroom. Anal shots, threesome's, facials. It's all there and I can't help but smile at the gesture.

"How did it go?" she asks, pulling out another videotape.

It's gay porn and apparently for her. She admires the cover and I try to avoid looking at it.

"Not well. Let's just say I'm going to seriously reconsider my career as an actor."

I don't say anything else about the experience because I don't see the point. It'll just discourage me further. We pick up sandwiches and eat on the road. Her mother continues to be insufferable and she needs to be home by three for no apparent reason.

"Why do they let you stay out only half the time?" I ask between mouthfuls of sandwich.

"Well, as long as they think I'm spending the night at your place, then it's ok if I beg."

"That makes no sense."

"Well, they think you're gay, so it kind of does."

"They what?" I shriek.

"They think you're gay. Don't get so butt hurt!"

"But why would they think that?" I shriek again, quickly dropping my sandwich into its wrapper, spilling lettuce on the floor.

"Does it matter?" Tawny asks, staring at me wide eyed. "Who cares? Even if you were gay, I wouldn't."

"Well, I'm not," I tell her, over-defensive and foolish.

"I know you're not, dumbass. My dad hates *Will & Grace* and my mom thinks Ellen's a cunt. So fuck them. At least it means we get to spend more time together, right?" she continues, still staring at me.

Her eyes are wide. I want to agree, to tell her it really doesn't bother me, but what kind of impression would that give her?

It's nearly three when I drop Tawny off. She kisses me on the cheek before she hops out and reminds me to give Jared his letter. I promise her I will. I leave only after she steps in the house.

The sun's almost set when I get home. So little was done with so much time and I simply want to smoke and watch MTV. I start stripping my clothes off, my regular routine, walking into the kitchen to get a beer. I flip my computer on so I can play a level of *Tomb Raider* and masturbate to Lara Croft.

The light is flashing on my answering machine in the hall and I stop to listen to my messages.

I never have messages. When I do, they're usually from my mother.

"You have nine new messages," the machine squawks at me.

It beeps twice and starts to play the first message.

"Jason, its mom. Call me as soon as possible. I need your help with something," her voice slurs from the small speaker.

I can tell she's been drinking; she sounds stern and determined.

Too calculated.

The second message is a little more frantic, twenty minutes after the first one.

"Jason, I'm having a problem with Brian. Please come over. I can't reach your sister."

The fact that she called Janine shows true desperation.

The third message is worse and much more for the fourth. By the fifth message she's in tears.

"Jason, where are you?! Brian's abusing me and I need you to come save me!"

There's grumbling in the background followed by a loud click. Silence.

The sixth message is Janine, wondering why mom is calling her. She dreads conversations with our mother and always uses me as her messenger. The last three calls are hang-ups, all in half hour intervals. I feel compelled to help, despite my better judgment. I redress and head back outside.

The closer I get to my mom's, the more I want to turn around and go home. The sun's completely gone and the air's crisp and inviting.

Brian's truck is in the driveway. All the lights are on and I can hear yelling from the street. I don't want to do this. I don't want to do this. I do not want to do this!

The front door's unlocked and the yelling blasts me when I step inside. I walk passed my old room and peak inside to see Jessica watching TV. Her eyes are red, swollen, and shrink-wrapped in tears.

My mom runs and throws herself at me when I step in the kitchen. She's wearing an old white t-shirt and blue jeans. The sobbing intensifies out of control. I hold her tight and she buries her face in my chest

"I want him gone! He pushed me! I want him to leave!" her voice booms.

Her bony arms are shaking and she wraps them tightly around me.

"Jesus Debra, you slapped me! **You** attacked me! It's called self defense!" Brian finally speaks up, stepping forward.

He's wearing exactly what she is with a John Deere hat placed tightly on his small head. A red hand mark is quickly darkening on his cheek.

"I have nowhere to go!" he continues, looking at me with worry in his eyes.

"Well, I guess that's your problem, isn't it?" I snarl.

I don't even know why I open my mouth. He doesn't have anywhere to go! My mother was the one who wanted him to move-in in the first place.

"I don't think this concerns you," Brian responds, stepping forward and straightening his back.

He barely comes up to my shoulders and the prospect of knocking him senseless makes me laugh.

"She wants you gone, so pack up your shit," I tell him without blinking. "Unless of course you want me to kick your ass in front of Jessica."

He contemplates his options for a second. He hesitates, only for a moment, and walks passed us.

"Jessica, pack some clothes. We're going to a hotel," he says as he heads for the stairs to the master bedroom.

I can't look at her, tears streaming down her cheeks. My old room has been converted into a little girlie haven and she's tightly clutching a teddy bear.

"Thank you, thank you, thank you!" my mother breaths into my ear as she reaches up and wraps her arms around my neck.

I hate when she leans against me like this and I want to throw her to the floor.

"It's ok," is all I say.

What I really want to tell her is to fix her own fucking problem. Clean up your own goddamn mess! Right when I thought I wouldn't have to do this for you anymore, you fall back on the one person that is always there. Not anymore. Not after tonight.

After ten long minutes, Brian comes back down wearing his boots and cowboy hat. He has a duffel bag filled with clothes slung over one shoulder.

"I'm coming back tomorrow for the rest of my stuff," he says to my mom, ignoring me.

She turns away, lifting her nose.

"Don't fuck with my shit," he decides to add in my direction.

"It wouldn't be worth my time," I snap back.

Jessica comes out of her room carrying a pink backpack overflowing with clothes and toys. She's dragging her teddy bear that's almost as big as she is and her hair's falling out of her headband. Brian doesn't give her the chance to say goodbye and quickly scoops her up. He slams the door and we listen to his truck roar away.

"I'm done with him. I can't do this again. I won't have some man interrogating me every time I go out for groceries!" my mother starts as she turns back to the fridge.

She fills a large glass with ice, a little Coke, and twice as much Jack Daniels.

"Honestly, who the fuck does he think he is?" she asks before taking a long swig of her cocktail.

"Mom, I don't want to hear it. Please," I plead.

She doesn't respond. She lowers her head and stares down at the counter. And now I feel like the asshole! I'm going to do exactly what she expects me to.

I walk to her and place a hand on her shoulder.

"It's gonna be fine," I whisper.

No response.

"Really. Give it time."

No response.

"I'm sorry. I didn't mean to be so harsh."

She turns and hugs me again.

"Thank you," she says, her weight dead in my arms. "Could you stay here tonight? You can sleep in my room. I just don't want to be alone."

She reeks of whiskey now and I'm a little too old to be sharing a bed with her. I'd rather not sleep in the same bed she fucked the short cowboy in.

"Sure, I'm gonna go have a smoke first," I say as I pull away.

"I'm gonna go get in bed," she slurs in response, heading for the stairs with her glass in hand.

I take the cordless phone with me as I step outside.

I light my Marlboro and dial Janine. I sit in a whicker chair and flick my ashes into the rose bushes. The other end rings four times and Heath answers.

"Hey man. Is your fiancé home?" I ask, smiling.

"Yeah, hold on a sec bro," he says in his normal jovial voice. I hear him call my sister's name and she picks up another phone.

"Where the fuck have you been? I've called your place four times!"

"I'm at mom's. Ever thought of calling here?"

"Very funny," she says, actually chuckling. "What happened?"

"The usual. Mom played the jealous game, had too much to drink, and pushed Brian's buttons. He pushed her back. He should've knocked her fucking lights out!"

We both laugh at the mental picture of my mom laid out flat, nose broken. Our conversation's short, like they always are, and she goes back to her evening with Heath.

I finish my cigarette and go inside. Maybe if I just leave my mom will never know the difference. I turn off all the lights and slowly walk up the steps.

She's already fast asleep. Her glass is completely empty and her breathing's already deep. I pull the blankets up around her and kiss her lightly on the cheek. I turn off the light and walk downstairs. I sit on the couch and watch some TV. I absorb all the familiar smells and noises, the things that remind me of being home. The things that are no longer mine. I drink a six-pack and by three I can barely keep my eyes open.

If Brian wants to come back and cause shit, so be it. I'm tired and this is no longer my problem. I lock the front door, climb slowly into my car, and drive home.

Home.

My home.

eleven

When Wednesday morning finally arrives, I face it with fear and anticipation. My cock's not any better and the secretions are far more severe. I'm so scared that I arrive three hours before the clinic opens just to be sure that I get seen. I sit outside watching the sunrise, smoking cigarettes and leaning against the hard stucco building.

A small crowd gathers, forming a loose line along the wall. Fifteen-year-old sluts, hookers, and Hispanic fags. I'm surrounded by people I would normally avoid and we're all here for one singular goal. I feel filthy and ashamed. I smoke an entire pack, Marlboro after Marlboro, and when the door finally opens, I run inside.

Each person is given a number as they walk in the door and I'm proud of my '1.' A large black woman hands me a clipboard without looking up and motions towards a row of chairs. I sit and fill out the form. I check 'No' for most of the questions:

Have you ever participated in anal sex?

In the past few months have you slept with an African?

Have you ever performed sexual acts with an animal?

I don't belong here. If I just wait and drink cranberry juice, maybe it will go away. My paperwork's filled out and I watch everyone else out of the corner of my eye. When I'm about to run for the door, my name's called.

"Jason..." the voice calls again and I slowly stand.

My feet feel like bricks and every step towards the large black woman feels like another foot in the grave. My head feels light and Kanisha, that's the name on her badge, actually looks at me this time.

"Sit," she says shortly, pointing to a chair in a small examining room.

She roughly wraps a cuff around my arm and applies pressure.

"I'm going to be taking some blood before the doctor sees you," she continues after writing my blood pressure down.

Kanisha continues to avoid my eyes and jabs me without warning. She fills three vials with blood.

"Alright. Dr. Kaushik will be with you in a couple minutes. Just take off your shorts and undergarments and sit on the examining table," she says while collecting her paperwork and blood samples.

Before I have a chance to ask why she quickly vacates, leaving me to my own devices.

I kick off my sandals and pull off my shorts. I'm not wearing undergarments. My skin goes cold in the sterile air and the hairs on my arms stand erect. I sit on the table and the crumpling paper makes me nervous. I slowly position myself, trying to get comfortable. I laugh, looking down at how pathetic and shriveled I am. I look at my reflection in the mirror above the sink. White t-shirt, nothing else.

After an eternity of waiting, the doctor finally graces me with his presence. He's a small Oriental man who avoids me like the nurse did. He walks across the room, sits on a stool and looks through my paperwork all before acknowledging my presence.

"What seems to be the ploblem?" he asks me, struggling with 'problem.'

"I think I have some kind of STD," I begin, wishing it weren't true. "It hurts when I pee and I've been having secretions."

"Sounds like you have Chlamydia," he comments, still not looking at me.

He stands and walks to a cupboard.

"I'm going to need samples of the fluid," he tells me, holding up a large Q-tip for me to see.

My head instantly goes numb and I feel like I might pass out. I stand up, leaning against the bed for support, and wait for the blow to hit.

"I need you hold it up for me," he says, annoyed. I look at him numbly, confused. "Your penis," he continues, disgusted.

So I stand holding my humbled dick and he rolls his stool over to me. He barely touches the head with his gloved fingers and slides the Q-tip inside my urethra. My breath is lost and the pain that ensues is unbearable. Like cleaning your ears with a huge Q-tip made of razors or wiping a hemorrhoid with steel wool, I am utterly humiliated. I feel like an exposed baby having his foreskin cut off, like a young virgin girl having her hymen ripped apart in front of her grandparents.

Dr. Kaushik places the Q-tip in a sterile baggy and instructs me to put my pants back on. I expect to see blood but there is none. He hands me two large pills, Penicillin, and says it will be gone in a week.

"If we find anything else, you will hear from us in about two days. Be careful, use condoms," he instructs, leading me out.

I feel lost in a bad joke. I cover my face with my large sunglasses and quickly run through the packed waiting room. I run to my Jeep and open a new pack of cigarettes. I inhale gratefully.

I still have the rest of the day with nothing to do before work. I had no idea how long this would have taken and now that it's over, I'm left with a multitude of options. I've considered registering for classes, finally dragging myself over to the community college campus. Before I start the car I notice a pay phone and suddenly get the urge to call Brandon. He'd mentioned going with me and I totally forgot.

"Hey buddy," I say cheerfully into the receiver when I hear his voice.

I found just enough change beneath my seat to pay for the call. I better make this fast.

"Hey," is all he says. I can hear music playing loudly in the background.

"Are you practicing with your band?" I ask, trying hard to be conversational.

"No, just listening to the new Rob Zombie CD," he says and the music abruptly stops.

"Well," I continue, wishing he would give me more to work with. "I was heading over to the college and I knew you wanted to go with me so I was wondering if you weren't busy if you'd maybe want to go." I feel stupid for being so nervous, for not just coming out with it.

We haven't spoken since my mother's party and I didn't imagine it would ever be like this.

"Sure," he responds simply. "I'm not doing anything else."

I offer to pick him up and when I hang up the phone, his words ring loudly in my ears.

I'm not doing anything else.

Is that the only reason he said he'd go? If there was something else better to do than hang out with me would he just blow me off? I didn't realize I was such a burden.

Brandon comes out to my car when I drive up. I had expected to go inside and see his parents but he hops in before I turn the ignition off.

"Oh. I wanted to say hi to your mom," I tell him.

"She's not home."

I want to push further, question him more but I keep silent. Both his mother's SUV and his father's truck are in the driveway.

Brandon is quiet for most of the ride. I talk about work and ask what he's been doing with his summer.

"Not much," he responds quietly, not looking at me. "I've been practicing with the band."

"That's cool. Are you gonna register for classes?"

"Not yet. I don't know what I want to do. I think I'll take a semester off. Maybe a year," he says.

It all seems like a chore for him, like talking to me is hard for him to do.

"Ok."

When we finally get to The San Soledo Community College, it takes nearly half an hour to find a parking space. With classes starting in a few weeks, the campus is crawling with people. Intersession courses, club meetings, and new comers buying books. I feel out of place, like a stranger who steps into church halfway through a sermon.

Brandon quietly follows me to the counselor's office and we wait in line. There are only two counselors manning the counter and the line gets longer and longer, outside and around the corner. We remain quiet and I'm starting to realize I did something very wrong. I have a faint idea of what it could've been.

"Next," the guy behind the counter says impatiently.

Almost an hour after we arrive and I'm finally being called.

"What can I do for you?" he asks impatiently.

He's only a couple years older than me, dressed much preppier in an A&F shirt, and is probably a student. He looks at me condescendingly, as if I am a waste of his time.

"I need to talk to a counselor about registering for classes," I say weakly.

"Do you have an appointment?" he asks quickly, turning back to his monitor.

"Sort of. I mailed in a card last September and someone was supposed to contact me. No one did."

"Did you call and make an appointment?" he asks again, taking off his glasses and placing his hands on the desk.

"No. I have to register and I don't know what classes I need."

"Let me get this straight. You supposedly put in some kind of card and no one called you. Then you decided it was unnecessary to make an appointment to see one of us. Then you wait until the last minute to even register! Have you even applied yet?"

I shrug, feeling more like a mouse than before. All of this was explained to me at one point. All the steps and procedures had been mapped out but I never bothered to pay attention.

"I'm sorry to inform you it's too late to meet with a counselor before classes start. You're on your own," he says quickly, washing his hands clean. "I do recommend that you look through that shelf of paperwork," he says while pointing behind me. "It has a list of all of our classes, majors, and transferable courses." He waits, and then adds, "Next!"

"Excuse me," I persist, my pulse raising and my face burning. "I really don't think that was necessary."

He doesn't respond, just stares at me.

"What kind of a counselor are you? This is your fucking job! I apologize if I'm not as informed about this place as you are but you don't need to be an asshole!"

My hands are shaking and I'm so frustrated I feel like I might cry. Brandon stands behind me, looking away. I turn and yell for the guy to fuck off as I kick the nearest door open.

I quickly light a cigarette, fumbling with the pack.

"Can you believe that?" I yell at Brandon when he exits shortly after me.

"I know. Jesus," he says unenthusiastically.

After I finish my cigarette I quickly run back inside and head straight over to the shelf. I grab paperwork for financial aid, class schedules, and a list of courses I would need for my basic two-year degree. Brandon's waiting for me when I come back outside and I silently lead him back to the Jeep.

"Are you hungry?" I ask.

"Yeah, but I don't have any cash."

"I'll pay," I say and burn out of the parking lot.

We go to the Denny's across the street and get a table by the window. It's just turning noon and the sun shines brightly on us from above and below as it reflects off the tabletop. We continue on in silence and my heart's still racing. Even after we order milk shakes and food, Brandon remains quiet.

"Ok, what the hell's up with you?" I demand after taking a drink from my strawberry shake.

"What are you talking about?" he mumbles into his straw, feebly attempting to sound unbothered.

"You've been quiet all day. What the hell? Is something going on? Did I do something?"

"Well..." he begins, looking away from me. "I wasn't sure if I wanted to say anything."

"Why wait?" I spurt, spraying pink all over the table.

"I'm worried about you."

"Are you joking?" I laugh, knowing exactly where this is going.

I'm happy I didn't tell him about the clinic I went to just hours ago.

"I think you should be careful. I think you're going to seriously hurt yourself."

"Really? Would you mind elaborating?" I ask, crossing my arms and staring at him.

Our food arrives but I don't touch my nachos.

"Your partying seems a little out of hand. I know you've been smoking pot and I just think you should be careful. It can lead to other things."

I laugh out loud. The fact that he's this worried about me is flattering but ridiculous. I'm in control. I feel in control. My restraint slips occasionally but never completely and I wish I could force him to see things differently.

"It's not funny. You weren't like this before. You party all the time and then you had sex with that girl. It just doesn't seem like you."

"Well, say hello to the new me," I retort, throwing my arms in the air. "I'm sorry you hold me on some kind of pedestal but I'm in complete check. Just because you're scared to do anything doesn't make it bad for me."

Brandon doesn't and eats his food quietly. I'm enraged and completely caught off guard. I'd never point fingers at him or tell him how horrible his decisions are.

"So, when exactly did you start feeling this way?"

"The night of your mom's party. Jenny and I felt out of place."

"Well, sorry if I didn't feel the need to go out of my way to include you. I thought you were big enough to do that on your own."

We eat in complete silence. I'm fuming and the rage keeps pouring in on me. I know Brandon has only the best intentions in mind but I feel violated. Irrationally, I feel violated. I give nothing but acceptance and love to my friends and now one of my greatest companions thinks I'm slipping down some inevitable slope. I'll show him. He'll see.

We continue on in silence to Brandon's house. I want to drop him off as soon as possible. I want to get rid of him and get ready for work. I put in a Marilyn Manson tape and blare it as loud as my little speakers will go. I don't want to give him the opportunity to talk. When we get to his house, he quickly jumps out. I can see his parents in the living room and I quickly turn down the music.

"I thought your parents weren't home?" I yell, glaring at him before he closes his door.

"I lied."

"Why would you do that?"

"Because they don't want to see you," he says sternly, glaring back. "After the shit you pulled with Jared and Tawny, my mom isn't really happy with you right now. I'm surprised Michelle is even talking to you."

He slams the door and walks away, not looking back.

I sit and stew, his words playing over and over in my head. I want to run up to the door, rush inside, and confront them all.

When I get home the first thing I do is call Tawny. I'm relieved when she answers the phone. I can't stand it when her mother yells for her.

"That's good news," she says enthusiastically when I tell her about the penicillin. "I'll keep my fingers crossed for the next couple of days too."

"Thank you," I say, breathing a sigh of relief.

I want to tell her what Brandon told me but I know it's a bad idea. They barely know each other and I don't need any more friends with hard feelings.

"When are you going to tell Morgan?" she asks.

"I have to work in a couple hours. I'll call her before I go."

"Call her now, Jason. She needs to know because she could be spreading what she has!"

"I will," I reassure her.

"Jason! Now!" she responds forcefully, refusing to take any shit from me.

"Ok. I will. I promise."

When we hang up I smoke two cigarettes back to back. When I light the third, I dial Morgan's cell number. I hate doing this to her, breaking this news. That night was neither of our bests and it's coming back to haunt us. With each ring I hope she doesn't pick up and right when I think it might go to her voicemail, she answers

"Hello?"

"Hey. It's me."

"Who's me?"

"Jason."

Long pause.

I can hear people talking in the background. Loud voices, like a TV.

"Umm, is this a bad time?" I ask, hoping it is.

"No," she says and I hear the voices fade away, like she's leaving the room. "What's up?"

"I have to tell you something..."

"Ok. What is it?"

I sit quietly with the phone to my face and drag slowly. When I'm done with this puff, then I'll tell her. When I'm finished inhaling, finished exhaling, new breath in, fresh air in.

"I have an STD. You gave me Chlamydia." The words fall out of my mouth easier than I thought they would.

"What?" is her immediate response. "Are you sure? How do you know?!"

"I went to a clinic because I was having problems. I haven't had sex with anyone else. I think you should get tested."

I give her the information about the free clinic and all I can hear is the muffled voices coming from somewhere behind her. She finally speaks up, sobbing.

"I'm sorry. I am so sorry."

"It's ok," I reassure her.

I'd love to say more, be mean and vindictive. Right now, today, that would feel good. But she doesn't deserve it.

"Just get it taken care of, ok?"

"Alright," she whispers, followed by, "Have you told anyone?"

"No, don't worry about it."

We quietly say goodbye and she gratefully hangs up.

My head hurts. My lungs ache but I can't help lighting one Marlboro after another. I've smoked two whole packs since this morning.

I try masturbating to a gang bang video, but I keep going limp because it stings so badly. After a half an hour I have blue balls. I resort to sticking a finger in my ass and I cum almost immediately, unsatisfactorily dribbling out.

I lie naked on the living room floor and watch the rest of the video, my cock and hand sticky from too much lube. I wipe off with a dirty t-shirt and get ready for work. I dread going because I'll have to see Michelle.

I hate myself for so many reasons.

TWELVE

With July ending the summer's nearing its peak. After my audition two weeks ago I've given up hope of ever becoming an actor. In every acting class I've ever taken, I've always been told to expect rejection. Well, fuck rejection.

And fuck Sheba.

When I show up for work today, Thursday, Dana announces that I'll be training a new busser. I've been wondering what the 'T' next to my name on the schedule meant. I'm impatient and unwilling to show every detail of my job but I begrudgingly tell Dana it won't be a problem. The new girl's sitting in the office filling out paper work, carefully rescanning it to make sure she didn't miss a thing.

Gwen's sixteen with the face of a twelve year old. She has curly, shoulder length red hair, and pale skin. She's much shorter than me and has breasts too large for her frame and age. I sit impatiently at the bar, waiting for her so we can prepare for the evening to follow. She sheepishly comes out of the office and hands her application and tax information to Dana.

"It's nice to meet you Jason," she says in a sweet voice. She has a wide smile, dick-sucking lips, and white teeth.

I'm instantly interested and know this is going to be easy.

"The pleasure's all mine," I say, shaking her hand.

She blushes, batting her eyes at me. *God, this girl knows what she's doing*. This is gonna to be a cakewalk. Maybe my summer isn't a complete failure because she's definitely do-able.

I go about the routine: turning on the lights, starting the stereo, making fresh iced tea, touring the stock room. I'm more than half tempted to do to her what I did to Michelle. Gwen follows me around like a lost puppy, eagerly asking questions and watching me intently. We chat intermittently, getting to know each other.

"So, what made you decide to work with us?" I ask, showing her how to fold napkins.

"I ate here a couple times with my aunt and uncle," she says simply, struggling to perfect her folding skills.

I reach over and help her, my large hands completely covering hers.

"Do you live with them?" I ask and know it's none of my business.

"Yeah. My mom abandoned me when I was nine and I haven't seen her since. I hope to save up money to go live with her. She's somewhere in Washington."

We continue to fold in silence. I struck a cord. Before I have an opportunity to apologize, people walk in the door and Gwen follows me back to the kitchen so I can show her the routine. After three tables, she's carrying the water and breads herself and I stand off to the side to admire my protégé.

The relief of not having to bus tables allows Dana to use me to stock her bar. She gives me a long list of liquor to retrieve from the cellar and I gladly carry a crate down. The air's damp and smells like cedar. Before I go about collecting my bottles, I pull a half empty carafe from the liqueurs and unscrew the cap. The chocolate flavored liquid was nearly full when I first discovered it. Brittney and I take turns sipping from it. We'll soon have to dispose of the evidence and find another.

After my third trip back from the cellar, the list is all checked off and the bottle's nearly empty. The bar's full and so is the dining room. Gwen chats with customers as if she's been doing this for ages and Rebecca already started a game of Hangman on the back counter. I hear the phone ring as I leave the cellar and Dana's looking for me when I approach with another full crate of booze.

"Your friend Jenny's on the phone. She sounds upset. Take it in the office."

I set the liquor down by the beer taps and quickly walk to the office. I haven't spoken to Jenny since my mother's party and I hope whatever's upsetting her isn't me. But I wouldn't be surprised.

"Hey, what's up?" I ask as I pick up the receiver and sit down at the desk.

"I have horrible news," Jenny whines and I can tell she's crying. "Do you remember Michael Duncliffe, from Sunday school?"

"Of course I do."

We grew up with Michael, attending the same church. His mother played the piano with the choir and was my sister's instructor.

"He died yesterday in a car accident," she barely gets out between gasps and sobs.

Jenny was close friends with his sister Sarah all through elementary school and always had a secret crush on Michael.

"Oh Jesus! That's horrible!" I honestly confess.

I've never lost a person close to me and the thought of someone my age dying makes me feel ill.

"His funeral's tomorrow. I need you to go with me."

This isn't exactly how I planned to see Jenny next, but I think I can make it through a funeral, as long as it's a closed casket. I've only been to one other funeral in my life, the mother of one of my mom's best friends, and I was nine. I was bored out of my mind and my mother kept giving me the dirty eye every time I fidgeted.

"Of course I'll go with you."

91

"Good. Can I see you? What time do you get off work?"

"I get out of here around ten. Come stay the night," I quickly offer. Maybe it'll give us a chance to talk about her quick departure from the party.

"I need to get out of my parent's house. They're driving me crazy! Can I go wait at your place?" she asks and I can hear the smile on her face.

"Sure. I left the door unlocked."

Gwen does an exceptional job and both Rebecca and Dana praise her up and down. She asks me for a ride home after I show her how to close down the dining room and clean up in the kitchen.

"I'd call my Aunt but she's probably sleeping already."

"No problem. It would be my pleasure."

"Unless, of course, you wanted to hang out or something," she adds, that sinful sneer reappearing on her face.

Of course I want to "hang out" but I don't think Jenny would appreciate the company. We go back into the empty bar to say goodbye to Rebecca and Dana as the clock turns ten. Dana's doing her routine paperwork and Rebecca's smoking, reading the newspaper, and having a glass of cabernet.

"Leaving already?" Rebecca asks.

"Yes. Gwen here needs to by home by curfew," I joke, taking a drag from her cigarette and sipping from her wine glass.

"None of that at my bar. I can get in big trouble," Dana yells, eyeing the wineglass in my hand.

If only everyone else knew.

"I have a funeral to go to tomorrow with Jenny, so I gotta get home too," I say and kiss them both goodnight.

They give their condolences and we finally make it out to my Jeep.

"I like the color!" Gwen exclaims as she hoists herself up into the passenger seat.

I actually stop to hold her door open.

"Yeah but red is definitely a bad color to speed in," I joke as I hop in next to her.

I pull out a cigarette and offer her one. I light a match and she gently holds my wrist as she ignites the tip.

"You know, it's more polite when you light yours first with a match," she says, blowing smoke.

"Why's that?" I inquire flirtatiously.

"Because the sulfur just burned my nose hairs!"

"Sorry!"

We talk the entire time it takes to drive her home. She's like a red haired Geisha, laughing at all my jokes and maintaining constant eye contact. Her ability to pay such close attention makes me nervous and I know I'm talking more than I should. When we finally arrive at her house, she lets out a deep sigh of disdain.

"Well, here we are. Thank you for the ride."

"It was no problem. I only live a few miles from here," I reassure her with a smile, actually surprised at how close we live to one another.

This is going to get me into trouble.

"I'll give you rides to work whenever you need them."

"Thank you. I'll see you later," she says, leaning over and kissing me on the cheek.

My hand's on the stick shift and her breasts brush against my forearm. They're firm and war. She smiles as she pulls back from my cheek and slowly gets out of the cab. The yellow streetlight above us shines brightly upon her and she walks away slowly, deliberately. She turns before walking in the front door, smiles shyly, and closes it behind her. Those ten seconds were so full of eroticism my heart's still pounding in my ears as I drive away and my crotch is quickly getting warm.

Jenny's sitting on the futon when I get home. I regret having told her to wait for me because after the excruciating drive home all I want to do is masturbate and fantasize about Gwen. Jenny's slumped over with a tissue in her hand, watching TV. She quickly stands as I enter the room and hugs me tightly, burying her face in my neck.

"Thank you so much for letting me come over," she whimpers.

I can feel warm tears stream down my neck and mascara's probably smeared on my white shirt. I hold her for a polite fifteen seconds and pat her on the back. I can feel her hesitate as I try to pull away but she reluctantly lets go.

"Don't worry. I can't stop thinking about it," I lie.

In all honestly I have no emotional attachment to the situation. I haven't seen Michael in years and we weren't exactly friends. Besides, I think funerals are a complete waste of time. Killing copious bouquets of flowers, crying over pictures, and flaunting a dead body is not in my opinion the best way to celebrate someone's life, even if it is lost.

I step in my bedroom to change into a pair of shorts and a Quicksilver t-shirt. Jenny follows me into the kitchen and I offer her some alcohol.

"I would love a Smirnoff Ice if you have one," she says while sitting.

She runs a hand through her long hair and moans deeply, exhausted. It's just her luck that Rebecca bought me a six-pack and I easily pop two lids. We sit quietly sipping our malts, the silence between us comforting.

"So, what happened to you at my mother's party?" I finally ask.

I don't let the sun go down on an argument and I rarely let something like this go unexplained.

"Just forget about that. I was being stupid and I just wanted to go home," she laughs, sipping from her cold bottle.

"You didn't go home. You went out with Brandon. You could have stayed you know."

"I know. I just felt like the fifth wheel at your mom's and Brandon was in the same boat."

"Well, I'm sure Morgan wouldn't have minded if you joined in," I add with a broad smile.

"Not funny. You haven't forgotten what happened last time, have you?" she asks, turning the tables on me.

"How are things with Jose?" I ask, downing what's left of my Smirnoff.

"We're over. I thought about trying again and we even talked about possibly having one of those 'open' relationships, but I just couldn't do that. Turns out I am a one guy kind of gal and I just don't have the dick he really needs."

I open two more Smirnoff Ices and we sit on the couch. Jenny has a crush on a member of N'SYNC, so she forces me to watch their concert on MTV. Following the show I'm subjected to a special about their sudden rise in fame. With my arm resting around her shoulder, she reaches her hand under my shirt and plays with the hairs just below my navel. Knowing each other for fourteen years brings a special kind of comfortability that often teeters on disastrous.

By the time the second program's over, I'm ready for sleep. My ass is numb from slouching and I gladly turn off the TV.

"I really need a shower," Jenny announces, standing and rubbing her cheeks.

The mascara that dripped down her face is now dry and flakes off onto her fingers.

"Do you want to join me?" she asks with out a moment's hesitation.

"Sure. I stink like bread and cardboard."

Jenny leads the way into the bathroom and that familiar sense of self-consciousness is slowly creeping back over me. I don't know why Jenny suddenly wants me to shower with her. I mean, we did almost have sex, but this is different. We'll be alone.

She closes the door as I step into the bathroom and looks at me, words resting on the tip of her tongue.

"What's wrong?" I ask, my heart pounding louder now, drowning out my own voice.

"Do you mind if we shower with the light off?"

"Sure, I don't mind I guess."

And I don't.

It won't be completely dark. The opaque window above the shower has no curtain or blinds and the street lamp outside will light our way. Jenny's not a super model by any means and even though she knows I won't judge how she looks naked, she doesn't even like to look at herself naked in the mirror. I turn the light off and we undress in the dark.

We laugh as we step into the shower and she giggles loudly as I stumble around her to turn on the water. It comes out ice cold at first, inspiring more laughter and Jenny grabs onto me in shock. Her face is bathed in a soft orange glow and I stare down at her as she smiles back up at me. The water quickly warms and we take turns under the showerhead. We fumble every time we have to switch positions and the shower curtain serves no purpose of stability.

"I'm glad you came over tonight," I confess while Jenny rinses her hair.

Her head is tilted back and her eyes are closed. I lean against the cool wall farthest from her and watch the water as it drips down her body. Thinking of what could possibly happen next makes my blood race and my cock harden.

"Me too," she says simply, ringing the water out of her hair.

She wipes the water from her eyes and finally opens them to see me staring at her.

"What?" she asks with a nervous chuckle, knowing exactly what's going through my mind.

I lean in and kiss her softly. What starts out as surprise quickly becomes the familiar and she eagerly kisses me back. The warm water pounds against her. I step forward, resting a hand on her shoulder, until I'm stopped abruptly by my hard dick. I poke her in the belly button and she starts to laugh at me, looking down with pleased surprise.

"Well, I can see what you're thinking about," she jokes.

"Yeah, well, can you blame me?"

Staring me straight in the eyes, she reaches out and takes a hold of me. Her hand resting around my hard shaft runs chills down my spine and I feel for the wall behind me. She steps forward vigorously and takes me by the wrist. She takes my right hand, shaking with excitement, and rests it between her thighs.

"We can touch each other," she says softly, pulling me in by the neck, kissing me.

I'm unsure of what to do and she can tell from the dumbfounded look on my face that I need direction.

"Spread the lips apart and feel me inside," she says plainly, coaching me along gently.

I slowly explore passed the pubic hair, stepping onto new ground and my fingertips are met with warmth. Jenny moans lightly, closing her eyes and never once letting me go. Her hand continues to rub me slowly and I'm starting to chafe.

"Put a finger inside me," she continues, her voice getting lower.

She kisses me deeply as I reach a finger inside her and her grip on my dick hardens the deeper my finger goes. She rubs faster and faster and I'm torn between continuing to obey her or interrupt her. I slide my finger in and out and it quickly becomes slick. The room's filling with steam and our bodies shine with perspiration. She moans even louder when I slip a second finger inside, her body pressed against mine.

"Rub my clit," she says, directing my hand upward.

My fingertips feel lost for a moment and I nervously stumble until they catch something stiff. Is this what they've always been talking about? This tiny piece of flesh that I can barely feel? I press harder, moving around, trying to feel it clearer.

"No, leave it covered," she whispers, looking me in the eyes.

I start rubbing her again, slower and gentler. Jenny's completely forgotten about my raging erection and both her hands are around my neck. We kiss deeply and slowly and right before she cums she rams her tongue deeply into my mouth. Her clit doesn't swell and nothing comes squirting out of her like I had always expected. She squeezes my hand between her thighs. Her body tenses and shakes and when she might pass out from pleasure, she finally reaches down and holds my hand still.

"That was perfect," is her only response and she kisses me softly on the lips.

After quickly rinsing with cooler water, we get out of the shower and dry off in the dark. I turn the lights back on only after Jenny is covered with a towel and we share my toothbrush. It's nearly one in the morning when we finally climb into bed, naked and refreshed. Within seconds of climbing under the sheets Jenny reaches over and takes me by the cock.

"It's your turn again," she says with a nervous smile, afraid of being disappointed.

It's been exactly a week since my penicillin and I quickly take her by the wrist.

"No," I say quicker than I want to and she stares at me.

I could let her continue with what she was intending on doing but the very slim and possible risks that are racing through my brain are too much to handle.

"What's wrong?" she asks, her face full of worry and her eyes wide with fear.

"Not yet. I... can't," is all I can say at first. "I got an STD." Her eyes widen even farther and I continue, "But I went to the clinic and it should be gone by now. I just want to be sure."

Jenny's no longer holding me. She rests a hand on her forehead, exhaling loudly.

"Morgan?" she asks.

"Yeah."

"Have you told her?"

"Yeah."

"Well, it happens," she says after a moment of awful silence.

A smile's back on her face.

"The condom ripped the first time Jose and I did it. I was terrified! I was so worried I'd get something. Or even worse, be pregnant."

"What did you do?" I ask, feeling the redness drain from my cheeks.

"Went to the doctor for a physical. They ran blood tests and I'm fine."

We sit for a few moments, mulling it all over. Her reaction is not at all what had I expected. So, when in Rome...

"Well..." Jenny starts to say and I cut her off with a kiss.

She receives me well and kisses me back. In an attempt to make it up to her, I push her flat on the mattress. I kiss her neck, her breasts, and her stomach. The light from the full moon outside is shining through my blinds, casting stripes across her pale body. I place my face where I never have before, a little lost again, my lips caressing warm, moist flesh. But I quickly find what I'm looking for and lick vigorously, continuously, and Jenny moans, writhes, and kicks until she finishes, lunging forward and pushing my face deep into her.

We wake up early the following morning. Jenny has a rare smile on her face and she glows like a woman served with two orgasms. I on the other hand have a tremendous ache in my groin. My balls have swollen to the size of kiwis and I want to drain them before we leave. But our time is running short, so I squeeze into an old black suit that fits me too tightly and Jenny zips up in a simple black dress.

"You look amazing," I tell her honestly.

She goes light on the eye makeup and the effect is astonishingly attractive. I quickly wipe bits of food off my Doc Martins and lace them up. The sun is already high when we leave and the heat is unrelenting. Jenny offers to drive and we put down the top of her Mitsubishi. I can barely hear the music on the radio and the loud wind makes conversation impossible. I don't want to talk anyway, I'm about to do something I hate more than anything.

Eternal Valley is an hour drive from my place. When we reach the top of the hill in the Santa Clarita Valley, driving south on the freeway, the cemetery comes into full view on the right. It takes up an entire mountainside and right away you know what it is.

I've been here only once before, when I was very young. My mother took me to show me where my father's parents were buried. I'll never know why she did that. I never met them. I've never asked why she cried so hard that day. She talks about them less than she talks about Richard, my father.

The security guard at the lavish front gate directs us to the chapel towards the top of the hill. We file in behind dozens of cars, slowly rolling passed hundreds of grave markers. The grass is so green and the trees are so lush that if not for the stones, it would look like something out of a Robert Frost poem.

"Jesus, could you pass me some tissues," Jenny says, pulling back her sunglasses and pointing to the glove compartment.

I know this is going to be a long day and I'm relieved when she asks for a cigarette too. I light two between my lips and hand her one. Tears are already rolling down her cheeks. We park in the nearly full parking lot and sit finishing our Marlboro's as the cloth cover folds over on top of us.

"Thank you again for coming," Jenny whimpers to me as we step out of the car.

The air is completely still and I'm relieved the service is being held inside. She slips an arm in mine and we follow the somber crowd. Michael's parents stand just inside the large double doors, with his sister, and they slowly accept condolences. Sarah instantly recognizes Jenny and they embrace, tears flowing over everywhere.

"I am so sorry," Jenny mumbles as she squeezes Sarah and unsure of what to do, I stand back with a hand placed on her shoulder.

Sarah also hugs me, as well as Michael's parents, who both recognize us.

"How's your sister?" Michael's mother asks, tears rolling down her cheeks.

"She's good, I guess."

"Say hello to her for me. This is... was... Michael's fiancé," she says while gesturing to a woman standing close to her.

I'm taken aback by the woman's startling beauty. She has dark skin with straight black hair and bright blue eyes. She accepts my hug and my apologies without an acknowledgement and goes on hugging Jenny the same, as if she were a zombie. She continues in this state as we walk away and I keep glancing back as we step into the sanctuary.

The sanctuary's full of familiar faces. Faces I haven't seen in years. Girls and boys I went to Sunday school with that have grown into adults, faint signs of who they were still discernable on their facades. There are a few people Michael went to high school with, distant relatives, and soldiers. Until today, I had no idea that Michael was in the Air Force. There are gentlemen decked out in their best, their faces solemn and their backs straight.

When everyone finishes filing passed Michael's parents and has seen enough of the pictures displayed in the foyer, the soft music fades to complete silence. The room is silent except for nervous rustling. The large number of bodies is rapidly raising the temperature. A chaplain steps forward to lead us into prayer and every face falls to the floor. My head is left up amongst a sea of reverence and I hold back guilty laughter. Even Jenny lowers her head and closes her eyes, squeezing my hand.

"And please Lord, let us remember Michael for the righteous man that he was. Let the pain in our hearts fade when we ponder on you. Give us the guidance we need to know that he is with you and when the time is right, we will all see him again," the chaplain finishes and the room is filled with a hundred whispered *Amens*.

He continues to talk about Michael and then introduces Donna, Michael's mother, who'd like to say a few words.

She slowly steps from the front row and stands next to her son's closed casket. She glances at the picture of him in his uniform and steps behind the podium.

"Thank you, everyone, for being here today," she starts.

Her voice quivers but never falters, strong despite the gale-force storm inside her.

"When Mike went into the service, I told myself that one day I might get that horrible knock on my door. I had to prepare myself for the fact that my son might die serving his country. So five days ago, at eight in the morning when I did get a loud knock on my door, my heart sank into my stomach."

She stops to wipe her eyes and turns from the microphone to blow her nose.

"Mike was a terrific son and grew into a beautiful man. He got off work late one night and drove home tired," she stops again, this time whimpering and bracing herself against the podium.

Michael's fiancé, in the front row being held up by her would be father-in-law, starts to break down and wale loudly.

"He would have been a perfect husband and an even better father. He will be missed. Nothing I could've done would have prepared me for this moment and I'd like a moment of silence for my boy."

And for over a minute all we hear is Michael's fiancé waling in a way I've never heard before, like an animal crying out in pain.

"Thank you and God bless," his mother says as she finally steps down.

A few other people speak; a high school friend, a distant cousin, even a fellow soldier. To see a man in all his regal glory cry is heartbreaking and my eyes quickly mist. The chaplain stands again to speak one final time. He speaks of life and its preciousness and my face starts to burn. He talks about giving ourselves to the Lord and that without him we are condemned to hell. How dare he use Michael's death as his platform! We're here to remember someone's life and he stands in front of us, spouting off his religious propaganda. Jenny wipes tears from her eyes and looks up at him with warmth and all I want to do is scream. We stand as he goes into another over drawn prayer and my legs are feeling weak from the heat.

"And before we gather graveside, Michael's parents request that we all pay our last respects by filing passed his casket," the chaplain finishes as two soldiers step forward to open it.

My heart starts to race and my mind goes blank as I watch in horror. I look to Jenny for support and all she can do is mouth *Sorry!* I want to run out the door but my legs would never carry me fast enough. Row by row, one by one, we all file down the middle and in front of the casket. Michael's mother is playing Amazing Grace on the piano. His fiancé cries even louder as she looks down at him and has to be carried out by his father. Our turn comes and I follow the man sitting next to me.

I feel like someone being led to my death as I slowly walk toward the open casket. I stop and stare down at him and can barely see him through the dots dancing in front of me. The body looks nothing like the smiling man in the picture. His hands are placed across his chest and look like they're made of plaster. His dark uniform's crisp and clean and makes the silk lining around him glow luminously. Jenny pushes on me and I follow out into the sunlight, unsure of whether or not I'm going to pass out. The tears are rolling now, stronger and fuller than I've cried in years and I run to the back of the crowd standing around the hearse outside. I lose Jenny and light a cigarette. I sob quietly to myself.

Once we're standing beneath the alcove, we're directed to the gravesite. A special acre has been set-aside for fallen soldiers. Some people drive to the other side of the cemetery. Jenny and I decide to walk, hand in hand across the grass.

"I'm so sorry. I thought it would be closed casket because, well... you know," she apologizes and I simply shrug my shoulders.

The tears continue to fall but I struggle to keep a straight face, squinting in the harsh sunlight. The sky is crystal clear but a soft breeze has started to blow, cooling the tears on my face and drying them before they fall to the ground.

A row of chairs has been placed in front of the open grave and the family's limo rolls up as we approach. The casket's already being carried over by six soldiers and Michael's family takes their seats. We crowd behind them and listen once more to the pompous chaplain pray another one of his self-righteous prayers. Seven soldiers fire their rifles into the air as another plays 'Taps.' The flag is lifted off of his coffin and folded. His mother holds her head high as they hand it to her, the soldier doing the honors crying through his condolences. Jenny begins to shiver despite the warmth and I place my jacket on her shoulders. She leans into me and I hold an arm around her. We all watch quietly as the ground swallows up the coffin, it's green lips and brown teeth devouring him whole.

The crowd files passed the family once more to hug them and comfort them. Michael's father steps forward, away from everyone, and stares down from the edge of his son's grave. The tears that subsided are now pushing their way to the surface and I can't watch him any longer. I quickly file passed the rest of the family, hugging them again, and in the distance I can hear Michael's father weeping.

"Ready to go?" Jenny asks, her voice exhausted and weak.

"Sure. Just give me a minute," I say without looking at her. "I'll meet you at the car," I tell her as I walk away.

The matching gravestones are not hard to find and I'm relieved the tree nearby covers them with a large patch of shade. One is older than the other and the elements have begun to age the color of it. The roses that were once bright red on its shiny surface are now a dark pink and I wipe it with my hand, the calcium scratching my fingertips. Robert and Mary, faithful husband and wife, devoted parents and adored grandparents. To think, I might have cousins somewhere that I'll never know. I'm kneeling above the stones when my thoughts are disturbed by a cough and I fall backwards.

A man sits on the bench next to the tree and glances up at me. I can't see his eyes through his sunglasses but he doesn't look at me long. He's wearing a t-shirt and blue jeans with old sneakers. He stands and puffs once more on what's left of his cigarette and flicks it out onto the grass as he walks away. He looks like he'd be in his late forties, a little overweight with brown hair that's long in the back. He glances at me once more as he reaches his truck and nods. He lights another cigarette and steps into the old beat up Ford. I recognize him from somewhere, from a place I can't quite remember, but before I have a chance to nod back or walk over to him, he's gone.

Jenny's sitting in the car waiting for me, the top already down.

"Are you ok?" she asks when I open the passenger side door. "You look like you've seen a ghost."

"I think I did. Let's get out of here, I'm starving."

We drive a few blocks to an In-N-Out and eat our food outside so we can smoke. We don't talk until the food's all gone and we both light up.

"Jesus, there's nothing better than a cigarette on a full stomach," Jenny moans with satisfaction.

I reciprocate with a loud belch and we both chuckle.

"Jason, there's something I need to tell you," she continues, staring at the table and flicking her ashes onto our empty tray. "I came back to your mom's party later on that night."

"Really? Why didn't I see you?" I ask, confused.

"Because I never came back inside," she answers and my confusion doubles. "Your mother was sitting outside having a cigarette and I stopped to sit with her."

Her eyes are darting back and forth.

"Now you have to promise not to tell any one about this," she begs, "especially your mom."

"Ok."

"Well, she was sitting outside in her bathrobe. It was really late and everyone had either left or was passed out. She and Brian had just had sex and she was smoking before going back inside to... you know, do it again. She was still drunk and I stopped to have a smoke with her," she continues and then pauses.

My heart's racing because I think I know where this is going.

"Well, she reached over and took me by the hand. She asked me to touch her and then placed my hand... there. I didn't know what to do so I just let her put it between her legs. It was only there for a few seconds until Brian came out, looking for her."

My mind is blank and I just smoke. I take three drags and let them slowly out before speaking.

"Then what?" I finally ask, looking at her.

"They wanted me to join them. I said I was tired and left."

"I'm not surprised," is all I can say.

Jenny holds my hand, apologizing. I reassure her that I'm not mad at her. We sit finishing our cigarettes and I'm overwhelmed with disgust and sympathy.

THIRTEEN

I finally give Jared his letter. It's been burning a hole in my pocket for weeks. I'd tell Tawny to deliver her own goddamn mail but I realized something. Jared hasn't spoken to me. Since the beginning of the decline, I haven't even seen him.

He hasn't returned any of my pages and I wonder if his mother's actually telling him I called. On my way to work, I'll stop by the store and deliver it in person. I'd hate to get Tawny's letter like this but he leaves me with no other choice.

"Hey buddy!" He shouts from behind the deli counter.

He smiles and actually seems happy to see me. He slips out and gives me a hug. Not a half-ass pat on the back, but one of those rare heterosexual male hugs where our crotches actually touch.

"How you been?" I ask after the obligatory pat, ending the embrace.

"Fucking busy as hell. There've been talks of a picket, so I'm working as much overtime as possible," he responds exhaustingly, wiping a hand across his forehead.

We stand silent for a few moments, both wondering who will ask the same question first.

"How's Tawny doing?" Jared breaks down, averting his eyes.

"Good. She's doing ok," I tell him.

He hasn't even gotten the letter yet and already knows the relationship is over. Well, at least he could have told Tawny.

"That's actually why I'm here," I continue and hand him the letter.

He eyes it quickly and looks at me, his eyes yearning for an explanation.

"Read it later. Give me a call sometime so we can hang out."

I give him another warm embrace and leave. My pulse is racing so fast my head's aching. I feel awful for being the bearer of bad news, but maybe he had it coming to him. Who am I to judge? I light a cigarette the second I step outside. I'm already sweating and my dark shirt is sticking to my back.

Like I always do, I get to work fifteen minutes early. I stand at the end of the bar, drinking a glass of water and tying my tie.

"You look exceptionally nice this evening!" Dana says, putting beer on ice.

She's always been kind to me and I've added her to my growing list of mothers. Maybe because I'm so disappointed with my own, I'm drawn to older women. She has no children and maybe the thought of making an impact in my life will be sufficient. Her husband's a drunken failure, moving from one job to another, and Dana confides all her hatred for him in me, in the safety of this place we both call our sanctuary.

Rebecca's waiting tables tonight and Michelle's bussing with Gwen, who blushes, giggles, and gets coy when she sees me. Michelle rolls her eyes. I'd never reveal this to her but I think she's jealous. The reservation book isn't very full and while the girls fold napkins and change tablecloths, I stock Dana's bar.

I take the crate down to the wine cellar three times before I'm finished. The bar isn't very busy and the news is on. As I finish unloading my last load, my eyes are met by a woman's at the bar. She's staring at me and then averts her eyes when they meet mine. She must have been sitting there the entire time, watching me lift bottles and put them away.

Her name's Susan. She frequented the bar with her husband when he was still alive. After he died, a year ago, she went into hiding. She's mildly attractive and in her early fifties. She looks like she could be the sister of Diane Keaton or Katherine Keener, with artificially dark red hair.

I smile at Susan as I walk passed her. She doesn't look at me but I know she saw the smile. She lifts her martini to her lips and sips as she watches Anderson Cooper.

I spend the rest of the evening seating tables, helping Rebecca carry plates, and serving cocktails. Michelle and Gwen get along wonderfully and I play a few games of Hangman when I get the chance.

I take a seat at the end of the bar shortly after eight. The dining room's only half full and I highly doubt I will have anything else to do.

"Want something to drink?" Dana asks when she sees me.

Susan's still seated at the other end of the bar, chatting with Dana between sips of yet another martini.

"Ginger Ale," I tell her as I watch the television, acting as if I care what I'm seeing.

I can see Susan out of the corner of my eye. She glances at me and quickly turns away. She continues in this fashion, glancing then turning away, until the urge must be unbearable. I turn to watch her pick up her glass and purse and walk down the bar to me.

She's wearing a dark red sundress that hugs her curves and sways in the breeze from her movement. Her body's still thin in its older age and her small breasts are held firmly in her bra. She smiles and I can smell opium.

"Is this seat taken?" she asks after already sitting next to me.

"Now it is," is all I say as I smile back.

I try to avoid the thoughts that are racing through my head but her flirtatious manner overwhelms them.

"I'm Susan," she says, extending her hand for me to shake.

"I know. I'm Jason," I say, taking it in mine.

My strong grip consumes her small appendage and my fingers brush against her wedding ring.

"I don't wear it on my left hand anymore," she says, glancing down at the delicate piece of jewelry.

"Oh," is my only idiotic response.

We banter back and forth. She bats her eyes at me and I smile, licking my lips and staring at her. She has the energy and grace of a girl half her age but I can still see gray roots growing out from under her dark hair. Michelle and Gwen take turns walking by us, glancing at me suspiciously. I don't care what they think; I have this woman's complete attention.

"I've seen you here before," Susan says as Dana hands her another cocktail.

Dana even glances at me, that imploring motherly look plastered on her face.

"Really?" I ask, smiling. "I've seen you here before too."

"That must have been a long time ago. Back when Peter was alive."

Susan grows silent after saying her husband's name. She tilts her martini glass back and downs the entire cocktail in one gulp. Her chest flushes and the redness rises to her neck and cheeks. She puts the glass down and runs a hand through her short curly hair. I'm completely and utterly mesmerized.

"Would you like another?" I ask.

I tell Dana to put it on my tab, a tab I'm sure I'll never have to pay. Susan thanks me and excuses herself, walking slowly to the restroom. The moment she steps out of sight, Dana takes me by the hand.

"Be careful," she says, looking at me with wide eyes. "She's lonely and fragile and kept talking about you."

"What was she saying?" I ask, hoping for the best.

"Just be careful," she warns and walks away.

Moments later Susan returns looking refreshed and rested. She smiles at me when she sits, her eyes squinting more than they should. She sips on her cocktail and we commence our flirtatious chatter.

"I came here for a reason," she says after a lull in the conversation, leaning in close.

Her voice is low and she glances around before continuing.

"And I found you..." she whispers after a pause.

A pause that hits the nail on the head. The line tickles my toes and slowly slides up to my groin.

I smile and feel my cheeks blush.

"What do you mean?" I ask, trying to sound coy.

"You're so cute," she says, laughing and laying a hand on my thigh.

105

The tickling sensation now warms my entire leg and rushes straight to the tip of my dick. My breathing's deeper and I fight the urge to kiss her.

"How much do I owe you Dana?" she asks, turning quickly away from me.

She pays the bill and hugs Dana across the bar. She waves goodbye to Rebecca and asks me to walk her out to her car.

"Are you ok to drive?" I ask, holding the front door open for her.

The night air's warm.

"I'll be fine," she says, glancing over at me.

The breeze blows a few stray hairs in her face and she doesn't lift a finger to move them.

"Well, thank you for the company. Maybe we can see each other some time, away from here."

"Sure."

"Here's my number," she says, pulling a pen and a small piece of paper from her purse.

She hands it to me and her finger lingers next to mine.

"Good night," I tell her, leaning in for the kiss.

Our lips meet and Susan steps into me. Her mouth tastes like gin and olives and I want to gag. I quickly finish and she smiles dumbly as she steps into her car. I watch as she drives away, flustered, surprised, and awe struck.

Michelle rushes up when I walk back into the dining room.

"What was that about?" she demands, her hands on her hips.

The dining room's empty and Gwen stands a short distance behind her, watching.

"Nothing. I just kissed her good night."

"That's sick Jason! She's older than your mother!" Michelle screams and I can tell this time she's genuinely jealous.

Gwen's aunt shows up to get her this time. We're all introduced and after she chats quickly with Dana, Gwen is whisked away. The bar empties shortly before closing and by ten we're all ready to leave.

"Do you want to go to the movies or something?" Michelle asks as we step outside.

Dana locks the door and hugs us both goodnight.

"No, there's nothing good to see right now," I tell her nonchalantly.

I have no idea what we can do and I blurt out the first thing that comes to mind.

"Let's go to the dam. If the water's warm enough, we can go in for a dip!"

"Are you serious?"

"Yeah, why not? The moon's almost full and it's eighty five degrees out!"

The gate at the entrance of the dam is closed, so we park along side the road and walk. It's a half-mile from there and the moon's covered by clouds. Our journey's nearly black. Neither of us have flashlights so we stumble along joking and laughing. When we reach the dam, the moon finally comes out. The water's illuminated and we stand above it.

"For such a mess, it looks so beautiful in the moonlight," Michelle says, staring down.

I climb a low wall and walk out across the dam. The structure's ten feet wide and sixty feet tall on the outside. The water is only five feet below me on the inside. Michelle follows and we sit in the middle, our feet hanging over the small lapping waves.

"So, you gonna jump in?" Michelle asks.

"Nah, I just want to sit here."

That's what we do. We watch the moon go in and out from behind the clouds and the bats as they fly across the star filled sky. I smoke a cigarette and Michelle doesn't complain.

"So, what's up with this new grandma?" Michelle finally asks.

"Very funny. She's real nice. That's all."

"Uh huh. Gwen has a thing for you too, Casanova," Michelle teases, laughing at me. "Just be careful."

We hear a truck in the distance and from across the water we can see the floodlights of a Park Ranger. It races along the edge of the water. Closer and closer it comes to us, heading towards the road we came in on.

"Maybe we should get our cars. We could get towed," Michelle says quickly.

Before I have a chance to respond, Michelle 's running back across the dam. She quickly jumps the low wall and runs up the road. I'm in far worse shape and I can barely keep up. I glance back once and blackness is all I see. We round corner after corner and right before I think my lungs might implode the entry gate comes into view. The ranger's office light illuminates our path. Just beyond the gate I can see our cars. Michelle turns back to me, smiling, relieved. I feel like a child playing hide and seek, narrowly missing getting tagged.

The roar suddenly inches up behind me and I turn to see light coming from behind the last bend. I grab Michelle around the waist and pull her into the bushes. I trip backwards and the green truck barrels passed as she falls onto me.

Michelle starts to scream at first but bursts out laughing when she realizes I was knocked flat. I try to laugh despite having the wind knocked out of me and we peak out from the bushes to watch what happens. The ranger drives over the exit spikes and gets out to double check the gate. With flashlight in hand, he walks over to our cars. He's not much older than me. He hesitates, taking a small pad from his belt, but puts it back. He doesn't leave us tickets and drives away.

"Ok, I guess we can take that as a sign to go home," Michelle says as she steps from the bushes, brushing leaves and dirt off her pants.

"I agree."

When we get back to the cars, she hesitates and curses loudly.

"I dropped my keys! When you pulled me into the bushes, I think they fell out of my pocket."

With more laughter, we slowly walk back to the spot we fell. I find them quickly. I walk Michelle back to her car and she hugs me goodnight. I turn down an invitation to hang out, making up an excuse to just go home.

I reconsider going to Michelle's after we pull away in separate directions. I haven't talked to Brandon since the day we went to the college and I wonder if he'd even want to talk to me again if I showed up.

When I do get home, after midnight, I fish Susan's phone number from my pocket and place it next to the phone. I didn't even have to ask for it. I wonder what else she would give up freely. I have a cigarette, stare at the numbers, and contemplate the possibilities.

FOURTEEN

I only wait three days to call Susan. I wish I had the willpower to wait longer, make her feel like I'm being cool and irresistible. I call her before I leave for work. The line only rings twice before she picks up.

"Hello?" she asks, her voice ringing sweetly.

The beautiful tone catches me off guard and I stumble on my words.

"Hi," I begin, nervously. "It's Jason."

"Well, you finally called. I was about to write you off. I just walked in the door."

"Good. I was wondering if you wanted to go out to dinner or a movie or something."

"I haven't been to the movies since, well, you know. I'd love to! When would you like to go?"

"How's Saturday?" I ask, glancing at my work schedule. "I get off at eight."

We agree upon a time and a theater and I say my farewell. I'm impressed with myself for dating an older woman. I feel I might be taking advantage of her though and I wish Dana hadn't said anything.

I don't tell anyone at work about Susan. I even turn down an invitation to play pool with Brittney. I have something else in mind, something that will end exactly how I want it to. I change out of my uniform the moment my shift ends and leave without saying goodbye.

Susan's waiting for me in front of the theater when I arrive. The mall isn't busy and the foyer's deserted.

"Hello handsome," she says when I walk up.

She kisses me on the lips, takes me by the hand, and leads the way into the theater. We stand at the counter for a minute, trying to decide on a film. She wants to see the new John Cusack thriller. I could care less. I pay for the tickets. I feel funny going about the regular formality of things with someone so much older but she seems flattered. She pays for a large Diet Coke and popcorn.

The theater's empty. The latest pop music hits are playing on the overhead speakers and advertisements flash across the screen. We sit close to the middle row. Sitting close to her I can smell the familiar Opium perfume again, faint and inviting. I take my time staring at her. She's wearing a black blouse and a pair of Levi's that fit too tightly. I feel like a bum in my old sandals and ripped t-shirt.

"When I was younger, I loved going to the movies and making out," Susan whispers to me as the lights darken and the previews start to roll. "We'd kiss for hours and hours..."

She leans in close. There are only ten other people in the theater now and I feel like they're all staring at me. I kiss her back, with a little less tongue and more restraint. She doesn't seem to notice when she finally pulls away and smiles at me.

The movie's awful and boring and I can't wait for it to end. Susan continues to hold my hand, rubbing her fingers against mine. She glances over at me, hoping for eye contact, for another excuse to kiss me. I stare diligently at the screen.

When the movie finally comes to an end, Susan doesn't get up with the rest of the crowd. I wait for her to stand but she just stares up at me. I have no choice but to relent and when I see the last person leave, I kiss her. I kiss her passionately, like her husband must have, hungrily and with energy. I grope her, kiss her face and neck, and squeeze her breasts with my large hands. She moans loudly, pulling me into her. We finally stop when the lights come on and we parade passed the cleaning crew, embarrassed and aroused.

The mall is completely empty when we leave the theater. All the shops are closed and the lights are off. The only other open venue is the Hamburger Hut near the food court and Susan drags me to a table by the bar. A sports show is still on and half the crowd glares at me suspiciously, knowing exactly what's going on. Before our waitress brings Susan her cocktail we bolt, hand in hand, laughing our asses off.

"Would you like to come over to my place?" Susan asks when we approach her car.

I'm not inviting her to my shithole.

"Sure," I answer, smiling and staring into her eyes.

She leans in and kisses me softly, without her tongue. She slowly turns and gets into her car, lifting her eyebrows at me for effect. It's almost pathetic how hard she tries, many years too old and out of practice. But I pity her. The sex will be easy even if it sucks.

The drive to her house is much further than I had expected. She lives on the out skirts of the valley, her nearest neighbor about a half a mile away. Her yard's filled with Joshua trees and cacti and most of her property is undeveloped. The front of her large house is all windows, staring down on the valley below. The night's completely still and dark, the lights providing a magnificent view.

Susan leads me by the hand through the front door and her lights automatically start coming on as she leads me through the foyer. The furnishings are elegant but simple and she knew exactly what she was doing by inviting me here. She steps down into the living area, a very tall room with windows that go up two stories, and turns back to me.

"This is my palace," she says with a proud smile. "It's the only good thing my husband ever gave me."

I follow Susan as she gives me the tour: the large garage full of her husband's motorcycles, the library with thousands of books, the very impressive kitchen, and finally the den. The den is a small dark room beyond the rest of the house with a large leather sofa and big screen TV.

"Would you like something to drink?" Susan asks after leading me there.

"I'll have a Jack and Coke," I say as I look around the room, soaking it all in.

I sit on the sofa and admire the walls adorned with awards and photographs. Susan's husband was quite the man: fishing, hunting, and golfing. He had done extensive work in the community and belonged to dozens of clubs. I feel out of place, minute to such an accomplished person. With his pictures staring down at me, I feel guilty.

Susan returns carrying two glasses. I can smell the Jack Daniels well before the glass touches my lips. The lethal combination burns my throat and I almost choke from the mispoured cocktail.

"Do you like it?" she asks after a few moments of silence, admiring me as I gaze around.

"Yes, I do. It's all very nice."

"Yes. Yes it is."

We sit quietly sipping our cocktails and I know the inevitable is coming soon. Susan takes one final gulp and downs her martini. She stands and runs a hand through her hair.

"I want to dance for you," she whispers, stepping over to the television.

She turns on the satellite, finds a station, and turns down the lights. I finish my drink and place a hand over my mouth to keep it down. My head is turning and I'm quickly getting dizzy.

Cher's "If I Could Turn Back Time" starts to play and Susan starts swaying back and forth. She looks seductively down at me, running her hands along her hips and breasts. I try to maintain a straight face, a face she might interpret as desire. Her rhythm is awful and her movements are awkward but she keeps smiling, even when she closes her eyes and raises her hands above her head.

She's like a car wreck, something I can't help but stare at. She unbuttons her blouse and slowly slips her jeans off. She stands before me in her bra and panties, unflattering even in the dark light. Her breasts are small and her bra sags. Her stomach's not as flat as it used to be and her belly sags just above her black underwear. Her knees knock together and her thick thighs lead down to narrow ankles. She continues to dance for me, getting closer and closer until it ends.

"Did you like that?" Susan asks, kneeling down in front of me as the song leads into another.

"Uh huh," is all I say.

I try to breath, try to stay calm, try to focus. She runs her hands down my chest into my lap and she undoes my belt. I kick off my shoes and she slowly slips my pants down. I'm nowhere near being hard and without hesitation she takes me in her wrinkled hands and quickly pushes me into her mouth. Her warm wet mouth.

My mind is racing and my stomach's flaring up. I get harder and harder until I'm so hard I think she might be able to bite me off. She works quickly, hungrily sucking on me and fondling my testicles. She fondles me so roughly I start getting sore. I lean back and place my hands behind my head, staring down at her in admiration. She can't get enough of me. After a short while, and a few embellished grunts, she stops.

I don't cum in her mouth or on her face, but she shines with satisfaction anyway. She leans forward and kisses me and her mouth is dripping wet.

Sour and fleshy, this must be what dick tastes like.

Susan pulls me down onto the floor and lies flat on her back.

"I want you to taste me," she says, closing her eyes and groping her own nipples.

This I have done before.

I pull off my t-shirt and lean down into her. I hesitate at first, unsure of what to expect but the dizziness encourages me. I lick her, lap at her, with determination. Her vagina feels just like Jenny's and despite their age difference, they taste exactly the same. I reach two fingers inside her and She groans loudly. A guttural, loud groan. She pulls at my hair, ripping out handful after handful. As she reaches the point of no return, I slip a third finger inside her. Then a fourth.

My heart's pounding loudly in my ears as Susan pulls my face away from her. I kiss her vigorously and she enjoys it. I'm inside her, pounding, pounding, pounding. I thrust out of control.

"Jason! Fuck! Jason! Fuck!" she screams, her body shaking out of control.

She wraps her legs around me and digs her well-groomed fingernails into my back. I fuck her over and over and she continues to cum over and over, soaking the floor beneath us. My body aches and my head starts to hurt so when she cums for the fifth time, I grunt loudly, stiffening my back. I fake an 'O' face and she jams my nipple in her mouth. I go limp, completely convincing.

"Did you?" she pants in my ear, running her hands through my hair.

I nod, exhaling loudly. I roll off and lie on the floor. My back's soaked in sweat and she twirls her fingers through my few sweaty chest hairs. With each breath I heave I'm filled with pride and my grin spreads from cheek to cheek.

After a few minutes lying together, I excuse myself to the bathroom. I walk completely bare across her house to the bathroom by the foyer. I stand before the sink, admiring my reflection in the mirror. My face is red and my hair's wet with perspiration. My muscles are tensed and toned and my cock's long and loose, impressive even to me. The toilet's next to a floor to ceiling window and I urinate proudly, hoping someone out in the large desert will happen by.

When I walk back to the kitchen, Susan's waiting for me. She's already sipping another large Martini and she hands me a fresh Jack and Coke. I drink it all with delight, this one not nearly as strong as the last. She quickly turns from me and reaches deep into a cupboard, struggling with something. What she pulls out amazes me and my mouth drops open onto the floor. A large bag of marijuana, what must be a pound. I'm hard again at the sight of it.

Susan leads me now into the living room, pot in hand, and we sit close together on another leather sofa, staring out at the valley of lights. I stick to my seat and my skin squeaks when I move. Without a moment's hesitation, she starts rolling a very fat blunt.

"Isn't it beautiful?" she asks me, staring out the large windows.

Her hands work quickly, pinching, rolling, and finally licking.

"Yes it is," is all I say, staring at the joint.

"I've always been good at this," she continues to herself, admiring her tightly rolled joint.

She lights it and inhales deeply. I light one of my cigarettes and we trade off.

"Someday I might make this place a restaurant. A line of tables along that window would be so romantic."

I nod my head and listen to her plans. Across the room I notice a vase on a small table. It stands alone and strangely suspicious by itself.

"What's that?" I ask, interrupting her ideas, puffing out green smoke.

"Oh, the vase? That's my Peter."

I try remaining casual and I simply nod. The question doesn't faze Susan and she continues to talk about...

her job as a school secretary...

her husband's landscaping business...

her past life as a young girl who died in the holocaust...

her son who's ten years older than me.

She talks and talks and talks about everything.

And I listen. The alcohol, the sex, and now the pot have made me a zombie and I struggle to remain coherent. Susan turns to me and asks about my family.

"I don't know my father," I tell her, getting my Marlboro back. "My mother raised my sister and me by herself, for the most part."

"Wow, she sounds like a nice person," Susan says without thinking, concentrating on the joint.

You have no idea, I think to myself. *She'd love to meet you.*

We finish smoking and Susan yawns loudly. I can tell my time to vacate is coming soon. She stands, stretches, and carries our empty glasses into the kitchen.

"I have to work early tomorrow," she says and I'm already in the den, slipping on my pants.

Susan stands next to me, nude, rubbing her hands along my shoulders. As I lean down to tie my boots, she kisses my back, licking my tattoo.

"We definitely have to do this again some time," she says, leading me to the front door.

I don't respond with words. I dramatically take Susan in my arms and kiss her. Her knees go weak and right before the kiss might make her crumble I turn and walk into the cool night air. I don't turn around, I don't even think about it. I'm a fucking man whose sole purpose in life is to spread my seed and she's staring at my backside, drooling over it.

I drive by Brandon's neighborhood on my way home. I'd love to stop and talk to him about it, to share with him what I just went through. I know it would be of no use though. If I talked about the booze or the marijuana, he'd write me off as an addict. I drive straight home, my windows down. I smoke the rest of a pack of cigarettes and sing along to an Avril Lavigne song at the top of my lungs.

FIFTEEN

I wake up early one morning in late July. I sit bolt upright, startled and afraid. The sun hasn't come up yet and its yellow rays are turning the dark horizon orange. I run over a list in my head of the things I'm supposed to do today and realize there are none. I have no plans with Tawny; she'll going to be buying school supplies with her mother. I don't have to work until tomorrow. For the first time in a long time, I have absolutely nothing to do and the feeling is sublime.

I don't go back to sleep. I get up and make coffee. I stand nude in front of a window, waiting patiently for the sun to peak. It's exhilarating, waiting like this. It slowly shows its face, shining brightly on mine. I close my eyes and hold my arms out to my sides as it warms my neck, then my chest, my belly, and then my groin. Within minutes I am bathed in warmth and shrouded by silence.

Complete and beautiful silence.

Not a car or a bird, not a single goddamn thing.

I take a shower and open the window above me all the way. The cool morning air rushes over my body and I get goosebumps even with the warm water pounding against me. I masturbate, rubbing large amounts of conditioner between my hands. I take my time, unlike I normally do, enjoying the slow rhythm of my touch. I'm in the shower for nearly an hour, rubbing myself, playing with my nipples, caressing my ass. When I finally cum I explode with such force my knees go weak.

After my shower I shave my face. I haven't done that in a week. I use astringent, cotton ball after cotton ball until my face is completely clean. I floss my teeth and brush them, taking my time. I slick my hair back and admire myself in the mirror.

No bags under my eyes.

No patchy facial hair.

No pimples.

As I walk to my room, I begin to think of what I can do with my free day. I slip into a pair of plaid pajama pants and get more coffee. I clean all the dishes in the sink. I have two pieces of raisin toast with calcium rich margarine. I pay bills. I clean Tigi's cat box and wash out her water bowl. I take a load of dirty clothes down to the laundry room. I do all the things I dread. I do them today because I want to, not because I have to.

After three hours of chores and silence filled with loud thoughts, I finally sit down to watch TV. I'm on my second pot of coffee and the overdose of caffeine is making me drowsy. I turn to re-runs of *The Real World* and when I feel myself start to nod, the phone rings.

"Hello?"

"Hi," a voice says sweetly back to me and the tone makes my heart skip a beat.

"Hey Gwen. What's up?" I ask, trying to sound as casual and cool as possible.

"I was getting kind of bored and wanted to know what you were doing today," she says sweetly.

I only consider, possibly, inviting her over. In all honesty, I'm enjoying the solitude and the quiet. So I lie, telling her I'm doing chores and that I have errands to run.

"That's cool. My aunt's not home so I can do whatever I want. I'll come over and help you clean up and then go with you on your errands." Before I have a chance to protest, she tells me she'll be over in fifteen minutes. No request for a ride, no leading for an invitation. When she hangs up, I can't hide a smile. I admire her drive, her childish persistence.

I clean up a little more, hiding more dirty clothes under my bed. I close the shower curtain. I check my breath and fix my hair. In almost exactly fifteen minutes, a knock resonates loudly on my door with cheerful, light, rhythmic taps. I answer it in just my pants, no shirt and no underwear. I pull them down low on my hips, my pubic hair peaking out and my lower abdominal muscles flexed.

Gwen greets me with a hug when I open the door. She's dressed like me in an old pair of green pajama pants, sandals, and a wife beater without a bra. Despite her casual attire her short hair is styled and light makeup is applied. She's playing the same casual game as I am and I hope I lose.

"So this is what your place looks like," she says, stepping in and admiring everything.

I'm surprised she remembered how to get here, based solely on descriptions. We only live two miles from each other. I see now how much attention she pays to me, how much she absorbs.

I give her a quick tour and she stops in front of the spare room.

"What's gonna go in here?" she asks.

"I don't know. I got the apartment without thinking about that. Probably roommates."

"Hey, I could move in!" she practically shouts.

I don't think she's joking.

"I've been talking to Brittney about it. She's been wanting to move out of her parent's house for a while," I continue, ignoring her.

An evening of wild fucking is one thing; being together on a more permanent basis is something completely different.

She admires my small room and lies on the bed. I'm happy I took the time to change the sheets.

"Comfy," she says, looking up at me. That flirtatious devilish grin shines across her face and pure lust lingers in her eyes. I can see her nipples, dark and hard, completely transparent through the thin shirt. I turn away, terrified.

Gwen gets up reluctantly, following me to the kitchen. She follows me out onto the patio. We joke about the wonderful view. She doesn't ask about my chores and I completely forget about the errands. We end up on the couch, each with a cup of coffee.

We talk about work and watch MTV. We don't get to talk like this at work. We never see each other socially. We lounge, my arm along the back of the couch and her feet on my lap. I massage them and she plays with the curly hairs on the back of my head.

I ask about her mother.

"She just wasn't ready. She was younger than me when I was born."

I nod, looking at her intently.

"I have a brother too. He lives with my grandparents in Oregon," she continues easily, as if this were a play, lines memorized and repeated from rote.

She tells me about her plans to leave and move to Washington.

"There's this guy I know, a tattoo artist. He's gonna be moving up there and said I could go with him."

"Is he your boyfriend?" I ask and wish at the same time that I'd paused first.

"No, not really," Gwen answers with a smile, egging me on.

"No as in 'not really' or no as 'in sort of'?"

"No as in 'non-exclusive'," she says, laughing at me. "I did sleep with him though. At my cousin's house, on an air mattress. We popped it."

We laugh. It's strange but I see things in her that I see in Susan. Their bravery and undeniable sexuality. They both wear it on their sleeves, a personality trait they're proud of. They have the same artificial red hair. But Gwen's roots are brown.

The Real World marathon ends and music videos start. A slutty Christina Aguilera video comes on and Gwen stands up to stretch.

"I made up a dance for this song with some girls I go to school with. Wanna see it?"

I nod, thinking about how when summer ends Gwen still has two more years of high school. She goes through a typical cheerleading dance with extra kicks and hip swaying for sex appeal. Despite her mature body and curvy figure, she still looks like a child. Her rhythm's on but her moves are awkward.

She stares at me and her eyes beg me to take her.

When she steps closer, her breasts bouncing a foot from my face, the phone rings. For my own good, I quickly get up and answer it.

"Hello?" I ask, winded.

"Hello there, Casanova," my grandmother's shaky voice shrieks, vibrating the phone.

"Hi Grandma," I respond, trying to sound pleasant.

She's calling from her over-priced haven in Prescott, Arizona. Never one to under do things, she was able to buy the house with insurance money she got after she lost her apartment complex in the 1994 Northridge earthquake. Thanks to insurance fraud, she got a lot more money then she deserved.

Thus, she was also able to pay for the much-needed face-lift I was never supposed to know about. The large, strategically placed, red hairpiece can't cover the scars that will never heal on her ever-thinning skin.

"I haven't heard from you in so long. Your mother gave me your new phone number and I wanted to say hello. How's your new apartment?"

"Nice. Small, but comfortable."

"Well, it's just you so I wouldn't let it bother me."

Gwen mouths, "Who is it?"

"My grandma," I tell her, not bothering to cover the mouthpiece.

"Oh, do you have a friend over?" she asks.

"Yeah, my friend Gwen is hanging out today."

"Hi grandma," Gwen shouts from the couch.

"Is she one of your sex friends?" my grandmother asks without pausing or accusing.

"What?!" I squeak, surprised something like that would come out of her old conservative mouth.

"You know. Is she that kind of friend?"

"No, no she's not," I answer, a little embarrassed.

"Oh well," she exhales, followed by a pause in the conversation.

"I need you to do me a favor," she continues. "Next week your grandfather and I'll be staying at the cabin in Oregon and I need another list of movies to rent."

Every summer they stay at their beach house and every night they rent a movie, all movies from a list I make on a yearly basis.

"Sure. I'll work on it today and mail it to you."

"That would be lovely. I would greatly appreciate it."

"Thank you for my graduation check by the way."

"Of course dear. I'm so proud of you," she answers sweetly, reveling in self-righteous bliss.

"How have you been?" I continue, obligated to act like I care.

"Good. I'm healing well," she says dramatically.

A year ago her doctor found a large tumor in her liver and more than half the organ had to be removed. He blamed it on her excessive smoking and drinking. She simply thought it was all a part of God's plan.

"I miss my wine," she complains but I can hear the unmistakable clink of ice cubes floating in Chardonnay.

"And my cigarettes," she continues and I hear her exhale loudly, the thick smoke leaving her mouth.

She still thinks I'm seven.

"And how's Grandpa?" I ask.

I barley know the man.

"Oh, he's good," is her only response. She could care less about him than I can and I pity him. His life will be much more peaceful when she finally expires.

"Have you registered for college yet?" she asks, quickly changing the subject.

College is extremely important to her and my mother always reminds me that I won't get my inheritance unless I get my degree. I don't want her fraudulent money. I hope they bury her with it.

"Of course. I start in the fall," I cheerfully tell her.

"Very good. I have one more thing to ask of you," she adds before hanging up. "Call your mother more often. She really misses you and is going through tough times without you or your sister at home."

"I will. I promise," I lie.

My mother has done it again: cried to hers. It's a constant struggle. I'll never be able to escape the both of them.

"Ok. Good. Say hi to your friend Gwen for me. I love you."

"Love you too," I say and hang up.

I'm now irritated and hot tempered. What business is it of hers? Who does she think she is? I'm half tempted to call her back and reprimand her for her years of selfish parenting. I know more than she thinks I do. I toss the phone back on the hook.

Gwen helps me make a list of movies I know my grandmother would hate: *Eyes Wide Shut, Basic Instinct, Wild Things, Pulp Fiction, True Romance*.

My poor, put upon, kept grandfather will get a kick out of it.

The sun that poured in all day is beginning to darken and clouds are rolling in. From all directions, they roll in on us until the only patch of blue is directly above. Like the eye of the storm, we wait for the downfall. We watch the *Weather Channel* and flash rain storms are expected.

The darker the sky gets, the longer Gwen wants to stay. She calls her aunt.

"I'm gonna stay the night over here," she says, lying about where she is.

As far as her aunt knows, Gwen's staying at her cousin's house. Then she quickly calls her cousin to make sure their stories coincide.

"You don't mind if I stay over, do you?" Gwen finally decides to ask.

I don't. This will hopefully lead where I want it to.

We make grilled cheese sandwiches in the evening and watch the rest of another season of *The Real World*. The perfect ending to a completely mundane day. After dinner we smoke and cuddle. My windows are still open and the rain has started to fall, bringing in warm, moist air. Without the use of alcohol or drugs, we find each other. Under a small blanket, in front of the bright television, we kiss.

I kiss her softly, gently. Gwen's the aggressor. Squeezed together on the couch, we hopelessly try to maneuver towards each other, lying side by side. When that proves impossible, I pick her up and carry her to the bedroom.

She submits to me. With calm breath and a smile on her face, she lies back and lets me do what I want... at first. I quickly slip my pants off and slowly strip her. Her skin is pale and soft and her groin is hairy, unkempt and virginal. I kiss her face and lips. She doesn't reach for me, just lies with her arms outstretched, hanging off the bed.

In the dark, she smells just like Susan. She sounds just like Susan. She moves just like Susan. When I was with Susan, drunk, she felt just like this. I kiss her breasts that are larger and firmer. I kiss her stomach that is flatter. I rub her thighs and her knees are bony, just like Susan's. I taste her and she tastes just like Susan.

When I place my face closer to her curly dark hairs, spreading her thighs wide, Gwen resists. She whispers No and holds my face away. Persistently I try again, holding her thighs open and shushing her. Gwen gives in to me, nervously holding my hair and squeezing her eyes shut. I do what I think I do best and I get the same reactions that I did from Jenny and Susan. After a few moments, Gwen is quivering and kicking, panting and tensing.

When I finish I lie behind her. I spoon her small form, completely encompassing her. I'm starting to harden, anticipating the best. It fits nicely down her butt crack, the tip resting between her thighs. She doesn't speak or move. She simply holds the arm I have wrapped around her.

The rain continues to fall outside, harder now. Thunder crashes in the distance and lightning splits the sky. Gwen jumps and her grip tightens. Her body shivers. I pull the blankets around us and hold her tighter.

"Thank you," she finally says, not turning to me.

"My pleasure," I whisper, kissing her ear and rubbing my cock against her.

It hardens more now, protesting.

"I only want this if you'll stay with me, exclusively," she says after another pause.

I'm surprised. Before she seemed so willing, so full of the desire to fuck. That shield's broken down now. I ripped away her security, exposing her raw and vulnerable. She wants a companion; she wants to latch onto me. She hooked me this far and right before the final pull, the curtain drops. I don't respond. I say nothing and my hard on dissipates. I simply hold her, warming her into sleep, unwilling to commit.

Gwen wakes before me in the morning. The clouds are gone and the hot summer sun is already in the sky, shining down through my open window. She pulls on a pair of my boxer shorts, the same ones Tawny wore, and pairs it with her wife beater. Before walking to the bathroom she peruses my CD's and pulls one out.

She picks up a picture I have framed on my nightstand.

"Who're they?" she asks, turning it to me.

I'm only waking but I don't even need to open my eyes. I know that picture by heart.

"That's my parents," I answer, rolling over away from them.

It's a blurry and badly taken picture from a wedding. My mother has big curly hair and her face is chubby from being pregnant with me. My father's next to her, the epitome of late 70s cool with long hair and a mustache. They were moving when the picture was taken and the only discernable feature is their smiles, eclipsing everything else. On the back is the date, in my father's handwriting. Handwriting exactly like mine.

This picture symbolizes something special to me. I stole it from a photo album when I was younger. I look at it, hoping that I was conceived out of love. I need to believe that I was meant to be because at one point, my parents actually loved one another. At one point, I belonged to a family.

I knock the picture to the floor when I get up and quickly walk out of the room. I walk into the kitchen naked and Gwen pours me a cup of coffee. We don't say much. She's listening to the new Linkin Park CD, rocking her head to the beat.

We watch an old copy of the *Pam & Tommy* sex tape. The video's worn from being watched too many times. Especially the cumshot.

The mood lightens and we talk for a little bit. The conversation is pointless because we're just trying to be polite. I wanted to fuck Gwen and she was completely disappointed in me. We take a shower but nothing happens. Before I go to work, I drop her off. She makes me stop at the end of her street, in case her aunt's watching. She kisses me on the cheek and gets out of the car.

SIXTEEN

My mother won't stop calling. I haven't seen her since we kicked Brian out and she's left me at least twenty messages in the past month. I don't know why I avoid her; I just find more important things to do with my time. She actually catches me on the phone this morning after my run and she's thrilled to hear my voice.

"My baby boy!" she squeals and the sound of her voice is like a nail on a chalkboard.

"Hello Mother," is all I can muster, sweaty from the 107-degree weather outside.

"Have you been avoiding me?" she asks and I can just picture her bottom lip sticking out.

"Of course not. I've been really busy," I lie, which is an excuse I wish was true.

"Well, since I haven't seen you in so long, I thought maybe we could go to dinner tonight when I get off work at the hospital."

"Sounds good. I don't have any plans. What time?"

"Meet me at Black Angus at 7:00," she says cheerfully.

She knows perfectly well that I don't eat red meat, but hell, it's free food.

I spend the rest of the day dreading dinner. I can't remember when our relationship started to become such a challenge for me or why I can't stand her. I loved her growing up. I genuinely did. She was my mother, my father, my confidant, chauffer and friend. In many cases, I was her best friend. She confided in me, often times in ways she probably shouldn't have. Now that I'm no longer forced to see her on a daily basis, I find the reprieve an extreme relief.

I sit around doing nothing really; drinking coffee, watching MTV, smoking, and trying some yoga. Just another lazy summer day. I value these days but not as much as I should. I know that my future summers will not hold these wasteful hours, but maybe the fact that I'm not thinking about the future is the entire appeal.

I leave the apartment around 6:30 so I have enough time to get gas. I have seven dollars cash and I'm not sure if I should buy a pack of cigarettes. A gallon of gas is $1.98 and Chesterfield's are on sale for $2.95. Two gallons of gas will last me a day or two. The cashier looks at me funny when I ask for so little but I keep a straight face, wanting to laugh at how stupid I must look.

I smoke all five of the cigarettes from my old pack on my way to dinner. I roar down the freeway and my smoke is carried out the open window. The evening air is warm and refreshing. I'm not at all looking forward to dinner. What will definitely start out civil and placid will inevitably become a shit storm, as it always does. I will do or say something and it will push her over the edge.

The edge is a place my mother has taken up permanent residence and base-jumping is now a hobby.

I arrive at exactly 7:00 and the sun will be setting in about an hour. The sky is a dark red and orange and the restaurant's outdoor lights have already come on. My mother's MR-2 is in the parking lot and I'm not surprised to see that she's not waiting for me in the foyer. As I walk up to the door and then the front desk, I'm going over the things I will and won't bring up during dinner. Susan, no. The apartment, yes. School, no. Morgan, I don't know. The clinic, definitely not. What Jenny told me? My options are running short and I hope my mother's the one with all the up-to-date news.

A cute brunette happily shows me to my mother's table, who spies me from across the dining room and stands up quickly to greet me with a bony hug. Her elbows seem sharper than usual and her arms get thinner every time I see her. Her graying red hair is up in an out of date scrunchy and she's wearing her favorite horse print scrub top.

"My baby boy! I'm so glad you found time in your busy schedule to see your mother!" she says loudly. Smiling at the young girl, she asks, "Isn't he handsome?"

The hostess just blushes awkwardly and walks away.

I pry my mother off and we sit down.

"You look nice," I lie.

Her hair is longer than she usually wears it and her bangs are combed back, sitting untidily on top of her hair.

"You think so? I desperately need a hair cut but Brian likes it long," she says, holding a long piece in her hand.

Everything must be fine again on the home front, but I'm not ready to bring it up. She's already half way through a Long Island ice tea and a cup of coffee is sitting in front of me getting cold.

"I ordered you a cup. I know how much of it you drink."

I put five packs of sugar into the lukewarm liquid and quickly drink it all.

"So, how have you been?" she asks, smiling at me widely and holding my hand, crushing it.

"Good. I've been busy at the restaurant."

"That's nice. How's Tawny doing?"

"She's good. She hasn't been able to do too much. Her mom's being worse now that she's out of school."

"That's too bad. I really wonder why she's so strict with her."

"What do you mean?" I ask while our waitress fills my coffee cup.

"Well, she has to have a reason for being so controlling. Did Tawny ever do something to break her trust? Has she ever told you anything?" she says bluntly.

It irritates me the way she assumes that it's automatically something Tawny did, that it must be her fault. I want to snap at her, but our waitress is standing there staring at us waiting for us to order.

"Oh, sorry. I have this coupon for the two New York steaks and appetizer platter," my mom says while digging through her gigantic purse. Coupon-clipping is her favorite pastimes. "Doesn't that sound nice?" she asks me as she pulls it out and hands it to the waitress.

"Can I also get a large dinner salad, with vinaigrette dressing?" I say after ordering my steak well done.

My mother has hers rare, which is always surprising considering she's a bleeding heart animal lover. I choose not to argue and I'll most likely not finish my steak.

"You're so handsome," she continues to remind me. "Just like your father."

She stares off into the distance, as if something is beckoning to her on the horizon. I hate her when she talks about the man I never knew and I dread the fact that I may never know whether or not it's true.

We sit quietly for a while, avoiding eye contact. I fidget with my coffee cup and she plays with her hair.

"Thank you again for my birthday party," she says out of the blue as our appetizer platter and salads arrive. "You grandmother was a little disappointed in you, though. She would have appreciated an invitation."

"She wouldn't have come, even if I did send one."

"I know. It's such a pain getting her to leave the house. The thought is what counts."

The thought is what always counts. That's the kind of bullshit philosophy I've come to expect from my mother. No real wisdom, just loose rules to live by.

Don't talk with your mouth full.

Cover your mouth when you yawn.

Don't do that or you'll go blind. Even worse, it might stop working properly.

My grandmother just wants reassurance that she hasn't been put out to graze. Mom quickly finishes her cocktail and is already starting on another.

"So, are you seeing anyone new?" she asks after starting into her salad.

I hate the way she lets the dressing sit on her lip, white and creamy. I want to lean over and wipe it for her because she won't notice it until she's finished.

"Yes actually," I decide to confess. "I met a woman at the bar."

"That's nice. What does she look like?"

"She has shoulder length red hair and she's tall."

"Sounds lovely," she responds proudly, always playing favorite for fellow redheads.

Brian always liked to joke "Red in the head, Good in bed," and would chuckle loudly at himself. I can see why he's so appealing.

"What does she do? Is she in school?"

"No, actually. She's the secretary at an elementary."

"Oh." My mother finally looks up at me, raising her eyebrows. "How old is this woman?"

"She's fifty-two," I answer a matter-of-factly, jamming a large bite of salad into my mouth.

My mother slowly sets down her fork and downs the remaining two thirds of her Long Island. She flags down a waiter.

"Can I get a Jack and Coke please?" she asks with a smile.

I can tell she'll soon be strapping on her goggles and jumpsuit.

"Well, I'm happy for you!" she finally directs at me, the alcohol glossing her eyes over. "There was a nurse I wanted to introduce you to though."

"Really?" I ask, not at all interested.

I can just imagine her talking me up to people that don't give a shit, showing off my high school graduation pictures.

"Yes! She seems like a girl you'd like. She's single, of course, with long black hair and a couple of tattoos!" she assumes out loud.

Wait, just because I have a tattoo I'm automatically going to be interested in this chick?

"But it's ok if you're not interested, I can just tell her you're already seeing someone," she pouts, sticking her bottom lip out.

"I'll come meet her if you want. Just give me a call and I'll come see you at work," I lie with a smile, finishing my salad.

The server doesn't waste any time picking up my plate and I order more coffee.

"So, how are things with Brian?" I ask, picking at what's left of the appetizers.

I have to get to the subject eventually and from the way her head is starting to sway back and forth, I know it will come out easily.

"Things are going well for once. After that one night, when you came and rescued me, he moved all his things out the very next morning," she says after finishing her salad.

Mom reaches across the table to hold my hands but I'm suddenly overtaken by the urge to drink coffee. She gets the point and places her hands in her lap. Our server comes back with the entrees and her Jack and Coke.

"Anyway, he and Jessica are living at his brother's house. We started seeing each other after some time off, but I told him under no circumstances can he move back in with me!" my mother continues while tearing into her slab of bleeding meat.

The sight of the blood mixing with her mashed potatoes makes me feel sick and I eat my vegetables in silence.

"Don't you think that's kind of stupid? You know, after what happened?" I ask, a little dumbfounded.

Honestly, she was desperate to get rid of him! I simply don't see the logic.

"No, I don't think it's stupid, and don't talk to me like that!" she spatters, pointing her fork at me. "I'm an adult and I'm not stupid. I love Brian! We just needed some time apart."

"Whatever. I just can't understand why you have such a taste for assholes. Think about it, every man you have ever dated was bad for you!"

"And that's my fault?! I can't help it if they seem to find me. But Brian is different, he loves me! I've forgiven him, just like Christ instructs us to!"

"Jesus, quit it with that! Then forgive him and forget him! You're smarter than this! There are so many men out there that'll treat you better and that don't have... baggage!"

My mother goes silent. She sets her fork and knife down and slowly finishes the bite of meat in her mouth. The cliff is looming and when our waitress returns to check on us, she orders another drink.

"I think you've had enough," I interject, worried. She only weighs ninety pounds and will soon be in a coma from alcohol poisoning.

"Don't tell me what to do! I'm your fucking mother!" she quickly yells, her eyes flaming rage in my direction.

She goes silent again and stares at her plate when the drink arrives.

I want to apologize. I know I'm right and I know that someone should try and talk sense to her, but I can't shake my sudden feeling of guilt. This always happens and I know it's because she's instilled this control in me that makes me feel like a fucking dancing monkey.

"I'm sorry. I just want the best for you and I don't think Brian's worthy."

"Why do you insist on these little stabs? Do you get pleasure out of hurting me?"

"Yes," I answer in a monotone voice. "I keep a little journal for every time I hurt someone. Cut someone off today, check. Piss off mom and make her feel like shit, check."

"You're not funny."

We finish our dinners in silence. My mother already finished her last drink and is enjoying her free fall. I just hope she remembered the parachute or else I'll be the one mopping up the mess. The check comes and I don't put up a fight when she reaches for it. I didn't want to eat here anyway, even though I finished the entire steak. We slowly walk outside and she stumbles every few steps, trying hard to regain composure.

"I'm going to drive you home," I finally say, away from any possible listeners.

"I can drive myself," she blurts out, quickly stumbling towards her car.

"No, I'm driving," I yell as I chase after her and reach for the keys.

"I don't need your fucking help. No! Leave me alone!" she screams, turning on me.

She lifts a hand to slap me and as it quickly approaches my face, I snatch her wrist. Her bones feel like balsa wood and if I wanted to, I could snap them.

"Listen and listen well. I'm driving you home and there's no fucking arguing! And if you try slapping me again, I will drop kick you and leave you here in the parking lot to get raped and robbed!" I scold, pulling her in close.

The animal's blood is coursing through my veins and I suppress the urge to slap her. I pull the keys from her hand and unlock the passenger door of her little MR-2. I push her inside and slam it closed.

I sit in the driver's seat with my knees straddling the steering wheel and quickly put it into gear. My mother's breathing hard next to me and I know she's about to explode.

"You hurt my wrist!" she whines while rubbing it.

"You embarrassed me!" I respond without looking at her.

"I don't care. I wasn't embarrassed."

"What if we saw someone we knew? What would they think of your behavior?!"

"I don't care," is all she says and then falls silent.

I hope Brian isn't at her house. The last thing I want is for her to sick him on me. I could drop kick his ass too, I reassure myself. This ride will be short but not short enough. My mother's completely silent, her breathing easier now. I glance over twice and she has her arms folded in front of her, staring straight forward.

A few miles from her house though everything changes. I can see her lunge forward twice out of the corner of my eye and then fold completely over. With her face between her knees, she starts to throw up. It isn't the slow, silent type either. She retches loudly, practically yelling as if she's being fucked hard in the ass. The smell is awful and I quickly roll down the windows. I pull over to the side of the road and she vomits the remainder of her dinner out the door.

After finishing she sits back, bits of food on her chin and in her hair. She mumbles loudly, incoherently.

"I'm so sorry. I didn't want to embarrass you. I'm so sorry. I'm just so lonely," she says, her head swaying back and forth.

When we finally arrive at her house, I help her out of the car. Brian's truck isn't here and relief actually waves over me. One less problem to deal with.

"I would leave him but then who would I have? I have nobody!" she starts to cry and I decide to carry her.

I lift her in my arms and into the house. It's completely dark and quiet, but I have no need for the lights. I know this house. I know it better than most. I know it better than Brian's fucking daughter does.

I turn on the lights in her room and go to set her down in bed. She lunges forward and I quickly take her to the bathroom. I help her down and she kneels in front of the toilet, hacking and vomiting. I kneel behind her, holding her hair back and lifting her body up. I feel for her and try to hold back but the tears come anyway. She makes me sick. Her weakness makes me sick and all I want to do it stick her face in the orange water.

We sit here for an eternity and when I feel her body go limp, I lift her back up. I help her walk to the bed. I pull off her old work shoes and tuck the comforter around her.

"Richard. I miss you, Richard," she whimpers as I kiss her on the forehead.

My father, Richard.

She only talks about him when she's drunk.

"Come back Richard, I miss you. I'm sorry...."

I want to lie next to her the way I did when I was little, let her snuggle up with me and talk about him. With a bottle of wine and an arm around me, telling me about my father.

Is it possible to miss someone you can't even remember? Is it possible for my loss to outweigh hers? Fuck her for missing him and not thinking of me. Fuck him, wherever he is. I need a fucking cigarette. I quickly leave, slamming the doors behind me, stepping out into the night air. I leave the windows rolled down in her car and begin my walk back to the restaurant.

seventeen

I'm grateful to see Brittney and I are doing a party together. We've been avoiding each other since the fourth. We've worked every weekend together since but she continues to avoid eye contact. We're doing a wedding reception on the patio and the weather's been warm in the evenings.

I arrive an hour early to set up the tables. Neither of us is old enough to mix drinks but we set up a beer and wine bar outside. Brittney shows up shortly after I do and as I set up the tables the bride's family puts up decorations.

"Hey," is all I say to Brittney when I approach her at the bar.

Her skin's nicely tanned, as if she spent the whole day outside.

"Hey. This is going to be a lot of fun," she responds casually, as if I were anyone.

As if I were just another busboy.

The guests start showing up on time and everything runs smoothly. There are a little over fifty guests and to my relief the DJ in the corner is actually avoiding country music. The line at the bar stays consistent and I keep myself busy clearing plates. I served the food buffet style, so only the two of us are needed on the party.

As the food slows and the cake's served, both Brittney and I are left with little to do. I finally step behind the bar and offer her a cigarette.

"Umm, I'll just take a drag off yours."

I hungrily light a Marlboro and she quickly takes a couple puffs.

"So, how have you been?" I ask, looking at her intently.

"Good. Really good," she says, looking back at me.

"How's Mark?" I ask.

"He's ok. I guess."

Brittney picks up the pack and lights her own. She inhales it deeply and blows the smoke out her nose, all the while staring at the smiling groom and bride. I pull out a box of food, leftovers I packed for myself, and offer her a bite of chicken piccata.

"No thanks," is her only reply and she pours a glass of wine for an elderly man who just walked up, placing her cigarette in the ashtray.

I step behind the patio, out of view of the patrons, and finish my piece of chicken. The back door of the restaurant opens and Susan walks out, followed closely by another woman. Her friend is younger and much more attractive.

"Hey handsome," she says as she kisses me.

I hold the box of food and hug her with my free arm. She's wearing a revealing blouse, without a bra, and a pair of shiny leather pants. They fit snuggly around her waist and taper down to her ankles.

"Dana told us you were out here," she continues and motions to the other woman. "This is my friend Diane. We work together."

I shake her hand politely and stand awkwardly, unsure of what to say.

"So, can you get us a glass of wine?" Susan asks.

"Of course. Just walk around the front of the bar and I'll be right there."

I step back behind the bar and Brittney barely notices me. Susan and Diane sit and smile at me.

"What can I get for you?" I ask.

This gets Brittney's attention and she glances at me.

"Just two glasses of whatever you have that's white."

I pull a bottle of Sauvignon Blanc from the ice and fill two small, clear plastic cups. They both thank me flirtatiously. I excuse myself, pick up a tray, and walk towards the tables. I know they're both staring at my ass and when I glance back, so is Brittney.

I clear plates of half-eaten cake. I pick up empty wine cups and beer bottles. I skillfully wipe crumbs from the tables. I do all the things that I have become good at. I exist here to make this wonderful evening run smoothly and despite how degrading it feels, it's very simple. I take cake to Susan, her friend, and Brittney. I set my tray down and eat with them as we watch everyone try to dance.

Susan talks to Brittney but she responds with half-ass answers. Brittney feigns laughter and smiles but won't even look at Susan. I don't know how she could know about us but I find it refreshing. I find her jealousy mildly affirming.

Well into the party, Susan and Diane stand to leave.

"Leaving already?" I ask casually, flashing my white smile that was perfected by six years of braces.

"Yeah. We have plans to meet some other girls for a movie. I just wanted to stop by and say hi," Susan answers. She pauses, and then continues, "What time do you get off work?"

"In about three hours," I say after glancing at the time on the register.

"Ok. Come over when you're finished. I'll have some dinner waiting."

Brittney definitely hears this and chokes on a mouthful of Coke.

I lean across the bar and kiss Susan. Not too much tongue but definitely not a peck on the cheek. I place a hand on her neck and gently brush my tongue against hers, our lips barely parting. She smiles as she walks away and Diane waves. I turn to see if Brittney was watching and she quickly turns away.

"So, are you and Susan seeing each other?" Brittney finally asks me when the reception is over.

I've already boxed up a large piece of cake and put it with the food I'm taking home. Brittney's behind the bar putting away unsold bottles of beer and I'm folding tables.

"Not really seeing each other, just sleeping together," I say simply and my confidence goes through the roof.

When I finish folding and putting the tables away, I sit at the bar to have a cigarette. I offer Brittney one and she accepts. The restaurant's still full inside and it's nearly ten o'clock.

"I wanted to tell you something," Brittney says after I give her a light. "Before summer started you asked if I wanted to move in with you. Do you remember?"

"Yeah. Of course I do," I answer and my hopes begin to soar.

Could she possibly be interested in taking me up on my offer?

"Well, I want to move in with you. With Mark."

I take a couple seconds to decipher what she's just told me. Brittney, living with me, sharing a room with Mark.

"I talked to him about it and he said he was cool with you and me living together. He'd just feel better if he lived there too," she continues, reading the expression on my face.

"I can't imagine why," I add and she smiles. A real, guilty, sinful smile, and I know for sure Mark doesn't know what happened between us.

"I accept. I think it would be great. We'd have fun living together," I say and her smile grows.

I know this will just make it easier for me to get in her pants.

There's a yellow note on the front door telling me to let myself in when I get to Susan's. Her hair's slicked back, accentuating her wrinkles, and her inappropriate leather pants have been replaced by an unflattering formfitting black dress. She's even wearing four inches heels that are skimpy and black with straps that wrap all the way up to her knees.

"Hey sexy," I say in a deep voice.

Susan quickly wraps her arms around my neck and jams her tongue in my mouth. I'm overwhelmed by the sudden presence of whiskey in my system. I kiss her with my eyes open and watch her at her best, trying so hard and not even coming close.

"You got here just in time," she tells me after our mouths detach.

Stepping away, Susan's hand slides down my chest, glides across my stomach, and rests on my cock. I'm starving but fuck the food, let's do it.

She pours me a whiskey and Coke and we toast in the kitchen. She slaved over pre-packaged fettuccini and frozen scampi. Warming the can of Alfredo sauce was the hardest part. She scoops the food onto two plates and leads me into the den.

I didn't notice the dining room before, which is now candle lit. Susan went as far as to sprinkle the table with rose pedals and we're eating on the nice china. This is overkill, her romantic foreplay. The TV in the den is turned to a cable radio station, a station for lovers.

"I thought tonight would be a little more romantic," Susan says as she sets our plates down, her eyes glimmering with hope.

"It's beautiful," is my only stupid response.

We sit close to one another and I get self-conscious, hungrily jamming food in my mouth. Susan takes her time, taking small bites and constantly wiping her mouth. She smiles at me, plays with my hair, and rubs my thigh. Ever so slightly her hand slides to my crotch and I'm reminded of the events to come.

"Do you like it?" she asks before sipping her cocktail.

"Yeah, it's really good," I say through a mouthful of food.

I definitely need to be drunk to get through tonight.

"That girl you were working with," Susan continues, setting her glass down. "She's really pretty."

I answer with an absent, "MmHm."

"Do you like her?" she presses, taking her napkin from her knees and placing it neatly on her plate.

"Umm, she's a friend," I slowly venture, unsure of where she's leading.

"She was kind of rude to me. You know, like she was jealous."

Susan turns away from me self-consciously. I stop eating and look at her.

"I'm sorry. It's really silly of me. You're young and attractive. I can't expect you to hold out... for me," she waves off, gulping the rest of her whiskey.

"We're good friends," is all I say and the subject is dropped.

"My friend Diane really liked you," Susan starts up again, her energy and vigor renewed. "She thought you were really sweet."

"You'll have to thank her for me." I lean in and kiss her on the cheek.

When we finish eating, I clear the table. While I rinse the plates, Susan walks up behind me, her heels clicking on the linoleum. She presses her body against mine and wraps her arms around me. Her hands slide from my waist to my chest and she pulls the pack of cigarettes from my breast pocket.

The lighter flicks in my ear and Susan places the pack on the counter next to the sink. I can hear the tobacco burn. I imagine the cherry glow. I turn my face to watch her blow smoke in the air. She places the cigarette between my lips.

I drag on the Marlboro while Susan hastily unbuttons my shirt. She untucks it and lets it fall to the floor. Her fingers caress my shoulders and back. My hairs stand on end. When she kisses my tattoo again I can feel it on the tip of my dick.

I turn around, leaning Into the sink. Susan kisses my neck and I keep smoking the cigarette. She continues kissing me and slowly drops to her knees. Within seconds my pants are around my ankles and my cock is sliding in and out of her mouth. I can't watch. I'm achingly hard and I want to stop her. I leave the cigarette between my lips, placing my hands on the counter for leverage. When I finally look down Susan's staring up at me, her eyes yearning. She's yearning for me to cum, to vilify her actions.

I quickly pull Susan to her feet and kiss her. The cigarette drops to the floor. I lift her body and step across the small kitchen to the other counter. I set her on the tiled surface and pull up her short dress. She moans loudly as I try to slip inside her but I can't. She isn't wet. I continue to try and Susan stops me, placing a hand on my chest.

"Not yet. Follow me."

Susan steps from the counter and pulls her skirt down. She walks from the kitchen and turns with her hand outstretched. As I take it I look back at the hole burned into the linoleum, my cigarette still lit.

Susan leads me upstairs and I can see into her bedroom. She continues to pull me through a set of French doors onto a patio. She hands me blankets and motions for me to step outside.

"Wait for me. I'll be right back."

I walk out onto the deck. It's positioned above her garage and I can see the city lights from where I stand. I can see my apartment. I can see where Brittney and I parked across the valley. I kick off my shoes and pull my pants and socks off. The cool night air invigorates my senses. I walk to the railing and stare out on my world.

Susan steps out into the moonlight, completely naked. She smiles and kisses me. She takes me by the hand and leads me back to where I laid the blankets. It is all like something out of a movie but *The Graduate* was never meant to be this romantic, it didn't even try. She lies on her back and pulls me on top of her. I slide in easily now and know exactly what she was doing inside, after she undressed.

I'm fucking a menopausal woman. I want to stop and laugh at how silly I must look. I'm not nearly drunk enough and I wish I had another cocktail.

I fuck Susan like before and like before she cums. She cums over and over and over. I'm beginning to think she's faking but the orgasms increase with intensity. After forty-five minutes I'm exhausted and nowhere close to finishing. I fall off her, my back soaked in sweat, my testicles low and swollen from slapping against her ass.

"I love you," she moans. "I fucking love you."

My hard on completely shrinks to nothing.

"I need a drink," I tell her, standing up. "Want one?"

"Of course. And bring your cigarettes."

I walk slowly into the kitchen. My balls hurt as they slap against my thighs and my knees are shaking. I mix two more whiskey and Cokes and light a cigarette as I walk back up stairs. I walk passed the cabinet where Susan keeps the pot and pause.

Susan gratefully accepts the cocktail and smiles at me as I light her cigarette. We lie on our sides facing each other. I try to maintain eye contact, try not to look down at her withered body. The bright moon makes that impossible and I find myself running a finger along her thigh, up to her chest. She takes this as an invitation and sets her glass down while rolling over. Without words she pushes her ass into the air, leaning forward on her elbows. She looks at me with determination in her eyes and I gratefully accept the invitation. I gulp my entire cocktail and swallow hard.

I position myself on my knees behind her and slide in easily. I awkwardly adjust to this new position, thrusting slowly at first. My legs are longer than hers and I continue to slip out. She patiently turns to me, placing a hand on my thigh and pushing my legs together. I bend my knees and she sits perfectly on my lap. I don't move while she leans into me, her cunt and ass slapping against my pelvis. She moans in ecstasy, writhing and shaking. She reaches back again and digs her nails into my thighs, pulling me deeper and deeper into her, until I can't go any deeper. And she cums. And cums. And cums.

I lie exhausted on my back again, my thighs screaming out in pain. I still haven't cum and Susan is enjoying another cigarette. Her legs are draped across my stomach and she massages my testicles, turning them over and over in her hand like coins in a change purse.

"I'm getting cold. I think we should take this inside," she finally says to me.

Susan stands waiting for me and we leave the blankets under the stars. My last cocktail pushed me far enough and my body feels like rubber. She leads me into the bedroom and flips on the light.

Her room is sparsely furnished, bare except for the bed and a single dresser. There's a portrait of her in the corner, maybe twenty years old at the time it was taken. She's lying on a bed with a large book strategically placed to cover her naked body. Her hair 's light red, it's natural color, and she stares longingly into the camera.

"My husband took that of me. I'll make you a copy if you want."

I fuck her in the bed. I fuck her over and over. I fuck her with the lights on and with the lights off. And she continues to welcome me, begging for more, every time forgetting that I haven't cum yet. We fall asleep some time around three in the morning, the room reeking of sweat and shit.

Susan wakes me shortly after eight in the morning. She's already dressed.

"I have to go to work. There's coffee in the kitchen," she says while kissing me.

She pushes her tongue into my mouth regardless of my morning breath and walks out the door.

Thank you it says. She leaves me four nicely rolled joints, all in line waiting for me to smoke.

I sleep for another hour and get out of bed. I collect my clothes from the patio, the hot sun burning my naked flesh. I pour a cup of coffee and slip my boots back on. I leave her a note, with my phone number, thanking her for the great night.

On my way home I drive by Brandon's, this time unable to control myself. I can hear him practicing with his band in the garage. I want to talk to him and apologize for being an asshole. I want to tell him he's probably right, that I appreciate his concern. Michelle's in the living room playing Monopoly with Ty and Eric and I wonder when they started hanging out.

I don't deserve it and I'm simply too afraid. I go home empty handed.

I'm not home long. I put the boxes of food in the fridge and I'm about to make coffee when my telephone rings.

"Hello sweetheart," my mother's says and I want to hang up immediately.

"Hello mother," I respond.

"I hope I didn't wake you," she says even though it's already ten o'clock. "I want you to come to the hospital so I can introduce you to that nurse I was telling you about. Are you still interested?"

"Of course I am," I say, scratching my crotch and thinking about taking a shower. "I'll be there in half hour."

I brush my teeth and fix my hair. I don't bother changing my clothes and I look nice except for the fact that my tuxedo shirt's wrinkled. I put my sunglasses on, light a cigarette, and walk back outside. I stop at a coffee shop on my way to the hospital and pick up an iced latté.

I park in the employee parking lot and my mother meets me outside. She's wearing her perpetual horse print scrub top with another gaudy scrunchy.

"My baby boy..." she whines.

She hugs me and hangs on me like she always does. She insists on holding my hand, gripping my arm as if I might run at the first opportunity. Every person that passes us is forced to hear about how handsome I am, about how smart I am, about how far I'll go in life.

We take the stairs to her floor. My mother drills me about what I've been doing. She even asks me about Susan.

"How's that 'friend' of yours?" she asks, annunciating the words so she won't have to elaborate.

"Good. Very good actually," I say, smelling Susan on me.

When we get to her department, she doesn't hesitate to talk me up to everyone. The sun's flooding in on the nurse's station and they all look up at us as we approach.

"I'd like to introduce you all to my son!" she exclaims, squeezing every last drop of blood from my hand. "His name's Jason."

I'm bombarded with introductions. I won't remember a single person after today, even if I were to come back and be re-introduced. It wouldn't be worth it. I just want to meet this girl.

I'm bullied into a seat and my mother suddenly plops down on my lap. I awkwardly look up at her but she doesn't even notice. I glance around and no one else seems to notice. Or at least they act like they don't.

Nurses come and go. Patients call up the desk and my mother continues to talk me up to the table full of women.

"Isn't he handsome?" is her world famous one-liner.

If we were all drunk, she'd be bragging about the size of my genitals.

"Umm..." I finally interrupt. "Where's this girl you wanted to introduce me to?"

"He hasn't met Katie yet?" one of the ladies asks, looking at my mother in shock.

"Not yet. I wanted to introduce him to you all first."

What she means is she wanted me to herself first.

My mother leans across the table, still sitting on my lap, and picks up the phone.

"Hi, this is Deborah over in North Tower. Can I talk to Katie?" she says into the phone, smiling back at me. "Katie? Hi, it's Deborah. Can you come down to my floor real quick? I want to introduce you to someone."

After hanging up everyone turns to me and smiles, as if I should be as ecstatic as my mother.

"I showed her your high school photo," my mother says, reaching into her pocket. "This one, with your theater polo on."

I cringe when she pulls it out. The photo's wrinkled and discolored and there I am, smiling in all my glory, the day after I got my braces off.

I continue glancing down the hallway, waiting impatiently for Katie to walk into view. I decide it might be better to get my mom off my lap the first time we meet but when I go to move her, see glances at me queerly.

"My legs hurt," is all I can come up with and I stand when she finds another seat.

I'm adjusting my shirt when my mother practically screams out in excitement.

"Jason, this is Katie!"

I expect a drum roll, a procession. I slowly look up and into the eyes of Katie.

My breath escapes me for a second, a short moment, but my heart is suddenly reaffirmed, awakened. Katie stands at the other end of the nurse's station, on display for us all. She has long black hair that falls well passed her shoulders. And green eyes. Green like the color of algae and limestone. She's tall and curvaceous, wearing all black scrubs. And when her eyes meet mine and her pupils focus in, I am immobilized.

"Hi," is all I can say and it's completely appropriate.

"Hello," is her only response.

All eyes gaze on us, glancing back and forth, waiting for the next move. My mother wastes no time.

"Isn't he handsome?" she says, wrapping her arms around me.

I reluctantly accept, shrugging my shoulders and limply hugging her back.

"Yes he is," Katie says casually.

"I told you she was cute," my mother says, looking up at me now.

The spotlight is shining on me, blinding me, and I simply stare at Katie because words can't suffice. Before I have a chance to rectify myself, my mother yet again takes it upon herself.

"Have you eaten yet today?" she asks me. "You look so thin."

"Umm, no. Not yet." *Not food anyway*, I think to myself.

"Katie, would you like to come down to the cafeteria with us?" my mother suddenly blurts out, taking me by the hand and dragging me down the hallway.

"Sure," Katie says and everyone watches the three of us leave.

The elevator ride down is quiet. Katie and I glance at each other, our smiles spreading every time. When the door dings open my mother takes us each by the arm and pulls us into the nearly empty cafeteria. I get a cup of coffee, as does Katie, and my mother gets an apple and hot tea. When we approach a table, she suddenly stops.

"I just remembered something," she over acts, slapping herself on the forehead. "I have some patients that need their meds."

She kisses me on the cheek and runs away before I have a chance to stop her. Katie and I glance at each other and laugh. We sit down anyway, just the two of us.

"I'm sorry," I say.

"For what?"

"For my mom. For the way she acts."

"Don't apologize. It's kind of sweet."

"Yeah and a little creepy," I say with a laugh.

She agrees and we both laugh.

We sit quietly, sipping our coffee and avoiding eye contact. I want to talk to her, ask for her phone number and ask her on a date. But the build up has been too much and I'm quickly buckling under the pressure.

"Well," Katie finally says after realizing I don't seem that interested. "I have work to get back to."

"It was nice meeting you," I say, wishing I would just say more.

"Yeah, the same here," Katie says, shaking my hand with disappointment.

She quickly turns and walks away.

With each step, I fight back the urge to yell for her to stop. I keep hoping she'll turn around and when she finally steps order the corner, I give up.

The sun is scorching hot when I step outside. I left my sunglasses in the Jeep and I can barely see it through my contacts. As I unlock the door, I hear my mother call out to me.

"Jason! Wait a second!" she yells and I turn to watch her approach.

"You can thank me," she says as she hands me a piece of paper. I open it and inside is Katie's phone number.

"What did you do?" I ask, disbelieving what she's capable of.

"I saw Katie in the hall and asked what she thought of you. She thought you were cute but uninterested because you didn't ask for her phone number. So, I got it for you," she answers, waiting for an enthusiastic response. I want to hit her, not thank her.

"Umm, thank you. I'll give her a call," I offer, not really wanting to give up an excuse.

I wish I had asked for the phone number myself. I wonder what Katie thinks of me now? Strike one.

EIGHTEEN

Katie.

Katie is all I think about.

Katie is all I fantasize about. Katie is all I lust for and when I masturbate, I masturbate for Katie.

She consumes my every molecule and my life's goal is to get her in bed.

I still haven't called her though.

Almost a week later and I haven't dared look at the phone for fear I might uncontrollably dial her number. I can concentrate on nothing else and my life may just end.

Tawny comes over on a night I'm not working. She helps me plan her going away party. She puts aside her newfound depression and self-loathing long enough to listen to me talk. When I tell her about Susan, she laughs harder than when I told her about my STD.

"Hell, at least you're gettin' some!" she says between snorts.

She calls me a 'whore' for getting so much pot and alcohol out of it and I hit her on the arm.

When I tell her about Katie, she smiles. She's genuinely beaming.

"Are you gonna to invite her to my party?" she interjects.

The thought had not yet passed my mind.

"Yeah," I say, suddenly reluctant. "I guess."

"Really?! Don't be a pussy this time!"

"I won't!"

"Jason, cut the shit! Have some fucking balls. She sounds really good for you and hell, if she wasn't in the least bit interested, she wouldn't have given your mom her number! Trust me!"

I know everything Tawny says is true and this time I don't want to be a pussy. I know what I want and I'm going to take it.

"What about Grandma?" she asks, smiling the way she always does when the joke is at my expense.

"I'll take care of Susan, that won't be a problem," I reassure her confidently. "I'm getting laid this weekend and it's gonna be with Katie."

Katie, like a bird piercing the silence, urging me forward.

The evening slowly drags by. Tawny brought a pack of clove cigarettes and to my surprise smokes them heartily. We drink a bottle of Sauvignon Blanc, courtesy of her mother. Rebecca agreed to let us have the party at her house. We call all our friends.

I leave a message for Brittney.

When I call Jared, he says he'd love to be there. To say goodbye.

I reluctantly call Michelle and she says she'll think about it.

Jenny acts overly excited to get the invitation.

Karen doesn't answer.

Tawny calls people we haven't seen since graduation and she's happy with the results. She even seems relieved when I tell her Jared will be there.

"Good," she whispers, rubbing her eyes. "I want to say bye."

We make a list of things to buy: food, alcohol, cake, alcohol, all while watching MTV, sipping wine, and smoking. This is what I will miss most about her.

Not the partying.

Not the nude sunbathing.

Not the sexual irreverence.

I'll miss the silence. The few moments where we have nothing to say and it doesn't matter. I'll miss my friend because she accepts me and loves me. I'll miss her because I have so little to say.

"I'm really going to miss him," Tawny says out of the blue.

Our lists are finished, the bottle's empty, and we're watching *Jackass* reruns.

"I feel guilty. I mean, did I lead him on?"

I have no answer for her. I just shrug.

"He's still an asshole but what did I expect would happen? Honestly?!"

Tawny leans in close, putting her arm through mine. I wrap a hand around her thigh, pulling her even closer and holding her tight.

When the re-runs end, I offer to pull out the futon for her.

"Would you mind sleeping out here, with me?" she asks, standing and stretching.

She peruses my small DVD collection and pulls out a violent zombie movie featuring a scantly clad former super model.

"I want to watch one of those woman empowering ones," she says.

We turn off all the lights and I bring out the brown comforter. I open the window next to us and the breeze blows gently in. I take off my shirt and keep my khaki shorts on. Tigi emerges from her hiding place and cuddles around my feet.

We smoke the pot Susan gave me. After three joints, the room's spinning and I quickly sink into the futon. The soft comforter absorbs my skin and soon I'll stare up at the world from my stuffed resting place.

I watch Tawny cry in the faint blue light. She doesn't bother to wipe the tears away and they roll thick down her cheeks. When she turns away from me I touch her. Like a blanket I wrap my arms around her, comforting her. She cries softly for me, only me, and I absorb it all.

I hear gunshots before I fade to black, dying men screaming and cars exploding.

In the morning we wake sleeping back to back. The sun is pounding down on us through the blinds I was too high to close. We laugh at the way our bad breath lingers in the air.

I make coffee. Tawny takes a shower. I take one when she finishes. I quietly masturbate, afraid to be heard. I think about Katie. I dress in an old pair of shorts and a white under shirt. We eat a breakfast of toast and Frosted Mini Wheat's. We smoke more cloves. Tawny inhales deeply, as if the burning, the killing, the dying air is relief to her.

We leave for the store. Tawny puts in a Placebo tape, complaining that I still don't have a CD player. She doesn't say much else. She doesn't even complain when I light a Marlboro like she normally does. She just lights a Djarum.

Tawny chases me with the shopping cart and squeals when I snarl at her. She carelessly tosses food in the basket, shoving the cart passed unsuspecting patrons. We laugh freely, like children, unaffected and unaware. Chips, dips, cake and candy; everything Tawny usually avoids she tosses into the cart with abandon. All for one last hurrah.

I volunteer to take all the bags up to the apartment. Tawny hands me a large glass of water when I finish my third and final trip up the flight of stairs, both arms full of grocery bags.

"What time is Rebecca expecting us?" she asks.

"I told her the party's starting at eight. That's around the time I get off work."

"Ok. I'll be there around seven to get it all ready. Is she picking up the alcohol?

"Yes."

"Can I have a key so I can come pick this all up while you're at work?"

"Of course," I say as I retrieve an extra one from the kitchen.

I don't know why I didn't give her the extra key a long time ago.

"I'll give it back on Saturday," she says, smiling at me as she shoves it into her pocket.

"Keep it," I say, pathetically attempting to be poetic. "For when you come back to visit."

Tawny leaves, waving to me from the parking lot. I watch until she's out of view. I watch her leave my apartment for the last time.

When I get to work, only five minutes early, Dana's in the office cursing and frantically making phone calls.

"What's wrong?" I ask, hanging up my keys and adjusting my tie in the mirror behind the door.

"Gwen quit," she breathlessly responds, dialing. "I called her house to see when she'd finally be showing up today and her Aunt said she ran away. I'm trying to find someone to fill in for her."

"I will," I say.

"Are you sure?"

"Of course I'm sure. How hard can it be seating people and bussing tables?"

When I pull my timecard, a small envelope's taped to the back. My name's written on it and sprinkled with purple glitter. Inside is a note, sprayed with perfume.

> Dear Jason,
>
> Goodbye. That's all I want to say to you. I'm never coming back and I'll miss you. Thank you for everything.
>
> Love,
>
> Gwen

The writing is hurried and messy and below her name is a smudged kiss mark. It's pink and smells like strawberries and when I kiss it, my lips feel waxy. I fold the note and place it in my pocket.

Rebecca's annoyed and Dana continues complaining about Gwen's immaturity. I mindlessly go about my duties and think about her the entire time. I hope she finds her way.

I'm bombarded and endlessly running back and forth to the front desk. The reservation book is completely empty and nearly all the tables are full, something unusual for a Wednesday night. Susan comes in to visit me and I spot her at the bar as I run to the kitchen.

"Hi," she mouths, waving at me.

Without thinking, I kiss her quickly on the lips and continue on my way. She's blushes and hasn't a chance to speak as I hurry away. Dana watches it all, eyebrows raised and mouth agape.

I don't get another chance to talk to Susan for three hours. By the time I slow down enough to approach her she's already had too much to drink. Dana's ignoring her and no one else at the bar seems to know she exists.

"Well, there you are," she says as I slide in next to her. "Glad you made time to see me."

"What's that supposed to mean?" I ask defensively.

Her voice is stern and hurt. I'm in no mood to deal with this.

"I've been here three hours and now it's time for me to go," she says, glancing at her watch. She tosses cash down on the bar and walks out.

"Wait," I beg, running after her.

I don't know why I try. I should let her go because that'd make this so much easier.

I grab Susan by the arm as she reaches her car. She turns as if she might hit me but stops to readjust the purse hanging from her shoulder. She looks at me, waiting for me to speak.

"What the fuck is your problem?" I scream, my arms raised in frustration.

"Why were you avoiding me? When Dana saw us kiss, she ignored me like I was some pedophile or something!"

"I was working! Grow up! What is this?"

Susan goes silent, staring down at the gravel. A chirping cricket is thunderous and I want to scream.

"I'm sorry," she finally says, stepping towards me with out-stretched arms. "I love you…"

I stop her. I hold her by the shoulders and she looks up at me with tears in her eyes. Tears of hurt and yearning. Tears of desperation. Tears of love.

"I can't do this anymore," I tell her and the words come out easier than I thought they would.

"But I love you…" she moans, continuing to reach for me.

I maintain my distance and her expression grows even more pathetic.

"I know you do. But I've found someone else. I'm sorry."

I don't want to see her cry. I don't want to kiss her again. I shouldn't have fucked her in the first place. I shouldn't have filled her void thinking I could just walk away. Her sex will never come unattached and I'll always be a reminder of what she can no longer have.

"Fuck you," she screams as I turn and walk away. "You're a fucking asshole!"

Before I walk back into the restaurant I turn and watch Susan stumble into her car. She gives me a dirty look and screeches her tires as she pulls out of the parking lot. From inside I can hear sirens whaling, brakes slamming and an officer's voice blaring over the commotion.

ΠΙΠΘΤΘΘΠ

Tonight's the night.

Tonight's the night.

Tonight's the night.

The night that drags on. Every second slowly fades into every minute, every minute quietly passing into hours. I find myself staring at the clock, cracking my knuckles impatiently.

"That won't make time go any faster," Dana remarks, annoyed.

With every table that I seat, I grow more and more weary. Eric and Brittney are working tonight, cordially getting along. Rebecca's home helping Tawny get ready for the party. I don't want to be here but I need the money. I have to pay a passed-due electric bill. I need more cigarettes.

Brittney borrows my cellar keys to retrieve a $75 bottle of wine. A bottle that only costs $25. While slowly seating an elderly couple, I watch her descend the stairs. Following close behind her is Eric.

I walk back to my podium and watch for them. I've lost my concept of time and they never return. I stare, transfixed by the hole in the floor. My curiosity builds to an uncontrollable level and I give in.

I step along the wall, supporting myself with the railing so the steps don't squeak. The door's ajar when I reach the bottom and I slowly peak around the corner. I hold my breath as if the least bit of air might disrupt the universe.

"Kiss me," he says, cornering her.

"No," Brittney responds flirtatiously, already holding the bottle of wine.

"Why not?"

"You know why..."

"That hasn't stopped you before."

"It's different now."

"Why? Because of Mark?" Eric replies with a laugh.

"Yes. I love him," Brittney says more sternly and I hate to hear the words come.

It doesn't stop Eric. He leans in and kisses her anyway. Brittney doesn't stop him, doesn't lift a finger to delay him. She closes her eyes and accepts him.

She wants this.

My breathing commences and my eyes grow wide. The molecules escape my lungs, roll across my tongue and fall from my partly opened lips. They put into play a series of events, a chain of movement that brushes against Brittney's eyes. They flutter. She opens them and stares at me from over Eric's shoulder.

Our gazes meet for a moment and time slows considerably. I'm suspended, dreading and unaware of the future. She continues to kiss him, knowing I'm seeing it all.

Eric remains oblivious and reaches a hand into her blouse.

I climb back up the stairs, this time inconsiderate of the noises I might make. I stomp the floor, imagining the dust fall on them. I'm eight years old again, jealous of the bigger kid that got the girl.

Back at my podium I watch intently for them. When they finally do resurface, neither Eric nor Brittney look in my direction. He quickly hurries to the kitchen and she runs off to open the bottle. I stare at her, praying she'll notice me. I want a response, an acknowledgement, a plea to keep her secret. She won't give me that satisfaction.

Ten minutes after eight Dana finally gives me the go ahead to leave.

"Alright already," she exclaims, her hand in the air. "Have a good time. Say goodbye to Tawny for me. And be careful!"

As I walk back to the kitchen, loosening my tie and unbuttoning my top button, I bump into Eric.

"Coming to the party?" I ask.

I don't want him there but I already invited him.

"Umm, I don't know. I already have plans. Maybe," he says as he steps around me.

As I walk into the office, the door bumps into Brittney. She's reapplying her lipstick, fixing the mess Eric made.

"Sorry," I apologize.

I pick up my keys and move quickly to leave.

"I'll be at the party in a little bit," she says, not taking her eyes off her own visage in the mirror behind the door. "Mark will be there a little earlier," she continues, glancing over at me.

"That's good. I can have a drink with my new roommate," I say to her, smiling now. "We can have some male bonding time."

She returns the smile and I'm relieved. She's reassured and I have ammunition.

When I get in the Jeep and place the keys in the ignition, I notice the napkin my mom gave me, the one with Katie's phone number on it. I stop for a second, transfixed by it. I pull it from the cup holder and run back inside.

Brittney's no longer in the office and I close the door behind me.

"Hello?" Katie's voice says after the third ring.

"Hi. It's Jason," I say quickly.

"Hey kid," she says and I feel foolish for calling. "What's up?" she asks casually.

"Nothing really. I just got off work and I was wondering if you had any plans tonight?"

"No. I'm just hanging at home."

"Well, we're having a going away party for my best friend. Interested?"

"Sure," she says. I can hear her shoulders shrug, her head tilt saying *Why not?*

I give Katie directions and she says she'll meet me there in half an hour. I run back outside and quickly head for Rebecca's. The ride is arduous and I keep thinking about Katie. What I'll say, how I look, how I can get her in bed. I'm wearing my lucky boxer shorts, black with white stripes. I should have trimmed my pubes. They're long and bushy, spreading hip to hip.

Katie hasn't arrived when I get there and I wait outside for her, smoking a Marlboro. While I wait Brandon shows up with Michelle and I stand awkwardly, watching them approach.

"Hey babe," Michelle says affectionately.

Brandon's deliberate and quiet, avoiding my eyes.

"Hey," is all I say at first. "I'm sorry... for what happened. Thank you for caring so much," I continue and the admission pains me.

Brandon quickly embraces me and I hug him tightly.

"No problem. It happens. I just love you man," he says into my ear, hugging me tighter.

The warmth of our friendship is renewed and I feel blessed. He offers to stay outside with me but I insist he go inside and join the festivities.

I flick my cigarette when Katie approaches. She pulls up in a white sedan and steps out confidently, looking around for me. She's wearing a white blouse that accentuates her full breasts and blue jeans that ride low on her hips. Her hair's pulled up tight behind her head and her long neck is illuminated by the streetlights. Her eyes captivate me. I walk slowly to her, wanting to run, to embrace her but when I get to my spot, my 'x' taped to the ground, I stand awkwardly with my hands in my pockets and smile.

"Here I am!" Katie says with a big smile.

"Yes, here you are," I reciprocate.

I lead her inside, her hand in mine as we willingly step across the threshold.

We're bombarded by a living room packed full of familiar faces. I slowly introduce Katie and I don't expect her to remember all their names. Michelle greets me again, with a hug this time, and embraces Katie too. Brandon shakes her hand. Jenny hugs me and quietly says hello to my guest. Jared hugs us both warmly, smiling to see me. Ty nods his head in our direction. Rebecca screams out her greeting and rushes over to us. Tawny does the same, excited that I finally arrived.

"Hi," she says, shaking Katie's hand. "I'm Tawny," she continues and her handshake continues into a hug and they both smile. "I'm Jason's best friend and I've heard a lot about you."

Katie looks at me sideways with a wicked smile and Tawny leads her off to the kitchen to get a cocktail.

I notice Mark sitting on the couch, quietly observing his surroundings. Our eyes meet and I smile, nodding at him. He waits a moment and returns the greeting, raising his beer bottle. I need a drink.

Tawny and Katie are already shooting back vodka when I find them in the kitchen. They both do it professionally. I catch up with a double of Tequila. Rebecca and I do body shots. John looks on, drinking a glass of wine.

We join the rest of the party in the living room. Katie and I squeeze onto the couch next to Jared and Michelle. Tawny sits with Ty and he puts an arm around her. Everything fits so perfectly and all the animosity I expected to feel in the air is gone. Before we get too inebriated to talk, Tawny insists on making a quick speech.

"I just want to say something really quick," she begins, holding up her beer. "Thank you all, for everything. This summer's been a memorable one and you've all helped make it that way. I'll miss you. Thank you very much Rebecca for the generous use of your home. And thank you Jason, for..." She can't finish her sentence and the words stick in her throat, something I would've never expect from her.

"It's ok," I whisper, hugging her tight. "Don't do this tonight. Not yet."

One by one, we all hug Tawny and quickly pass around shots.

The music gets louder.

The lights get darker.

Katie and I get drunker.

We say very little to each other but I continue to catch her staring at me. I bathe in the attention and intend to return it ten fold.

Brittney arrives still wearing her uniform and she hugs Tawny. They share tears and Brittney gives her a gift. Mark's happiness to see her looks forced. She kisses him on the cheek and I wonder if Eric will be showing up. I wonder if Mark can smell him...

I continue filling Katie with alcohol. The air gets warm and she unbuttons the top two buttons of her blouse, exposing her breasts even more. I can see her lacy bra and the thought of sticking my face between them makes me hard. She notices and continues to lean forward, pushing them in my direction.

"It's getting hot in here," I whisper in her ear and lead her into the backyard.

I light a cigarette and offer her one, which she turns down.

"You have nice friends," she tells me as she sits in a chair, crossing her legs seductively.

If only she were wearing a skirt.

"Yeah. I do don't I?" I answer.

I watch them inside. Rebecca brings out her deck of Uno cards again and everyone congregates around the dining room table. I laugh when I think about how long **this** game will last.

"Thank you for inviting me," Katie says after licking her lips, swallowing a mouthful of beer.

"My pleasure. I'm just glad you were able to come. And I want to apologize again for my mother."

"That's ok. I know it can be hard to ask a girl for her phone number yourself," she laughs with a wicked smile. "My mom thought it was so funny that you weren't picking me up," she continues, waving the smoke out of her face.

"I'm sorry," I say quickly, feeling guilty. "I just thought it would be easier..."

"It's ok. I didn't mind," she interrupts.

I flick my butt over the back wall.

We take a shot of Southern Comfort in the kitchen with Brittney and Mark. He continues to pour himself another and another. Brittney scolds him and he ignores her.

Michelle and Jared are sitting together again, laughing and enjoying each other's company. They seem almost normal again, almost like what they used to be. I find it hard to see them apart now and I wonder what's transpired since I spoke to them both last. Brandon seems out of place but is making the most of it sitting next to Jenny. Rebecca explains the rules for the fiftieth time, incorporating shots into the game. A large bottle of Vodka is placed on the table with shot glasses and the cards are passed out.

John turns up The Verve playing on the computer in the corner.

Mark takes more shots, even though he's not losing. Brittney continues to reprimand him, her temper rising. Katie keeps staring at me, waiting for something.

Mark finally gets up and stumbles on his way to the bathroom. He walks towards the front door and when he starts making heaving noises, I quickly get up to help him.

We stumble outside and he throws up all over the lawn. It gets on my shoes and all over the front of his shirt. He tries to lie on the ground but I drag him to the sidewalk where it's dry and he can throw up into the gutter.

"Hey roomie, just let it out," I say, patting him on the back.

I step back to give him room, lighting a cigarette, and he speaks to me.

"I know what you did. I know what you did with Brittney."

He's propped up on his elbows, his face hanging inches off the ground. He doesn't look at me and continues to spit up bits of food.

"She told me. She told me what happened."

I consider my options. I drag deeply and kneel down next to him. I blow the smoke in his direction.

"I'm not fucking her," I say simply, glancing back at the door.

Brittney steps outside, purse in hand.

"But Eric is," I whisper, standing as she approaches.

Mark looks up at me, about to speak but is interrupted by more vomit that he heaves into the gutter. Brittney stands next to me, staring down at him.

"I'm gonna take him home," she says, exhaling loudly.

"Yeah, well, I have a date," I say, brushing it off.

I help Mark into Brittney's Honda and he doesn't thank me. He sits quietly, staring straight ahead.

"See you later, roomies," I say one last time and close the door for him.

The card game is still underway and Tawny bitches about the smell of vomit that followed me in.

"Sorry," I apologize, kicking off my shoes and throwing them outside.

The game continues on for another hour until everyone loses interest. Jared and Michelle leave together, hugging Tawny before they go. Brandon follows them, embracing me one last time. Jenny leaves with him, whispering something about giving him a handjob but I'm too distracted to pay attention. Tawny goes up stairs to smoke a joint with Ty, yelling down at me one last time about picking her up in the morning. Rebecca starts to clean.

"Looks like I won," Katie jokes, left with the fewest cards.

"Hey, don't be a bitch," I joke, scolding her.

She stops and stares at me.

"Don't ever call me that. That's one thing you'll never call me again."

I sit quietly, awkwardly, and we both turn in different directions. I hope I didn't strike out.

"I'm sorry. It was only a joke."

That answer seems sufficient and she continues to collect the cards.

"I've been wondering something," I begin, laying my balls out on the table for once.

"Yeah..." she responds and I know *she knows* what I'm about to ask.

"If I tried kissing you, would you push me away?"

"Why don't you try?" she says.

I want to try. I ignore my fears, my irrational feelings, and lean in. I don't know what to expect and I don't care. Our lips meet and she accepts me. I kiss her softly and slowly pull away. She continues to stare at me and I know she wants more. I hold her face and kiss her again, deeply. My tongue's in her mouth. My hand reaches from her face to her neck and I squeeze it lightly, feeling her breath enter and leave, her pulse beating beneath my fingers. It slides to her shoulder and I can't help but brushing up against her breasts.

I stand and lead her by the hand to the couch. She lies down and pulls me on top of her, between her legs. I continue to kiss her, caressing her breasts and massaging her thighs. I can hear Rebecca still cleaning in the kitchen.

"You two can stay the night if you want to," we hear her call out.

Katie and I both stop and weigh our options.

Not here. Not like this.

I stand up quickly and say goodbye to Rebecca. My cock continues to stiffen as we walk outside.

"Follow me," I say, kissing Katie again.

I'm way too drunk to drive and I watch Katie's headlights all the way to my apartment. I try to maintain stability while hurrying. There are no other cars out tonight. I watch her headlights, reassuring myself that this is actually happening. A night that is solely ours.

We hurry up the steps, rushing in the front door and racing to the bedroom. I turn on the bedside lamp and both Katie and I throw our clothes on the floor. I turn the CD player on and slide in the new Norah Jones CD Rebecca made for me. She falls on the bed in matching white panties and bra. I stand above her in my boxers, letting her admire me. Letting her wonder what I have to offer her. I slowly lower myself on top of her and she wraps her arms around my neck, kissing me deeply.

I skillfully reach a hand behind her back and unclip her bra in a matter of seconds, impressing even myself. She slips it off her arms and I kiss her nipples, licking them, sucking them. She moans loudly, reaching for my boxers. I slip them off and she holds onto me.

I continue to kiss her breasts and her neck. I suck on her, leaving purple bruises and small bites marks. She slowly rubs my cock, her fingers lightly caressing the head. My testicles brush against her and she's wet, warm and inviting. She rubs my dick against her clit and I remain semi-hard. I'm frustrated but unwilling to stop. She rubs harder and faster, moaning loudly into my mouth as I kiss her.

I enter her the way I am and slip out. I feel foolish, embarrassed, and I wish I hadn't drank so much. Katie seems not to notice or mind. After ten unsuccessful thrusts I pull away. I kiss her body all the way down to her moist crotch. I push my face into her, as deep as I can go. She spreads her legs wide for me and pushes me in. With each convulsion of her body her thighs tighten on my head until I can barely breath. I'm dizzy when she cums, her body shaking and her back arching.

I lie next to her as she breaths deeply, descending.

"Fuck," is all she whispers, over and over again, looking at me.

I smile in gratification. I try not to think about my shrinking dick.

"It's ok," Katie says, sitting up.

I sit up and she climbs onto my lap. She sits between my knees with her legs wrapped around me.

"I want to watch you," she says, kissing my neck and chest.

She spits on my cock and the warm saliva instantly hardens me. I grip it and she bites my nipples. I hold her neck and her back and she caresses my balls, squeezing them. I kiss her, sucking on her tongue. She licks my lips and I can feel it in the tip of my dick. As I start cumming, she holds me tighter, rubbing her cunt against me. I rub my fist against her and we cum together, semen bathing our abdomens and dripping from her chest. I cum so hard I want to cry and I bury my face in her neck and she holds me.

TWENTY

I can hear the phone ringing in the distance but I'm no way interested in answering it. The dark horizon's beginning to turn a light purple color and I know the sun will soon peak out from behind the shrubbery and Joshua trees. Katie's still beside me, tucked against my chest with her head resting on my shoulder. The semen on my chest and abdomen is dry. I haven't fallen asleep. I lie here dazed and completely content.

I hear the phone ring again and it jars something loose in my head. I turn quickly, forgetting that Katie's still asleep. My alarm clock reads 5:45 a.m. and I know exactly who's calling me. I quickly jump from the bed, almost knocking Katie to the floor, and rush into the kitchen.

"Where the fuck are you?" a voice screams back at me menacingly.

I let her down again.

"I'm walking out the door right now," I stammer into the phone, hanging up and tossing it back onto its jack.

I rush back to my room and dress quickly in the pale light that's starting to get brighter. Katie's still asleep and she turned away from where I lay. I throw on a t-shirt and a pair of jeans. As I slip on sandals, I kneel over Katie and kiss her on the cheek.

"I'll be back in a couple hours," I whisper and kiss her again.

She mumbles and I hope she's still here when I get back.

The air outside is abnormally cold, much cooler than I remember it being. The early morning is silent and still and I can see faint signs of my own breath as I lock the front door and start down the stairs. My heart starts to beat loudly and as I reach the bottom step I'm completely aware of the fact that I'm still drunk. I light a cigarette as I hop in the Jeep and the leather seats melt to my warm ass. I wait a moment, pushing on the gas, warming her.

I wish I'd brought a jacket or at least a sweater. My truck offers absolutely no protection from the elements and the heater barely warms my feet. The sun's slowly peaking over the horizon, shortening shadows and waking all the birds. It'll be warm soon but until then I must endure the cold wind that carries my smoke out the open window. Tawny will ream my ass for being late and I don't need a speech about my smoking. Hopefully I have gum somewhere.

Fifteen minutes after her call I arrive like a bat out of hell raging up her dirt driveway. As I pull up I see her sitting on the front step, sunglasses on and accompanied by a very mad face. I quickly jump out and load her things into the back seat. Before I can say a word, she cuts me off.

"Don't say a fucking thing," she scolds in a hushed voice.

I close the passenger door behind her and hop into the driver's seat. I can see the silhouette of her mother in the kitchen window watching us. Like the dark force constantly in her daughter's life, she stands unmoving with a cup of coffee in her hand, not wasting the energy to wave her only child off.

I drive quickly down the driveway and up the dirt road that leads to the freeway. The loud roar of my engine is all I hear, and feel, and the absence of voice is torture.

"I can't fucking believe you! I reminded you like seven times and you still forgot!" Tawny screams at me as I pull onto the freeway and race towards the carpool lane. "And don't drive like an idiot either!" she screams frantically as I pull in between two semi-trucks.

The hour and a half long ride to Burbank is busier than I had expected and I hide the nervousness that Tawny might miss her flight. She sits stone-faced, her arms and legs crossed, staring straight ahead. It's not until someone cuts us off that she decides to speak up, loudly.

"Son of a bitch!" she screams at a piece of shit Honda that crosses the double yellow and abruptly slows down in front of us, causing me to slam the brakes.

"Hurry up and cut him off! That stupid mother fucker!"

Under the circumstances, I choose not to argue. 'Road-rage' is the word in the dictionary that would have Tawny's picture under it, so I cross the double yellow. My 'Heap' roars as I gas it, pushing the clutch to the floor and jamming it into fifth gear. As I pass the passenger side window, I can see a Spanish woman staring straight ahead, obviously avoiding eye contact. Unlike my usual self, I sneer and quickly cut the car off.

The Honda comes within an inch of hitting me, smoke rising from its wheel wells as it's brakes lock. The cars lined behind it all do the same and honking rings out behind me like a bell choir. Tawny giggles loudly, slapping my shoulder. I smile widely at having made her happy. The incident doesn't sit well with the driver and he again crosses the double yellow line, rolling down his window as he approaches.

"What's your fucking problem?" Tawny yells out her window before the man has the opportunity to say anything.

He's in his mid forties and Hispanic. He opens his mouth again to speak but is shut down.

"How about you go back to Mexico and re-learn to drive before you kill an American!" Tawny continues, her face turning crimson.

This new insult of his heritage doesn't sit well with the passenger either, who leans over to yell out the driver's window.

"Fuck you Bitch!" she screams, her accent very thick and muddled.

"How about you go make a baby and rob me of my taxes, cunt!" Tawny responds with the ease of a drunken sailor, flipping them off.

She grabs a handful of change from my cup holder and hurls it at them. The shower of coins hits their windshield and hood, bouncing all over the freeway. The man swerves back and forth in his lane and I quickly down shift into fourth, hauling ass away. We laugh hysterically the rest of the way to the airport, almost forgetting about my tardiness.

We arrive thirty minutes before the flight is scheduled to leave. We park in the nearly empty parking structure and I carry all her luggage as we run towards the terminal. The air outside is quickly warming and the air conditioner is on full force in the small terminal. After gazing up at the flight schedule, Tawny quickly spies her flight.

"You're in luck, butthead. The plane's been delayed an hour," she exclaims with a smile, finally looking me in the eyes.

I smirk and quickly cover it up, eternally grateful to whomever intervened on my behalf. Both our bodies relax. We check in and drop off her luggage.

We find an empty table in the middle of the long corridor, outside a café. We can smell coffee and hear music playing.

"Want anything?" I ask, pulling out my wallet and making it obvious that it'll be my treat.

"Water. And something to snack on."

I wait in line for an iced coffee and grab two small trays of pre-packaged sushi. When I sit back down and hand Tawny her water and sushi, she laughs loudly.

"Oooh, crab with a K. How nutritious," she says, reading the label.

"Hey, don't get picky!" I scold her playfully.

"I'm just joking Poopy. Thank you very much for thinking of me!" she responds apologetically, patting my hand.

It lingers for a moment.

"I saw your mom in the kitchen as we were leaving," I finally speak after we both start eating our sushi.

We're forced to eat with forks instead of chopsticks and we both mix our wasabi with soy sauce.

"Yeah, she was actually up before I was. She was sitting at the kitchen table, drinking coffee and reading the paper," Tawny says with a hint of disappointment in her voice.

"I made some tea and sat at the table across from her. All she said was, 'Good Morning'!"

"Fuck her!" I blurt out with a mouthful of food.

Tawny laughs. It's forced and bothers her.

"I just don't understand. What have I ever done for her to be such a bitch to me? She didn't even hug me! She just told me 'Be Good'," Tawny continues, mocking her mother's authoritative tone. "Thank God I saw my Dad last night. I was afraid if I went in to say goodbye this morning, she might see me cry and laugh!"

We silently eat our food, wanting to say so much but not knowing where to start. I want to thank her. I want to thank her for being my friend, for making my summer so exciting. I think of all things that recently happened and one event suddenly pops into my mind.

"Did you talk to Jared last night?" I ask urgently, as if I might forget what I was going to.

"Yeah. I got to say goodbye right before he left with Michelle," she says with a smile.

Tears that welled up in her eyes are now pouring down her cheeks.

"He said he was sorry and that he'd miss me. He even thanked me for showing him such a good time! I always knew it had to end, but not like this."

I reach across the table and place my hand on hers. She squeezes it hard. The tears have smeared what little eyeliner she was wearing and a smile's spread across her face.

"Thank you. Thank you for everything," she tells me.

Those six words speak volumes and in my silence I acknowledge the same by holding her hand. When I finally find my voice and as the words are about to escape my lips, the overhead speakers interrupt me.

"Flight 97 for Seattle, now boarding. Flight 97 now boarding," a man's voice echoes down the terminal around us.

The announcement catches us off guard and we quickly throw out what's left of our mediocre sushi. I pick up Tawny's carry-on bag. We walk briskly down the terminal, hand in hand and silent. The gate for Flight 97 isn't a very long walk and a line's already started to form.

"Well, I guess this is goodbye," Tawny says as she turns and hugs me.

She tightly wraps her arms around my neck and jumps up to wrap her legs around my waist. I hoist her up and hold her tightly in my arms, not wanting to let go. I can feel her tears on my cheeks and they're running down my neck. She holds me tight, gripping my hair and whispering, "I'll miss you."

Slowly she steps down and smiles.

"I'll miss you too," is all I can say and I kiss her on the cheek.

She walks away. Her walk is brisk and bouncy at first but fades. Her confidant swagger ceases and by the time she reaches the gate, her swaying rear is belittled to a slow walk. I watch, wanting to say more but not having the words. She shows her boarding pass and as she walks down the corridor she turns and blows me a kiss, her fingers lingering in the air. I catch it and close my fist around it.

I don't stay to watch them close the door behind her and I don't want to see her flight take off. I'm surrounded by people crying and kids whining and all I want is a cigarette. A fucking cancer stick and a cup of coffee. I walk away quickly and step out into the hot summer day. The air is stifling now and I light a Marlboro, shielding my lighter from the breeze. I buy a cup of iced coffee from a short Indian woman whose face is beading with sweat. I walk to my car and quickly leave, refusing to turn back and watch as Tawny's plane leaves the ground.

TWENTY ONE

The sun's already high when I finally get home from the airport. My cheeks sting with dry tears and my contacts hurt from the sun, despite my sunglasses. I turn off the engine and sit, finishing my cigarette, unsure of what to do next. The summer I've waited so long for is now ending and in just a week I'll be starting college.

I sit in quiet reflection, yearning to remember all the details of the events that have recently expired. I long to have Tawny next to me, laughing her big laugh, teasing me the way she always does. I knew from the moment I left the airport I would never have her in my life the way she's always been. We've spent nearly every day for the past two years together, inseparable, but I no longer have the security of that controlled environment. The reality of the world around me started to haunt me as I drove those busy freeways home, alone.

I slowly step out and breathe in the warm air, flicking my cigarette butt. The sky's clear and the air's perfectly still. The wind has finally ceased and the stillness is saddening. I make my way towards the stairs that lead up to my apartment. I walk the steps in the shade and feel the hint of a chill that's not too far away. The chill that signals the end of summer and the end of all the smells that will now be forever different. My knees will start to ache soon and all summers to follow will never be the same. No more lazy days in the sun, no more late nights without care. No more "summer breaks" or virginity to lose.

As I reach the door, I wonder if Katie is still inside waiting for me. I quickly turn to see if her car's still there, surprised at myself for not having already noticed. And it is, in the same exact spot she left it.

I open the door and step into the harsh blackness. All the blinds are still drawn and my vision is gray and wavy, my eyes still adjusting to the darkness. The air is cool and refreshing and I quietly set my keys down on the counter. Bright light streaks the floor in front of my bedroom. I open the door to find the window still open and Katie on the bed.

The sunlight pours in like a flood and reflects off my white sheets, casting light on the ceiling. She's lying on her side facing away from me, the sheets low on her hip. Her long black hair is in disarray, spread clumsily across my pillow. A tattoo on her back peaks out from beneath the sheet and I can't resist smiling, wondering what else I missed last night.

I undress as quietly as I can and drop my clothes on the floor. Katie doesn't move as I lie on the bed behind her. I gently push her hair out of my way and lie close to her. I carefully wrap an arm over her and our palms find one another's.

I'm overcome by a feeling of desire, a feeling of belonging. I want to wake her and talk to her. I want to wake her and fuck her. I want to wake Katie and make love to her.

"I think I'm falling in love with you," I whisper, completely unaware that I might really feel that way.

I interlock our fingers and pull her even closer to me. I fall back asleep and will sleep the rest of today with the sun warming our naked bodies.

ABOUT THE AUTHOR

Jesse Lee was born in 1983 and raised in Southern California.
He graduated from Vasquez High School in 2001
and Antelope Valley College in 2008.
He still lives in the golden state with his wife and son.
This is his first novel.

Contact him online at
www.myspace.com/cooldaddy